Spencer Edwards:

Emperor of the Galaxy

Spencer Edwards:
Emperor of the Galaxy

Alex Prior

Matador
Unit E2 Airfield Business Park,
Harrison Road, Market Harborough,
Leicestershire. LE16 7UL
Tel: 0116 2792299
Email: books@troubador.co.uk
Web: www.troubador.co.uk/matador
Twitter: @matadorbooks

ISBN 978 1805141 402

British Library Cataloguing in Publication Data.
A catalogue record for this book is available from the British Library.

Printed and bound in the UK by TJ Books Limited, Padstow, Cornwall
Typeset in 11pt Adobe Garamond Pro by Troubador Publishing Ltd, Leicester, UK

Matador is an imprint of Troubador Publishing Ltd

This book is dedicated to Jamie, Emma, Louise, Matt, Clara, Rosa and Padlins. Carpe Diem.

Prologue:

More than a hundred thousand years ago, the Galactic Council of Inhabited Worlds was established to bring peace and stability to the cosmos. For all this time it has endured, dealing with disputes and conflicts as they have occurred, bringing different species together, balancing trade and the sharing of technological advancements across countless worlds.

Throughout the millennia, the Galactic Council has been led by a leader selected for their wisdom, intelligence, diplomacy, vision and experience.

Until now.

The Grand Hall of the Galactic Council built many aeons ago on the central government planet of Eloim III, has been in session for more than a century in a failed attempt to select a new Galactic Emperor.

Factional disagreements and infighting have erupted once more. The Zylaxxians, a warlike barbarous race whose empire was reduced in size by the Orion Treaties five hundred years ago, are once more in the ascendant. They have schemed to place their duplicitous leader, Haxenaar, as the prime candidate for succession.

In a desperate bid to break the deadlock, the outgoing Emperor, Volaria the 18th activates a long-forgotten clause in the Galactic Constitution that states, 'In the event of no agreement being reached to certify a clear successor, a sentient being shall be selected at random from any of the known inhabited worlds of the galaxy'.

The vast omniscient Artificial Intelligences of Eloim III hold a record of every single living sentient lifeform in the known universe. At a tumultuous session of the Galactic Council, they are asked to select a successor, from the quadrillions of beings known, seemingly at random.

On the rather primitive cosmological backwater of Earth, fourteen-year-old Spencer Edwards life is about to change, forever.

1

Life:

'Spencer, Spencer! Are you out of the bathroom yet?' The exasperated tones of Spencer's mum rang loudly up the stairs.

'One minute! Nearly done!' Spencer looked at his reflection in the toothpaste-flecked mirror. Hmm. A spot had erupted on the side of his nose, and that downy hair on his upper lip made him look like he had just drunk some cranberry juice. He ran a brush through his hair once more and decided that looked sort of okay though. Spencer sighed. He wasn't likely to be talent-spotted by a modelling agency, but he was just about passable in an incredibly ordinary kind of way. At fourteen years of age, Spencer was of average height, average build, and (even his mother would admit) average looks. He was never going to be a boy band heartthrob, but to be fair that wasn't one of his ambitions anyway. Come to think of it, Spencer didn't really have any particular ambitions right now, other than winning the heart of Amy Heartly and nailing a BattleBlast tournament on his Nintendo.

It was just coming up for 6pm and Spencer was almost ready to head off for his date with Amy. This was his big chance. More than two years after the biggest crush of Spencer's life had suddenly hove into view that second morning at high school, as a vision of raven-haired gorgeousness chewing gum and looking bored, he had finally succeeded in convincing her to join him for a burger (provided they split the bill she said), at Yumburger, the third most popular fast-food eaterie in town.

That's not to say that he hadn't made some progress over the years. Amy had, he was sure, come to quite like him, or at least tolerate him. He was polite, made her laugh, and had listened when her parents went through that messy divorce. At times he had thought there was the danger of simply ending up as friends, but much to his delight, Amy's friend Debbie Skelton had told him last week to 'Get a bloody move on and ask her out you hopeless muppet.'

So after psyching himself up for the best part of three days, he had. And in what was undoubtedly the romantic highpoint of his life so far, she had said, 'Go on then, yeah. Take me somewhere nice. Not the kebab shop.'

The battle fleet was assembling twenty parsecs out from the binary stars of Mizar and Alcor. Vast ships, each the size of icebergs, drifted through space, while flecks of light flitted between them like tiny fireflies, each a small craft attending to the needs of its master. The light from the twin stars rippled over the enormous hulls, picking out contours both smooth and jagged, and at times reflecting intensely like a flashgun.

This was the war fleet of one of the greatest powers in the galaxy, and it represented the unstoppable might of civilisations that many millennia ago took to the stars and colonised the Milky Way.

Amy looked beautiful. Spencer had rung her doorbell twice until her mum had answered. She gave him one of those unbelievably embarrassing smiles that only parents whose daughter you are about to take on a date can. After being invited to step inside 'Because she is *still* getting ready', Spencer had waited awkwardly until Amy slowly descended the staircase, fashionably ripped jeans and leatherette jacket making her both immensely desirable, yet with a touch of attitude that Spencer had so come to like.

'C'mon then! Let's get moving, I'm starving!'

The heavy cruiser squadron manoeuvred in tight formation around the small stray moon that had been released from a nearby planet's gravity well sometime in the past few million years. Artificial Intelligences aboard each attack ship coordinated their weaponry in what was not only a test but also a demonstration to other species of their gigantic firepower and readiness to use it.

In perfect synchronisation, the twenty or so ships unleashed pulses of pure energy which slammed simultaneously into the hapless celestial body, causing it to flash a vivid blue and then shatter into a myriad of fragments as forces far beyond anything ever witnessed on

Earth ripped apart the atoms of the rocky planetoid and removed it from existence.

Spencer was trying not to stare too intensely at Amy. She certainly was hungry and had quickly polished off a Yum 'N Tum Special TumBuster. She had laughed pleasingly at his jokes, and Spencer was acutely aware that their knees were touching under the table.

'That cow Lisa Catchpole in 9R was slagging me off to her mates the other day. I told her that if she didn't shut her big mouth I was going to shut it for her.' Spencer smiled sympathetically and nodded. Amy and her friends were a complicated bunch and seemed riven by infighting and rivalry. But it was also apparent that whoever was out of favour one week could easily be the flavour of the month the next.

Spencer was listening carefully, but also thinking hard about how to make sure Amy understood that he liked her. Not just liked, as in a *friend*, but really, really liked, as in a *girlfriend*. He could feel his nerves jangling as he envisioned that moment later on when he might try to hold her hand, and she would pull away, a look of horror on her lovely face.

'I like you, Spencer.' Amy kicked his ankle under the table. Spencer looked up into her eyes, bright and smiling. 'I do, you know.'

Spencer's head swam, 'I, I, er, do you, Amy? Really?' She nodded, clearly expecting him to say something.

'Well, that's great, because I, you know, really, really like you too Amy.' As he said the words, Spencer realised he probably wasn't going to go down in history as one of the great romantic poets, or even as a poet at all (to tell the truth he didn't get poetry), but Amy seemed satisfied with his response.

'So you're my boyfriend now, right?'

'Yes, yes, definitely! Definitely yes Amy.'

'Good, that's sorted then. You can snog me later.'

Spencer thought he might pass out. In fact, he was certain he would pass out, or at least screw it up. Amy though seemed perfectly happy and reached out to touch his hand, an amused smile playing on her lips.

Spencer reflected that it was pretty clear that females held all the cards, well the best ones anyway, in matters of the heart. Still, he smiled to himself, he wasn't complaining. In truth, he felt like punching the air and giving himself a high-five before lapping the tables, but he didn't, as that probably wouldn't have been very cool at all.

Onboard one of the behemoth battleships, a single imposing figure stood inside an immense dome filled with the holographically projected alien faces of dozens of species. Star charts and data streams flowed from his hands and swirled in the space above his head, spreading out to fill the cavernous darkness, shimmering and mutating into diagrams and simulations.

Some of the virtual attendees asked questions, some shared their own schematics, and some simply watched in silence, their inscrutable gaze never wavering from the being who stood holding court over them all.

The walk home had been beyond Spencer's wildest dreams. True, he had managed to step in something rather unpleasant, and his efforts to scrape it off on some nearby grass had been

5

a cause of some amusement for his new girlfriend, but they had held hands all the way home (apart from the scraping bit), and she had at times leant her head on his shoulder. As they reached her little road, filled with terraced houses and parked cars, they had stopped and she had pulled him to her. 'Come here then…'

Amy definitely tasted of gum, strawberry flavour, and in that moment Spencer knew he loved her more than anything.

Later that evening, lying in bed, he allowed his imagination to take him to far-off lands, on conquests to save his fair Amy from the clutches of an evil knight and his nefarious intentions. Spencer won the day every time and rescued his beloved.

More than four thousand light-years away, two servants of the Galactic Council were receiving their instructions.

2

Eloim III:

Eloim III is widely regarded as a beautiful world. With a circumference of just over 20,000 miles, it is a little smaller than Earth and much less densely populated. Gravity is also about a fifth less than that of our home world, and huge nature reserves span continents. The seas and lakes are clear and sparkle in the bright light from the K-Class star it orbits at a distance of approximately two thirds that of the Earth to the Sun. K class stars are a little cooler than our sun, but due to the closer proximity of Eloim III, the climate was not dissimilar to our own world. The slightly reduced gravity had led to the evolution of enormous trees, often over a hundred metres tall, and many large species of animal, some recognisable as cousins of Earth fauna, others entirely different and fantastical.

Scientists long ago discovered that Eloim III was one of the predominant cradles of galactic life and civilisation.

The conditions here had led to the eventual evolution of advanced bipedal humanoid beings, more than a million years before similar species had emerged on Earth. It was originally considered a wonder that evolution would lead to similar life-forms throughout the galaxy, but, as more and more inhabited worlds were discovered and began to communicate, it became apparent that given enough time, evolution on many planets, though by no means all, would eventually lead to comparable end results, with variations caused by local factors such as climate and gravity (for example the people of Lorasta average nearly three metres tall as their gravity is considerably lower, whereas the inhabitants of the enormous planet of Voohale in the 47 Tucanae cluster barely reach a metre, are extremely stocky, and have no discernible neck but four arms).

Colossal orbital mirrors, managed by the climate Sentinel AI, moving imperceptibly at Lagrange points above Eloim III's surface, gently moderated the global climate to ensure that all life was protected and able to flourish free of extremes of temperature and weather. The planet's energy is harvested from solar panels and the white solar paint that adorns the majority of buildings – essentially turning them into free and self-sufficient energy collectors. As a result, the entire planet is virtually pollution-free, and the damage caused by the excesses of ancient ancestors, on their journey toward enlightenment, has long since been cleansed from the ground and air.

Eloim III is also an ancient world. Fossil remains had shown that life had evolved there more than six billion years ago, and in the aeons since had evolved into many astonishing and wondrous forms. The planet had long been a source of intense scientific study, but many millennia ago agreements had been reached to protect the ecosystem. Of the number of cities and settlements, housing a global population of approximately 400 million sentient beings, the large majority were involved in either scientific research or diplomatic service and governance, for Eloim III housed the Grand Hall of the Galactic Council. This monumental edifice, built many millennia ago, stood at the centre of galactic civilisation. It was here that the many species and races of the known galaxy met to discuss, debate and reconcile differences in an atmosphere that while difficult at times, was mostly respectful and cooperative.

The Grand Hall itself was built from a white marble-like stone containing traces of precious metals that made it twinkle and shimmer. Soaring spires pierced the blue sky, reaching heights of more than a kilometre. The immense building was perched on a spectacular granite upland, with the city of Se'henva spreading out at its feet for several miles.

Airborne transports darted around the skies above the city, some small and for personal use, others larger and with a variety of purposes, all part of a complex aerial ballet whose AI choreographer was hidden from view. Amongst the artificial skyships flew incredible creatures, as large as pteranodons but resplendent in vibrant multi-coloured iridescent plumage, seemingly at peace with the bustle of technology. Eloim III is, therefore, a near-perfect synergy of nature and technology, where both co-exist harmoniously.

But on this day, all was far from serene in paradise. Inside the Grand Hall of the Galactic Council, events were taking place that jeopardised the safety of the entire galaxy, and would shape its future for generations to come.

Volaria the 18th, Emperor of the Galaxy and Leader of the Grand Galactic Council for the past three centuries, stood behind her virtual lectern at the centre of the huge chamber. Her gaze swept the myriad rows of delegates, each representing a planet, or colony, solar system, or trade bloc, federation or one of the many peoples and races that came together at this most special and auspicious place.

This was not going well. The usual calm of the chamber was absent, replaced by a frisson of discontent.

'Friends, I stand here today, before this esteemed body that has now been in session for so many years to make a frank admission. We have, despite our efforts, been unable to reach an agreement as to my successor. Where once there was harmony, we today face increasingly disparate needs and agendas.' She glanced at the Zylaxxian delegation, who stared back with open hostility. 'My time, as Leader, must be drawn to a close and a new chapter must be opened.' There was a general murmur of agreement.

'It is clear, that there is no one amongst us who can command a consensus of support. So', Volaria paused so that her next words might have increased impact, 'We have no choice but to refer to the ancient texts and founding principles of this council.'

The chamber fell silent. Every eye and photoreceptor was trained on her. Volaria knew that the next words she spoke would put in place a chain of events that could not be undone by any being present, and would lead to the immediate appointment of the new Leader of the Galactic Council.

The Zylaxxians looked as if they were about to object once more, as they had countless times in the past decades, but Volaria raised a hand toward them and summoned all her authority in that moment, 'Enough. We must reach a resolution.' She paused briefly.

'You will be aware that our ancestors, countless years ago, foresaw that one day we may reach this impasse. In their infinite wisdom, they made provision in our constitution.' She paused again, the chamber was silent. 'I now call upon the Artificial Intelligences of this Council to make themselves known.'

'We are here.' A clear voice, ageless, genderless, calm and sonorous, filled the hall. 'We stand ready to assist.'

'Sentinels, I now call upon you to perform a most solemn duty.'

'We are ready.'

'AI, how many sentient beings exist in the known galaxy at this precise point in time?'

'4.76234 quadrillion'.

'By the power vested in me, from our founders and through the Galactic Constitution that has sustained us for so many millennia, I ask you to select one sentient being from that number at random.'

'It is done.'

'Then tell us, who will be the next Emperor of the Galaxy?'

3

Visitation:

Spencer had fallen into a happy sleep. The high emotion of the evening had taken its toll, and as his eyes had closed, heavy with fatigue, his last thoughts had been of Amy. The small digital clock by his bed slowly advanced until it read a little past 2 am and outside, in his street, all was silent and still save for a couple of cats having a disagreement over territory.

'Awake. Awake, Spencer Edwards of Earth.'

A gentle voice intruded on his subconscious as Spencer became increasingly aware of his shoulder being shaken. Eh? What? This was an odd dream.

'Awake. You must awake.' The voice became more insistent.

Spencer blinked, and as his eyes began to focus, he perceived two figures standing in his room, one was leaning over him, insistently rousing him from his slumber.

Reality snapped disturbingly into place. 'What the…?' Spencer panicked and immediately pulled himself away from the creature's touch, shrinking into the corner of his bed where the two walls met.

'Sir, please do not be alarmed. You are at no risk. We mean no harm.'

In the dimness of his room, Spencer began to make out the forms of his visitors. One appeared to be quite tall with long flowing hair a bit like a heavy metal fan and was standing by his door, perhaps to keep look out. The other, now stepping back from his bed, had a clear, wide-eyed face, open and calm, but somehow not human.

'Who the hell are you, and what are you doing in my bedroom?' Spencer's voice shook with the shock, and he would later freely admit, fear.

'I am Aila 632, and this is Nomo.' The being gestured toward the tall figure by the door.

'What, what are you?'

Aila 632 looked blankly at Spencer for a moment, then a flicker of understanding passed across her extraordinary face. 'Ah, I see. I am an artificial life form.'

'A robot?' Spencer gasped.

'Well, that isn't a term we use much as it means 'slave' and is considered derogatory, but yes, I suppose in your understanding I am such. We prefer the term Synth.'

'And what do you want with me?' Spencer was struggling to take the situation in. He felt sick.

'Sir, we need you to come with us. The Galaxy needs you.'

Spencer's head was swimming. What did this thing just say? "The Galaxy needs him?" This had to be some kind of intense dream. Maybe the whole evening with Amy had somehow overloaded his brain circuits. Yes, that had to be it. Or there was something wrong with his TumBuster burger – perhaps it was the cheese.

'Wait! Are you… aliens?' Spencer gasped.

'Well, that's very much a matter of perspective. To us, you are the alien.' The Synth thing responded calmly.

'Where do you want me to go? Are you kidnapping me?' His voice seemed to come as a squeak.

'Oh no, sir! Nomo and I will give our lives to protect you. We need to take you on a journey, but it will take only moments. We will later return you here, and it will be as if almost no time has passed. Now come. We must get going.'

'I'm not going anywhere! I have school in the morning, and I'll be missed.'

'You will be back in time, I promise you, sir.'

There was something about the sincerity of this life-form's voice that was strangely reassuring. Spencer found himself resisting a little less.

Nomo crossed the room and tapped a badge on his chest. Within moments a single point of light appeared, steadily growing and expanding into what became a swirling tunnel of soft light – reds, blues, purples and all shades in between. Spencer gasped and felt his knees begin to buckle. Aila 632 gently but firmly took his arm to steady him and guided him from his bed toward the glowing whatever it was. 'Hang on a sec,' Spencer grabbed a hoodie and his joggers from the back of his desk chair and quickly pulled them on before Aila 632 steered him into the glowing portal. 'You won't feel a thing.'

That, Spencer quickly learned, wasn't entirely accurate.

4

Volaria:

For a moment, Spencer felt like he was falling. It was very much like that sensation you get when a rollercoaster crests the top of a peak and begins to drop back toward the next trough. Lights flashed before his eyes and there was a strange whooshing tone as if a high wind were blowing through trees. And then he was standing in a large chamber, with curved walls that glowed softly. The floor beneath his bare feet was cool, but not cold. He could see no lights, yet the room was evenly lit.

Standing at his side, still gently holding his arm, was Aila 632, and he became aware of the impressive presence of Nomo, right behind him, almost guarding him.

A door opened in the far wall of the room. Well, it didn't exactly open, as there wasn't a door there, but it appeared and then a willowy figure, dressed in what Spencer would have considered to be some kind of Cosplay outfit entered and crossed over to them.

The woman had hair that tumbled over her shoulders. Her face was mid-brown and she had dark eyes. Spencer couldn't begin to guess her age, but she had a certain authority that was unmistakable. She looked rather like Cleopatra in his school history books, except with blond hair.

Her eyes met Spencer's and she smiled, her small mouth with delicately formed lips making an almost perfect bow.

'Welcome, Spencer of Earth. I am Volaria the 18th, Emperor and Leader of the Galactic Council. I expect this has all come as a bit of a shock.'

Spencer nodded, his voice cracking as he tried to process his situation.

'I…I…what…'

'Please sit down Spencer. You have nothing to fear from us.' Volaria gestured toward the floor and a seat immediately extruded itself. Aila 632 guided Spencer to it, sat him down, and then, with a small bow, stepped back.

The chair seemed to form itself around Spencer, and for a second he felt unbelievably tired. This dream was so intense.

'Spencer, we have brought you here because we need you.'

'Who needs me?'

'We do. Everyone. Every species. Every planet.'

'I don't understand.' Spencer really didn't.

'You have been selected to be my successor. You will be Spencer 1st, Emperor and Leader of the Galactic Council.'

Spencer began to laugh. 'This is ridiculous! None of you are real. This is just some crazy dream stuff going on in my head. I've had enough. I'm going to wake up, at home, in my bed, right now!' Spencer strained his mind, his eyes closed as he concentrated on banishing the hallucinations. '5…4…3…2…1… and I'm awake!' Spencer snapped his eyes open to see Volaria, Aila 632 and now even Nomo gazing at him in curious concern.

'Spencer, this isn't a dream. You are not asleep. You are not in your bed. Come.' Volaria beckoned him toward the far wall, and Spencer felt the chair gently rise and lift him to his feet before melting back into the floor. Gingerly he stepped forward as Volaria waved toward the solid stone wall.

As she did so, the wall vanished to be replaced by a brilliant vista of a sunlit landscape stretching toward the horizon. Spencer felt a warm breeze ruffle his hair, and in the distance, he saw mountains rising from a deep blue sea. Everywhere were trees and plants of infinite colours and hues, and Spencer had the overwhelming impression that he was being afforded a view of paradise. 'It's beautiful!' he gasped.

'Welcome to Eloim III, Spencer. This is the seat of your Government, your power, and your responsibility.'

The room swam and Spencer felt his knees buckle once more, moments before he passed out.

*

'Spencer…Spencer…' His mum's voice was reassuring. Spencer's mind began to wander slowly back toward the present. Thank goodness, he thought hazily. And then, Amy! School. Homework. The thoughts were jumbled but began to coalesce. He opened his eyes.

Aila 632 was looking at him closely. 'I've scanned him.

He's fine, just a bit overwhelmed.'

No! Spencer sat up. No! He wasn't at home. And that wasn't his mum's voice he had heard.

'I want to go home!'

Aila's synthetic face did a good approximation of sympathetic concern, and she turned to look at Volaria.

'Spencer, we will not keep you here against your will, but please, I must explain the situation to you fully, and only then ask you to make a decision. Will you be so kind as to let me do that?'

There was something about Volaria's earnest tone that compelled Spencer to give a slight nod.

'Okay, I'll listen, but do you promise to take me back home after?'

'If, after you have heard what I have to say, that remains your wish, then we will of course comply.'

That seemed fair. Spencer suddenly realised that he didn't fear these strange people, just the circumstances. It was a lot to take in, but he felt his nerves begin to subside. He stood, shakily, and then his knees steadied. 'I'm listening'.

For the next half-hour, Volaria told Spencer the most incredible tale he had ever heard in his life.

5

A Short History of the Galaxy:

'For a hundred thousand years, the Galaxy has been at relative peace. There have been disagreements, even costly wars, but despite these trials, galactic civilisation has mostly prevailed and when peace has been disrupted, the Galactic Council has managed to negotiate a return to harmony. This is how it has been for so long that few now have any knowledge of the dark times before the Council was born out of conflict, rage and violence.' Volaria paused and sighed.

'Our historians and some leaders do study the ancient records, but for the vast majority of the sentient beings that inhabit the thousands of worlds, such matters are so far in the distant past that they have, perhaps understandably, become complacent. After all, countless generations have never experienced anything other than peace and prosperity.'

As Volaria spoke, an entire wall dissolved into an enormous screen showing scenes and images from what

Spencer quickly realised were many different planets and civilisations. There were planets much like Earth and Eloim III, others that seemed heavily industrialised, some that were mostly ocean worlds, some of ice, and some pockmarked with active volcanoes. There were colonies in space – inhabiting giant artificial environments inside spheres and cylinders, others on-board incredible city ships, and still more spanning asteroid belts where the asteroids themselves were tethered together to form what to Spencer looked like spiderwebs stretching across incredible distances, the filaments apparently acting as transport links for craft moving between the colossal rocks.

There were planets where the crust was made of crystals, with mountains that refracted light as if they were gigantic prisms; Planets wandering through space, not part of any solar system and thus completely dark, but where the inhabitants had constructed gigantic subterranean cities; and even planets that lay within the corona of stars, their entire surface screened from the radiation and heat by some kind of force field.

'These are just some of the inhabited worlds of the Galaxy, Spencer. And just the other side of that wall...,' Volaria gestured toward the far end of the chamber, '...is the Grand Hall of the Galactic Council, filled with representatives from all of them.'

'I have led the Galactic Council, as Emperor, for more than three of your Earth Centuries Spencer. It has not been an easy time. I have managed to hold the Council together as one species, the Zylaxxians, have become increasingly belligerent and aggressive. They resent the Orion Treaty, signed two hundred years before I took office, for restricting

20

them in their expansionist desires. The Zylaxxians have always been a warlike race, one of the most difficult members of our Galactic Family, and yet we have so far managed to work with them and maintain the peace.' Volaria paused, and her voice became sorrowful. 'But I fear I have failed. Only recently the Zylaxxians have moved their battle fleets into interstellar space, and begun to annex other planets outside of their own systems. They justify this as a need for resources and living space, but that is simply just an attempt to hide their true intent.'

'Which is?' Spencer asked, struggling to make sense of the sheer scale of this story.

'I believe the Zylaxxians intend to take control of the Galactic Council, impose their own Emperor, and declare martial law.'

'Why?'

Volaria hesitated. Then appeared to make up her mind. 'You have the right to know, so I will tell you. Until not so long ago, the almost limitless distances of space between the countless galaxies in the Universe remained untraversable. Our Galaxy is approximately a hundred thousand light-years across. The technology required to be able to travel those distances, still formidably complex, was developed many millennia ago. But the distances between galaxies are thousands or millions of times greater still, and thus intergalactic travel has forever been out of reach. Our astronomers have studied the known Universe for generations, and come to realise that life exists almost everywhere within it, but there had never been any contact with an intelligence from another galaxy until recently. Our scientists detected a message from the galaxy you know as

Andromeda, which lies approximately two and a half million light-years from our own.'

'Light years? I've heard the term but can you explain it to me?'

'Of course, it's very easy to understand. The speed of light is approximately 300,000 kilometres per second or a little over 1 billion kilometres per hour in the vacuum of space. That's pretty fast, but even those velocities are nowhere near enough to make travel across the galaxy feasible, let alone to cross the universe.

Spencer recalled something from science class with Mr. Doyle. 'But nothing can travel faster than light though, can it?'

'No, you're technically right Spencer, one of your own Earth scientists realised this, Einstein I think his name was, about a century ago. However, there is a way around this by changing the way you travel distance. We use something called the Multi-dimensional Inter-phasic Drive, or Multi-drive as it is usually known. This makes use of the dimensions outside of the four we usually inhabit – length, breadth, depth and time. Put simply…'

'Yes, please keep it simple,' said Spencer who felt his brain was already beginning to hurt.

'Put simply,' Volaria continued, 'it enables a ship, to jump out of our four dimensions, enter alternative dimensions where distance and time are essentially different and unconnected to our own, and then re-enter our reality at a different place. The journey is almost instantaneous but does require incredible amounts of energy so ships can't keep skipping around the galaxy continually, they need to pause to recharge their M-drives after a jump.'

'Okay, that kinda makes sense,' said Spencer, 'but if a ship can move almost instantly to another part of our galaxy, then why can't it move to another galaxy altogether?'

Volaria looked at him, perhaps slightly surprised and even a little impressed by the question.

'That's a very perceptive question, Spencer. The answer is simply one of power requirements. Shifting a craft into interdimensional space requires, as I mentioned, a lot of energy. The bigger the ship, the more energy, and similarly the further the jump, the greater the power levels needed. Trying to jump too far, without sufficient energy levels could leave a ship stranded in interdimensional space for a while, or even permanently.'

'Scientists long ago calculated that the amount of energy required to jump to another galaxy was far beyond the capacity of any ship or craft to generate.'

Volaria paused, her tone and calm countenance betrayed her concern. 'That is perhaps, until now. Intelligence operatives believe that the Zylaxxians may have found a way to channel enough energy into a ship, or fleet of ships, to make the jump. We don't yet know how advanced their plans are, or any of the details.' She shook her head sadly. 'The Zylaxxians have always been a militaristic race, their industry and technology geared toward expansion through conflict. Their history is one of aggression and bloodshed. If they are in the process of developing such technology, it is likely they will use it not for exploration or peaceful contact purposes, but for conquest.'

'We believe their goal may be nothing less than intergalactic war with the Andromeda Galaxy. We have no idea of what that could mean, but we fear there is a chance that the Andromedan's capabilities may be significantly in advance of ours. Once provoked, they could retaliate with devastating force, laying waste to huge swathes of our galaxy, that you call The Milky Way, but we know as Valius.' She paused, and her face became grave.

'So you see Spencer, what is at stake here is potential inter-galactic war, and the destruction of countless planets and civilisations.' She stopped and looked Spencer directly in the eye. 'And it is now up to you to stop it.'

6

Why me?:

Spencer looked deeply into Volaria's sincere eyes. He no longer thought this was a dream. Quite incredibly, he felt "real". The room felt real. His companions were, he was now certain, absolutely real too. He surreptitiously pinched his thigh to double-check. Yep, that hurt!

But Spencer had just one question he had to ask. 'Why me? Why would any of these races possibly listen to me?' He hoped his voice hadn't sounded too squeaky.

Volaria smiled slightly. 'Because, Spencer, you come with no history. You are from a planet that has not yet joined the Galactic Council. You have no preconceptions, no bias against any species here, no knowledge before this moment of the great peril our Galaxy faces. Anyone else, from any of the known inhabited worlds, would be seen as compromised and far from impartial. Your very naivety makes you the only being currently on Eloim III who would not offend or be objected to by others.'

Spencer thought on this for a moment. On the one hand, it was almost a little offensive, and yet he could see the sense in what he was being told. Just an hour or so ago he had been blissfully asleep dreaming of Amy. Yet here he now was, on another planet, and being asked to lead the Galaxy through dark and difficult times. Oh, what the hell!

'I'll do it. Or at least I'll try.'

As Spencer heard himself say the words, he was already questioning his sanity, but the look of relief and even admiration on the faces of his compatriots was surprising and rather flattering. He smiled, trying hard to exude a confidence that he absolutely did not feel.

'Spencer, the Galaxy will owe you a great debt. Your nobility and heroic sacrifice will become legend across countless worlds, and your wisdom will shape the cosmos for millennia to come.' Volaria spoke the words earnestly, her eyes never leaving Spencer, who wasn't entirely sure he felt comfortable with any of that, especially the "sacrifice" bit. Still, he had gone along with it this far, and he didn't feel he could back out now without letting a lot of people down, including those in this room.

'Well, I guess we'd better get on with it then.' He said, trying to sound cheerful.

'Yes, but let's get you properly dressed first.' Said Aila, and within seconds Spencer's hoodie and joggers were replaced with a well fitted, smooth dark blue jumpsuit with gold and silver highlights and a crest upon his left breast that appeared to show the Milky Way, or Valius spiral as he now knew it to be named. Spencer looked down at it in amazement. The suit felt like it was moving, tightening and loosening in various places Spencer didn't feel inclined to mention, and dark black sneaker type shoes seemed to grow out from the hems of the suit and form around his feet. Aila smiled at his look of alarm. 'Don't worry, the suit is adjusting to you.'

'It feels a bit tight... no it doesn't, it feels quite warm, no...' Spencer tailed off in confusion.

'Give it a few more moments and it will be finished. The suit is intelligent and can even mimic a range of other garments, but more than that, it will protect you. It isn't indestructible, but it is resistant to extremes of heat and cold and can withstand multiple attack modes. The crest contains many features I won't go into now, but if you tap it twice and say 'Home', it will open the Space-Time transit tunnel and return you to Earth, but, and this is of paramount importance, although you will return home within minutes of the time you left, events will progress here at their normal pace. We can bend time in one direction, specifically for you, but not for the whole Galaxy. If you go home for a day or a week, events here will move on by a day or a week by the point at which you return.'

'Eh? How does that work?'

'It's complicated, and we probably don't have time to explain it right now, but you'll understand soon enough.'

Spencer definitely didn't like the sound of the 'attack modes' Volaria had mentioned, but the return to Earth bit was very reassuring, although rather confusing in terms of the time displacement thing. Perhaps sensing his trepidation Aila sought to reassure him, 'Don't worry, all leading dignitaries wear a similar suit, Spencer, it is standard practice.' Spencer smiled weakly.

'Fitting now complete,' said the suit. Spencer did

a double-take. 'It is my pleasure to clothe you, and trust that you are now both comfortable and approve of your appearance.' A mirror materialised in front of Spencer. He certainly looked quite, well, what was the word? Sleek?

Aila then stepped forward and handed Spencer what looked like a Smartphone. It was completely black and smooth, with no obvious buttons or controls at all. 'This is Bradlii, your AI. Pop it in your pocket, here.' She showed Spencer a virtually imperceptible flap that fitted the device perfectly to the right-hand side of his torso.

'Now you are ready', Volaria pronounced, 'Just follow my lead.' I will introduce you to the delegates and do most of the talking. Just say something like, 'I am deeply honoured to accept this role at this challenging time, and I will work tirelessly to unite the worlds and peoples of this Galaxy. Aila will be at your side, and will prompt you if you need.' Spencer nodded, his mouth dry. He wasn't very good at public speaking and had been on the losing side of a number of debates in History class.

7

Death and Life:

Spencer took a deep breath and followed Volaria and Aila through the opening in the wall that had appeared from nowhere. The tall form of Nomo followed behind, and Spencer found his silent presence somehow reassuring. Within moments the small group was striding down a gently sloping walkway toward a central podium someway off in the distance. Spencer immediately became aware of the vastness of the auditorium, and as he looked around he could see endless banks of creatures, many probably humanoid, others less so, stretching away on all sides and above and below. The Grand Hall of the Galactic Council reminded him of an enormous football stadium, but fully enclosed and almost spherical. It was also virtually silent, but Spencer was sure he could feel the eyes, or whatever they were, of thousands of delegates boring into him.

He did his best to walk confidently and hold his head

up as mum had always told him to do. Spencer felt a sudden pang of homesickness, what on earth was he doing here? He was just an ordinary kid, with a new girlfriend he reminded himself. Amy, what would Amy be doing right now? Would she be proud of him? Or think he was an idiot for getting involved in any of this? Probably the latter.

They reached the podium, and Volaria took her position behind a softly glowing lectern. Aila gently steered Spencer to one side, her hand resting delicately on his arm. It calmed him a little as he gazed out into the immense hall. The details of the delegates were hidden in semi-darkness, but there was no doubt the attention of every being present was focused solely upon him and Volaria.

'Esteemed delegates and all council members. I stand before you today to complete my most solemn duty, that of the passing of power from me to the new Leader of the Galactic Council and Emperor of the Galaxy.' There was a barely audible murmur from the auditorium.

'As you know, in accordance with the Galactic Constitution, a new Emperor has been selected. I have spent some time with him, and I am now certain that he will lead you with wisdom, humility and determination, as I have tried to do these past three centuries.' Volaria paused, and Spencer was acutely aware of the total silence that engulfed them.

'I present to you, Spencer Edwards, Emperor of the Galaxy.' The spotlight on Volaria dimmed and the intensity shifted to Spencer. 'Step forward a pace,' Aila whispered to him, 'And speak.'

Spencer took a deep breath. He felt his leg begin to tremble, but then steady as the suit appeared to sense this and stiffened, providing extra support.

'Delegates,' his voice was hoarse. He swallowed hard. A soft voice said 'This is Bradlii, listen and repeat after me.' Spencer almost froze but then lifted his head up and swept the Grand Hall with his gaze. The whisper continued and Spencer relayed every line. 'Delegates,' his voice was steadier now, and Spencer summoned up all his courage. 'I stand before you with one commitment. To do all that is in my power to honour the faith placed in me by my predecessor.' He gestured toward Volaria who was regarding him with approval.

'I have only recently learned of the role I am now to take, and the peril which the galaxy now faces, but I pledge to you that I will work tirelessly to bring peace and harmony to all the worlds once again. I will not favour one species over another, and I will lead with honesty and faith so that together we are united, for the benefit of every sentient being in the cosmos, be they humanoid, or er, something else. I speak as the new Leader of the Galactic Council and as Emperor of the Galaxy. I ask for your support and I challenge you to follow me toward a new peaceful and prosperous dawn for every world and every species.' He paused and became aware of a growing response amongst the delegates, some started to clap, others made trumpeting sounds from orifices in their heads, while others still seemed to be buzzing with approval.

'We object!'

The deep, guttural voice rang out across the auditorium, cutting through the growing noise and once again the hall fell silent. Spencer stiffened, Aila whispered, 'It's the Zylaxxians, Haxenaar himself!'

A light illuminated several delegates seated close to the podium. One was standing, the heavy coarse horned features of his humanoid face twisted in what was very recognisable fury.

'This boy has no place here! The Zylaxxian Executive does not recognise his legitimacy, and gives notice that for the common good of all members, I, Haxenaar, declare myself to be the true Emperor of the Galaxy.'

Pandemonium broke out and Spencer saw the huge figure of the Zylaxxian leap toward the stage, followed by several of his entourage. He appeared to be holding something in his hand that he raised toward Spencer.

The next two seconds would prove pivotal in the fate of the entire Galaxy.

Aila pulled Spencer aside and at the same moment, the formidable figure of Nomo threw himself in front of Spencer, directly between him and Haxenaar. There was an intense flash and Nomo disintegrated in front of Spencer's eyes, a blood-curdling scream emanating from him as the molecules of his body were quite literally torn apart. Spencer felt his feet lift from the floor and he was carried backwards, held tightly by Aila who rapidly picked up speed.

Another flash, and Volaria, her face still turned toward Spencer, seemed to freeze in shock and then her elegant form was shredded as she met the same terrible fate that had befallen Nomo.

In the ensuing chaos, flashes and screams rang out across the auditorium, and Spencer saw dark silhouettes, presumably Zylaxxians, cutting down other delegates with their weapons.

Haxenaar was advancing on the podium as the wall

at the back of the stage opened and Aila, now moving far faster than any human could, sprinted into a lit tunnel, with Spencer still carried securely over her shoulder.

Explosions seemed to follow them into the tunnel and shouts and cries rang in his ears as they accelerated toward a lit doorway. Aila didn't slow down for a second, and once through, the door sealed itself instantly with a hiss.

Aila stopped dead. The deceleration was almost painful. Spencer's head was spinning as Aila gently deposited him in a seat that emerged from the floor. In his confusion, Spencer started to perceive that he was now in what appeared to be some kind of control room. At a console a couple of metres in front of him he saw a seated figure huddled over screens.

'Zan, launch now!' Aila's voice was clear and urgent. A screen appeared to one side, hovering in mid-air, showing what looked like Zylaxxian troops hurtling down the tunnel outside. One stopped and adopted a kneeling position, a weapon something akin to a bazooka on his shoulder. There was a flash and a split second later a shattering explosion. The soldiers advanced again, picking up speed, moving in a tightly coordinated way.

Spencer's seat moulded around him and gripped his thighs.

'Launching in three… two… one…' The figure in front of him called out.

There was a moment of almost imperceptible calm, before the ship, for Spencer had realised that was where he now was, accelerated brutally. He gasped and felt his suit respond, tightening at his waist. He recalled reading somewhere that flight pressure suits worn by fighter pilots on Earth did something similar to force blood up toward the brain in hi-G manoeuvres. It wasn't very comfortable, but Spencer didn't black out.

The wall in front of him had turned transparent with monitoring data, status information and trajectory overlays moving rapidly around his field of view. The ground below was rushing past at an almost impossible speed as the ship hurtled toward the horizon. 'Hold on!' Aila was standing next to him, seemingly unaffected by the extreme acceleration of their craft.

Suddenly the ship tipped up, and the sky filled Spencer's view as the craft went vertical, its speed still increasing. The dull roar in the distance increased in intensity and the light blue sky quickly darkened as their altitude increased, until it turned black as they left Eloim III's atmosphere. Spencer felt his stomach pitch as the planet's gravity suddenly flicked off before weight returned in an instant. 'Gravity on,' said the pilot loudly.

The expansive viewscreen flipped to show an image of the world they had left behind, rapidly receding. 'Here they come!'

Three points of light appeared around the curved edge of Eloim III, obviously on an intercept course with the craft Spencer was aboard. The viewscreen zoomed to show menacing vessels, bristling with what looked to Spencer like some kind of weaponry, with blue waves of energy rippling around these needle-like protuberances.

'Incoming transmission,' Aila informed them.

The face of Haxenaar appeared in the middle of the control gallery. 'Spencer Edwards of Earth. This is not your battle. Surrender immediately and I guarantee you will not be harmed and can return to your pointless life on your insignificant home planet. Resist and you will be destroyed. You have ten seconds to comply.'

Spencer felt something inside him begin to boil. What was it? Oh yes, anger! This was the bastard that had killed Nomo and Volaria right in front of him. He last felt this way when he had stood up to that bully in Year 7, but it was even more intense in its ferocity.

He looked at the holographic image of Haxenaar, and their eyes met, virtually.

'Go to hell!'

The apparition's mouth twisted into a hateful sneer, 'I was hoping you'd say that!'

Energy arced out from the pursuing ships, flashing across the void toward them.

'Multi-drive coming on-line,' the pilot shouted, and at that moment the cabin seemed to split into two overlapping images that stretched and intertwined in a spiral of glowing matter. With a visceral snap the space in front of the ship flexed and stretched like the surface of a balloon as their ship punched its way through and all went quiet.

The hunched back of the pilot relaxed, and he turned to Spencer.

'Welcome to *The Infinity* sir, we're glad to have you aboard your personal starship. My name is Zan.'

8

Homework and Bradlii is a Smartass:

Spencer flopped down in his bed, the exhaustion was almost overwhelming. Just moments before *The Infinity* had entered the Androsep system, more than a thousand light-years from Eloim III, Bradlii and Aila had suggested that Spencer use the portable worm-hole device to return to his bedroom and spend a day in his regular life. After all, they assured him, *The Infinity* would be safe for a while, and they needed to contact numerous other races to begin to formulate a strategy. Bradlii, who was evidently far more than a Smartphone, had come with him, snuggled in the smartsuit which had immediately transformed itself into a pretty decent impression of his favourite hoodie and joggers as he emerged from the wormhole and into his rather untidy bedroom.

It was barely 7 am and his alarm clock started beeping. Thoughts started rushing in. School. Amy. Homework?

Damn. Breakfast. Hungry. Amy. *Amy.*

This could be one of those cheesy 'And then I woke up and it was all a dream' moments you often saw in movies Spencer thought to himself. Except he knew it wasn't.

'Bradlii, how smart are you?'

'Pretty smart ,Spencer. What do you want to know?'

'Bet you can't tell me if I have any homework due, can you?'

'As a matter of fact, I can.' Did Spencer detect a trace of smugness in Bradlii's voice?

'Go on then…'

'Your history homework on the rise of Nazi Germany is due today, you missed the maths and French that was due in yesterday.'

'Oh hell! 'How can you possibly know that Bradlii?'

'As I said, I'm pretty smart.' The AI retorted. 'I tapped into the online homework system your school uses, bypassed the security encryption, and took a look at your account. I have to say I don't think you've been putting enough effort in recently.'

He had to be kidding! Spencer had an AI more advanced than anything on Earth in his pocket, and it was already telling him off.

'Bradlii, don't get on my case. Don't forget I am Emperor of the Galaxy, right?'

'Yes, you are. But you are also a fourteen-year-old schoolboy from Earth. Don't you forget that either.'

Spencer's eyes widened. 'And you can drop that stroppy look right now.' Said the increasingly annoying AI.

'Okay Bradlii, but what am I going to do? I have to get that homework in, and I also need to look after Mo for an hour later before mum gets home from work, and I really, really want to see Amy.'

'Don't whine, Spencer. It's not seemly for the Emperor of the Galaxy to whinge and moan. Hmm… alright, I'm going to help you with the homework just this one time and I expect you to make extra efforts in the future.'

Spencer could hardly believe it. This was worse than his stepdad and mum's ticking offs. 'Okay, okay, just this one time. What can you do?'

'Give me a moment. Processing. Done. The maths and French have been completed and turned in online. The history needs to be a hard copy.'

The printer connected to Spencer's laptop whirred into life and began its work. A minute or so later Spencer was clutching what was an impressive looking essay on Germany in the 1930's.

'Have you just copied this from the Internet, Bradlii? My school checks for plagiarism sometimes.'

Bradlii sounded almost offended. 'No, I have not copied it! That is an entirely original essay with one or two rather novel insights of my own into the political machinations of the Weimar Republic in the pre World War 2 period. I drew on the work of three thousand two hundred and sixty-seven authors and their collective published works to produce it.'

'When did you do that?'

'Just now of course. When it became clear you probably weren't in a position to do it yourself.'

Spencer began to grin, perhaps there were going to be benefits from being the Emperor of the entire Galaxy.

'And you can wipe that smile off your face, I'm not making a habit of this.'

Damn.

Breakfast was the usual barely organised chaos. Mo managed to drop his toast onto the floor, jam side down of course. Although he was only four, Spencer expected better of him. Mo was always happy to see him though. Hassan, his stepdad ruffled his hair (Spencer didn't mind that too much) and wished him a good day at school before heading off to the insurance company where he worked. Mum looked tired as usual, but made time to fuss over him a bit and chide him for his untidy bedroom. 'Spencer, please put your dirty washing in the bag and the rest of your clothes away in the wardrobe, not on the floordrobe!' It was a family joke that she made frequently, but Spencer smiled as he usually did. His mum had always been there for him, and he loved her dearly, even if she could be quite annoying at times.

As he headed out the door, he realised he had left his phone in his room, so told Bradlii he had to pop back and get it.

'No, you don't. I've taken over the role and function of your device. I can replicate it perfectly.

'Wow, that's very clever, Bradlii, but I can't get you out in front of my friends as they'll ask me what model you are, and, well, that could be awkward.'

Bradlii emitted what sounded like a resigned sigh. 'Get me out of your pocket.'

Spencer did and had a moment of confusion. He was holding his phone, complete with diagonal scratch to the screen.

'Yes, it's still me, Spencer. I've simply mimicked the form of your primitive device, see?'

The phone quickly morphed back into the smooth black lozenge of Bradlii, before once more resuming the appearance of Spencer's rather worn handset.

'That's very cool, Bradlii.'

'Yes, that's me. Cool.' Came the sarcastic rejoinder. 'Oh, and I have something called a text message from someone identifying themselves as Amy. She says she lurves you babe and is looking forward to seeing you at school. Shall I respond?'

Spencer wondered why he had to have a massively advanced AI with such an attitude problem.

*

School was school. It was okay. Spencer didn't actually mind school too much. He got by. Never at the top of the class, always somewhere in the middle. He liked most of his teachers, apart from that sadist who took them for PE and rode a bike alongside them when they did cross-country, shouting all the way.

Lunch was the first time he really got to see Amy, and she grabbed his hand and pulled him round the corner of the science block. 'Miss me?'

Spencer had, a lot. Even though by earth time he had only been with her in YumBurger last night.

Amy smiled coyly and planted a kiss on a delighted Spencer.

'Mmm…mwah! Have a good afternoon babes, I'm at my Auntie's tonight but I'll text you, yeah?'

And then she was gone, and Spencer realised he was grinning like an idiot.

'She's definitely into you Spencer, although I struggle to see why.'

'Shut it, Bradlii. Who asked you?'

9

Astren and the Firecats:

Androsep is a colourful planet from orbit and possesses a warm, temperate climate. As a result, it is teeming with a major ecosystem quite different from that on many other planets. There is ice at the poles, large oceans, and thick clouds that roam throughout an atmosphere rich in oxygen and moisture.

In many ways, the planet has a lot in common with Earth in the Eocene period, when mammals were flourishing and took a myriad of forms across the vast continents that were their home.

The Infinity had entered a geosynchronous orbit. That, as Zan patiently explained, meant it was fixed in a particular spot above the planet far below. As Androsep turned, so did *The Infinity*, at exactly the same speed – tracking above a large continental land mass in the equatorial region.

Spencer had returned to the ship an hour beforehand,

much to the relief of Aila and Zan who confessed they were concerned that he might not come back.

It was true, Spencer had had his moments of doubt, and it was fair to say a complete crisis of confidence. He still felt that this was all some kind of gigantic, galactic size mistake, but he also felt flattered in a strange way. Here he was, an ordinary Earth boy, suddenly thrown into the most extraordinary situation that anyone from his home world had ever experienced.

In truth, he realised, he was already in possession of knowledge far, far beyond that of any human who had ever lived. He, Spencer Edwards, knew the answer to the question that humanity had pondered so long – are we alone in the Universe?

If only they knew! Far from being alone, the Galaxy was brimming with life. One day, humans would join the Galactic Council, and discover, to their absolute amazement, that it was once led by a fourteen-year-old boy from Earth. Thinking about that made him smile to himself.

Aila spoke, 'My sensors are showing some interference from the planet's magnetosphere so instead of holoprojections I suggest we take the Lander. I will accompany as security, and you Zan as a cultural liaison.'

Zan turned to Spencer, 'Androsep is a fascinating world, with a harsh environment. Its peoples are renowned as fearsome warriors who prize loyalty and integrity above all things. If you befriend an Androsian, as they call themselves, you have not only a friend forever, but a powerful ally who will sacrifice their life to protect yours, for they consider such a death to be the most perfect and honourable possible.'

'We have come here because we need allies, Spencer', said Aila, 'And the Androsians are no friends of the Zylaxxians who they regard as scheming and deceitful. Our aim is that we might be granted an audience with a spiritual leader named Galen, and while his people usually avoid taking sides in a galactic conflict, we know that there have been times in the ancient past when they have intervened decisively in times of strife. Our hope is that we can persuade them, now is such a time.'

The Lander looked a little like a smaller version of *The Infinity* – streamlined and with a clear glass crystal cockpit and windows that the larger ship appeared not to have – relying mostly on internal virtual displays and holoscreens. Zan explained that most pilots and passengers liked to be able to see reality with their own eyes, not through display systems as they landed on a planet. Spencer could see some sense in this, as impressive though *The Infinity*'s holographic displays were, there was something more immediate, more real, about simply looking through a window, even if it were so clear as to appear invisible.

As they approached the Lander, standing softly lit in its hanger, a door materialised in the side, and steps extended to meet the floor. Inside it was, Spencer thought, rather cosy. It wasn't claustrophobic, but instead warm and welcoming. The seats were plush, made of that unknown material that moulded itself around you, and it smelled new. Spencer remembered going in a friend's Dad's new car once – it smelled like that. It also looked expensive – much like *The Infinity* itself – everything was just beautifully finished, control panels, screens, interior fittings, chairs, it all just seemed to blend together seamlessly and tastefully.

As if sensing his thoughts Zan said, 'Not all ships are as nice as yours, Spencer! As Emperor, your starship truly is the top of the line in everything. I was brought up on a freighter, making Bismuth runs between systems. That ship was dirty, smelly, cramped and always on the verge of falling apart.' He sighed wistfully, ' I still loved it though.'

There was a faint hum as the Lander came to life, soft screens glowing beneath the clear crystal canopy. Spencer felt an almost imperceptible change in attitude as the craft left the hangar floor and became airborne. At once the wall in front faded and the full majesty of Androsep hove into view. Spencer gasped at the spectacle, it was so vivid, and then he gasped again as the Lander left *The Infinity* and tipped over to point straight down at the planet below.

'Whoooaaaaa…' Spencer felt as if he were at the top of a rollercoaster about to drop, suspended in that moment of sheer exhilaration mixed with abject fear, before the Lander did indeed begin to plummet toward the Androsian surface.

Within moments they began to penetrate the thick atmosphere, and Spencer recalled those science lessons when his class had been shown the return to earth of the Apollo space capsules bringing astronauts back from the moon in 1969. Those crafts had glowed with white heat as their protective shields burned off, slowing the cone-shaped spacecraft from more than twenty thousand miles per hour to a few hundred before enormous parachutes were deployed, and they splashed down safely in the ocean.

The Infinity Lander, on the other hand, didn't seem to be slowing down at all, and Spencer felt increasingly uneasy as the cockpit window was engulfed in flame. Zan reached forward and pressed an icon on one of his control panels and the canopy went dark to be replaced with a holoscreen showing a clear view of the planet, spread out from horizon to horizon. 'We'll switch back to realview once we are clear of the entry burn.'

A minute later Spencer could see tremendous mountain ranges rising up through the reddish clouds, and rivers and oceans stretching as far as he could see. The Lander began levelling off, and at a few thousand metres above the surface, they began tracking over the landmasses as the Lander seemed to home in on a pre-set destination. Aila examined a display on her forearm, 'Hull temperature nominal, speed three thousand metres per second, we are hypersonic and slowing…'

'I'm going to set down a few kilometres from the city, and we'll walk,' said Zan. 'Even here we need to be careful. We are unannounced and we need to keep a low profile. It is quite possible that the Zylaxxians have some spies or at least sympathisers here as not every Androsian is quite as honourable as the best of them. And a sudden appearance from the Emperor could be relayed back by QEComms before we've even had a chance to contact Galen.'

The Lander began to slow and Spencer felt the deceleration tug at him, before Zan, having found a suitable clearing, flared the craft and set it down gently in the middle of a forest glade next to a tumbling waterfall.

'Outside temperature forty degrees, humidity 100%, relative gravity 140%,' intoned the shipboard computer.

'Er, forty degrees? Isn't that like very, very hot?' Spencer didn't do heat very well. Like most boys his age, he was prone to being a bit sweaty at the best of times.

'It is a little warm for your species, yes Spencer,' said Aila, 'but the smartsuit will deal with it.' The hatch materialised and for a moment Spencer felt a blast of sticky heat, before miraculously, the suit seemed to adapt and a bubble of cool air formed around his head. Weirdly, he also felt heavier and staggered momentarily until Aila reached out and steadied him. 'You weigh nearly half as much again here, Spencer' Bradlii chimed in, 'but the suit will help out,', and it did. The weight seemed to fall away and Spencer stood up straight. 'The suit is compensating for your lack of muscle mass, and acting as an exoskeleton to support you.'

'Thanks, Bradlii. I can't tell you how much I appreciate that.' Spencer hoped his voice conveyed just the right amount of sarcasm.

'Come on,' Zan was consulting his own AI, 'it's this way about five klicks.'

It soon became clear that the suit was also reducing the effort of hiking over difficult terrain. At times it almost felt like Spencer was walking on air, and he seemed able to jump and move with an ease and agility his PE teacher back on Earth would never have believed.

Zan, a few metres up ahead, suddenly paused and held up a hand for quiet. 'We are being watched.' He whispered, his concern evident.

It was then that the attack came at a truly ferocious speed. Spencer became aware of a rushing through the forest from all directions and then creatures with blazing red coats and eyes that seemed to flash and burn were all around and amongst them. 'Firecats!' Spencer, down!'

For a moment time seemed to slow down and Spencer saw Aila once more move to place herself between him and danger, but this time the threat was coming from everywhere. A firecat leapt upon her, trying to close its bone-crushing jaws around her head, and she heaved it away. Then another attacked, and another, and then… a blur. Something was fighting the creatures. Spencer thought he saw a girl wielding some kind of sword, but she was moving at impossible speeds, like a cross between a ballet dancer and a kung-fu master. Backflips turned into lunges, which turned into roundhouse kicks, punches, parries and sword thrusts. She was a whirlwind of flashing blades, feet, fists and flowing red hair.

Within a minute or less it was all over, and the beasts loped back into the forest screeching horribly, but their saviour was kneeling on one knee, head down and breathing heavily. With concern, Spencer could see blood trickling from cuts and lacerations on her arms and legs. Slowly she stood, and taking a deep breath she raised her head and her gaze swept over them. She was a little taller than Spencer, but then many people were, and perhaps aged seventeen or eighteen, well in Earth years anyhow, and quite muscular. Deep red hair tumbled to her shoulders, and the tops of her arms and the left side of her neck sported intricate tattoos that appeared a little Celtic to Spencer's untrained eye. She was dressed in a russet leather jerkin, something that seemed very much like a skort, with leather bindings on her shins. Sleek fitted boots with sharp polished metal points completed the ensemble.

To Spencer, she looked somewhat Amazonian and undeniably rather impressive.

Spencer spoke first. 'Thank you. You were incredible. Awesome. Wow.' It had sounded better in his head, and inwardly he groaned. He definitely had to work on his gravitas.

The girl nodded. Then a little smile seemed to twitch at the corners of her mouth before her face became stern. 'You could have been killed. This part of the forest is firecat territory.'

'So what were you doing here?' Spencer asked.

'Hunting firecats of course.' The girl seemed rather amused that he should ask such an obviously stupid question.

'I'm Spencer, and this is Aila, and that's Zan over there. We are in your debt.' Yes, that sounded a bit more Emperor-like. 'Who do I have the honour of meeting?' Nailed it.

'Astren, of the tribe Aclides.'

'Well Astren of the tribe Aclides, we are very grateful for your help and we must attend to your injuries. Aila, can you help?'

The Synth moved over to Astren, and after a moment's hesitation, the patient offered her arm. Aila's fingertips glowed a soft blue, and she gently passed them over the cuts and grazes.

As Spencer watched closely, the skin seemed to move of its own accord under Aila's touch, and he realised the cuts were closing. It was quite incredible to witness, but then Spencer was slowly becoming used to the incredible.

Astren looked at them suspiciously, but then found the good grace to thank Aila. 'Where are you heading?'

'We are trying to get to Aclides City, we need to meet with Galen,' Zan said. Immediately Astren's eyes widened and then quickly narrowed. 'Why do you seek Galen? Do you know him?'

Zan stepped in before Spencer could speak. 'We cannot say, but his wisdom and help is greatly needed by those who are both honest and of good heart.'

Astren didn't look convinced.

Spencer gave her what he hoped was a reassuring smile. 'We mean no harm, and as you can see, there are only three of us. We have risked a lot coming here, hell, if you hadn't stepped in at least two of us could have been killed. We really do need to see him, so if you can help, I hope you will.'

Astren looked from one of them to the other, as if weighing her thoughts. 'Well, clearly you aren't a threat because you don't know what you are doing...' Spencer nodded encouragingly.

'Follow me. Stay close, move quietly, and if another attack comes, get out of my way.'

Eventually, they made it to the fortified gates of Aclides City without further incident, and at a command from their saviour, the gates swung open to reveal several armed guards, this time carrying weapons that were significantly more substantial than swords.

10

Haxenaar:

The Zylaxxian High Fleet Commodore visibly quivered before Haxenaar as he delivered his news. 'We've lost them, sire. They engaged their Multi-drive before we could disable them and long-range scans can detect no signs within a five hundred light-year radius.'

Haxenaar sat silently, his gaze fixed firmly on the hapless Zylaxxian cowering in front of him.

'We have our spies and operatives searching for any indication of where they might be, and I am confident that it won't be long before we get some kind of information we can act upon.' He swallowed.

Haxenaar was not renowned for his accommodation of failure, for failure this undoubtedly was.

The enormous domed chamber was softly illuminated by the glowing holographic faces of numerous Zylaxxian military commanders, who looked down on the proceedings with a studied lack of emotion.

Haxenaar shifted his attention to the holoimages. 'This boy, a pilot and an android have managed to elude a distinguished fleet commander and some of our best pilots. Not only have they escaped, but we now have no idea and no prospect of certainty as to how or when we may find and eliminate them.' He spoke softly, but the fury and menace in his voice were clear.

'We are poised to take control of the Galactic Council, to finally bend the Galaxy to our will, to fulfil the destiny that has been denied to us for centuries by the cursed Orion Treaty, and yet we have been thwarted by an adolescent schoolboy from a primitive and worthless planet nobody has even heard of.'

He stood, his huge frame, more than two metres in height would have been impressive under any circumstances. Right now, for the Commodore who quailed before him, it was terrifying.

'The price of failure is a high but just one. We know that, and it is something all Zylaxxians learn from an early age. We do not tolerate incompetence, for tolerance is a weakness and Zylaxxians are not weak.' His voice was soft, almost gentle, yet his eyes burned with anger and resolve.

The Commodore summoned whatever courage he had left, and stood straight, looking Haxenaar directly in the eyes. The Zylaxxian leader nodded slowly, both understood what came next.

There was a sudden flash, and with one savage blow Haxenaar's glowing blade, shaped not dissimilarly to a scimitar from Earth, sliced the Commodore cleanly in half from his left shoulder to his right hip.

Purple blood erupted from the remaining torso, spattering Haxenaar in an arc that covered several metres before the legs collapsed and the lower half of the Commodore fell to join the rest of his cleaved body.

The holographic faces registered nothing, Cold eyes looked down on the scene, they had all received and understood the message.

11

Family and Amy Smells Nice:

It was Aila who had suggested that Spencer return home for a little while, and he had readily agreed. Leading a now complicated double life was, Spencer realised, actually pretty exhausting. The portable wormhole corridor had once again bent time and returned him to his bedroom, just minutes after he had left.

Spencer collapsed onto his bed and despite the tumultuous events of the preceding... what was it? Twenty-four hours? Forty-eight hours? Time was beginning to become deeply confusing for Spencer, but of one thing he was certain. He was absolutely knackered. Within moments he was asleep, and if anyone could hear him, which they couldn't, snoring softly.

*

'Spencer, Spencer! Are you out of the bathroom yet?' The exasperated tones of Spencer's mum rang loudly up the stairs as they did most mornings. Spencer wasn't in the bathroom though. In fact, he was still fast asleep in bed.

Footfalls on the stairs, and then the curtains being pulled apart. Spencer groaned, and then slowly blinked his eyes open.

'Morning my little cherub!' She knew he hated that. But this morning it wasn't quite so annoying.

'Mum! I'm so glad to see you!'

Spencer's mum looked puzzled, 'Okay, well I'm glad to see you, Spencer, and I'll be even more pleased once you are up and downstairs in your school uniform eating breakfast.'

Spencer struggled to his feet, and then, on impulse, gave his mum a big hug. For a moment she looked startled, and then pleased, and then gave him a fond hug back. 'Bad dream was it, Spencer?'

He nodded, not wanting to let go, and then stood back. 'I'm okay, and feeling better already. How's Mo?'

'Downstairs supposed to be waiting for you.'

Mo always smiled whenever he saw Spencer. Spencer was his hero, and until now Spencer had only needed to be a hero to Mo. Over some own-brand breakfast cereal, Spencer reflected on how he now had to be a hero to the entire galaxy. It was still so daunting that the moment he began to think about it he could feel his stomach lurch and that horrible queasy sensation when you are about to be sick started to rise within him.

But the Androsians hadn't seen him as an impostor or a joke. Somehow he had managed not to trip over his own feet, or make a total fool of himself. Incredibly, they seemed to believe in him. Spencer chewed thoughtfully while Mo threw some rice crispies on the floor. Perhaps, and here was an entirely new thought for Spencer, he wasn't a complete loser. The notion cheered him considerably, until Hassan came in, looking worried.

'Everything okay darling?' Spencer's Mum had returned and was busy vacuuming up the detritus surrounding Mo's high chair.

Hassan signalled for her to join him in the hallway. Spencer was worried. Hassan was usually pretty cheerful and easy-going, yet this morning he looked far from happy.

There was animated whispering coming through the door, but Spencer couldn't make any of it out. Then Hassan and Mum came back through. 'I'll tell him.' Now Spencer was getting very worried.

'Hassan's company are making redundancies. It's the blasted pandemic last year. They haven't recovered.'

Spencer looked at Hassan, who just looked sad. Oh no!

'It's true, Spencer, lots of companies have been restructuring since Covid, and cutting costs.'

'But it won't necessarily be you being made redundant will it?' Spencer tried to find a glimmer of hope for Hassan.

'No, but the division I work in is being targeted the most. I haven't been there all that long, and I'm afraid, Spencer, that in these circumstances it is usually last in – first out.'

Spencer didn't know much about employment matters, but Hassan explained that because he had only been employed there for a relatively short while, it would be cheaper for the company to make him redundant than it would be for employees who had been there years.

'But you love that job!' Spencer blurted. This was all so unfair. Hassan genuinely did enjoy working there and Spencer knew he was a hardworking man, always punctual, always diligent. The bloody pandemic had been a miserable time for so many, but he had hoped it was all in the past now. It seemed he was wrong, Hassan was to be another casualty of the cursed virus, just in a different way.

On the walk to school, Spencer felt helpless and angry. His was just an ordinary family, like so many others. When his dad had left he had only been a baby and it had been some years before Mum had met Hassan. For a long time it had been just him and Mum, but then Hassan had started to visit. A big man with a ready laugh and a sweet nature. It hadn't been too long before he felt like on one of the family, and then Mum had taken Spencer out for a pizza treat and told him that she had come to love Hassan, and she hoped that Spencer wouldn't mind too much if Hassan came to live with them.

Spencer was aged about nine by then, and Dad had been gone a long time. He already thought of Hassan as a father figure, and it was clear that Hassan was very fond of him. Spencer hadn't minded at all. Mum was happy, Hassan was happy, and he was happy. And then Mo came along a couple of years later and he was hilarious. Spencer loved his little half-brother, and although there were quite a few years between them, they got on like a house on fire.

'Bradlii, what can I do?'

'I'm not sure what you mean Spencer, can you be more specific?'

'What can I, can we, do to help Hassan?'

'I'm sorry Spencer, I'm not sure there is anything we can do.'

'I'm supposed to be the Emperor of the Galaxy, right?'

'You are the Emperor of the Galaxy, Spencer, no *supposed* about it.'

'Okay, well then, can't I issue some command?'

'Oh I see,' said the AI, apparently detecting that this was not a time to be insensitive. 'I'm sorry but it doesn't work that way. Nobody on Earth knows your true identity, and the Galactic Council has no official presence or relationship with your planet yet. Even if it did, I am not sure you could, or should intervene in such a way.' Bradlii actually sounded quite sympathetic.

Spencer glumly walked on until he reached the school gates to find Amy waiting for him.

'Hiya gorgeous!' she squealed. Spencer immediately felt his face turn crimson. Amy sped over to him and flung her arms around his neck. Some of Spencer's mates looked on, either amused, a little embarrassed, or, perhaps, a tiny bit envious. Despite his worries about Hassan and Mum, Spencer brightened. Amy just didn't care what others thought, and Spencer loved that about her because all too often he felt that he did care, and worried just a little too much.

On impulse, he kissed her. A few wolf-whistles almost spoiled the moment, but Amy was clearly delighted. She punched him on the arm.

'Oi! What was that about?' Her happy mood was infectious in a good way. 'You can do that again after school, she whispered.'

The bell rang, and the school day started. Lessons came and went. Lunch was its usual mediocre culinary non-delight, and then it was home time and Amy and Spencer walked hand in hand down past the canal.

'What's bothering you, babe?' Amy asked after a while, so Spencer told her about Hassan. 'Aww, that sucks big time. Wish there was something I could do.'

There wasn't of course, but being with Amy, and just walking together, was very comforting. For the first time in a while, Spencer wasn't thinking about the rest of the galaxy, just the two of them, down by the canal, and that she smelled really nice.

12

Galen:

Galen was unquestionably old, but given that Spencer didn't know his species, it was impossible to take a guess at exactly how old he was. Long, silvery hair flowed from his crown and temples, framing a thin face with, Spencer thought, kindly eyes that gave the impression of both wisdom and great intelligence. He was dressed simply in a green smock, a talisman hanging from his neck by a coloured cord. He looked, to Spencer, somewhat like a cross between a shaman and a wizard.

Galen exuded a certain calm that Spencer found very reassuring. The chamber, high in an impressive stone building that Astren said was the seat of the local government they had been shown to was simply furnished, but with a large window that gave a panoramic view of the city below. There were signs of advanced technology, but Spencer gained a strong impression that this was a society not dominated by it. The city itself was entirely surrounded by a high wall with ramparts and battlements. At some point in the history of this planet, there must have been conflict, but perhaps that was in the more distant past, Spencer thought hopefully.

'Please be seated, my friends.' The voice was quietly authoritative and a little dry. Galen waved toward what looked very much like large beanbags. Spencer and Zan sat down, and after a moment's hesitation, Aila followed. The bags gave a soft rustle and formed around them, and they were supremely comfortable, Spencer noted. Astren stood by the door, apparently feeling the need to guard it alongside a strapping youth of perhaps nineteen who had been introduced to them as Qarak.

Zan, acting as the cultural liaison spoke first. 'Thank you for granting us this audience, Galen. I am Zan, of Hylea, this is Aila, and this…'

'I know who he is,' said their host softly. 'Greetings Spencer Edwards of Earth. I am honoured by your presence.'

Spencer didn't know what to say. 'Er, thank you, and I am honoured by you. Of you. To be here with you. Sorry.'

Galen smiled gently. 'So much weight on such young shoulders, eh Spencer?' His eyes seemed to see right through him as if his soul was being searched. Spencer felt something begin to break a little within him.

'I haven't got a clue what to do. Only yesterday, I think it was yesterday, I'm not sure, I was at home. I have a girlfriend, Amy. A family. A psycho tried to kill me, and I have homework.' It all started to tumble out, his voice cracked, and Spencer felt like he was about to start blubbing, but somehow he didn't. Galen just gazed at him, sympathetically.

Out of the corner of his eye, Spencer thought he saw Astren looking disapprovingly in his direction, so with an effort, he pulled himself together and cleared his throat.

'I'm good. I'm just a bit tired. It's been quite a lot to take in, but I'm fine now. Sorry.' Spencer felt he seemed to be apologising a lot, and wondered if that was that striking the right tone for an emperor.

'There is nothing to apologise to us for, Spencer,' said Galen soothingly. 'You have already endured a lot, and there is much yet to come.'

Spencer almost recoiled at that but bit his lip. He was done making a fool of himself for the time being. 'Tell me,' he said.

'I cannot tell you what I do not know, but I can perhaps help you understand the path that lies before you and prepare you a little for it. Come, there's something I'd like to show you.'

Galen rose, and they followed him to a door that slid back to reveal what was very obviously an elevator of some sort. Once inside, Astren's finger hovered over a button embossed with a symbol Spencer didn't recognise, but he presumed it represented a number. At a slight nod from Galen, she pressed it.

Underneath his feet the floor dissolved and Spencer plummeted. He almost screamed until he realised that firstly he didn't feel sick, and secondly, he and his compatriots were falling at precisely the same speed, in perfect formation, in an entirely controlled yet high-speed descent. It was, Spencer realised with a start, actually almost fun.

After a few seconds, he felt himself begin to slow, as invisible hands seemed to gently grip him, decelerating them until, with an imperceptible bump, they alighted onto a smooth stone floor and a door slid open, revealing a large terrace area bathed in reddish sunlight.

Spencer realised he must be grinning, as his companions were staring at him with a mixture of amusement and curiosity. 'That was cool! I'd quite like to do that again!'

'I expect anti-grav elevators are quite "cool" if you've never ridden one before. But perhaps later, Spencer?' suggested Aila politely.

The terrace was built from large slabs of impossibly smooth deep grey rock, and so precisely fitted together that the joints were almost invisible. Spencer guessed it was at least a hundred metres long by about half as much wide. There were other Androsians here too, engaged in what was certainly some kind of martial art, but it was unlike anything Spencer had ever seen on earth. The speed and precision of the sparring were far beyond anything human, and it was apparent that these Androsians possessed physical abilities that would be considered extraordinary by anyone who witnessed them.

At a sign from Galen, the twenty or so chidwas (which he was told was the name given to trained fighters) moving as one instantly formed into a single unit, ten Androsians wide by two deep. They stood completely immobile, eyes fixed ahead. Spencer did a quick head count, there were eleven females and nine males. He guessed their ages ranged from around mid to late teens (Earth years), and each was dressed slightly differently in attire that was clearly intended to facilitate unencumbered movement but seemed to provide little obvious protection. On their feet, Spencer noticed, they wore smooth single piece shoes that encompassed their feet up to their ankles. He would later learn that these were made of an intelligent composite that adapted to the environment the wearer was in.

'This is my current class, Spencer. One of the finest I have ever trained. Every single one of them would give their life for you.'

Spencer was staggered. They didn't even know him. He felt a turmoil of emotion, but mostly he felt like a fraud. The idea that others had such high regard for his position was something Spencer found very difficult to comprehend.

'They would be honoured if you would inspect them,' Galen continued.

'I don't know how, or what to do.' Spencer felt extremely uncomfortable.

'Just walk with me, smile a little, nod and maybe speak to one or two of them.'

Spencer followed the sage and together they began to inspect the formation. Spencer continued to feel ridiculous, but he tried to muster as much authority as he could and looked each of the troops in the eyes with what he hoped was an encouraging and approving smile rather than a lop-sided leer.

Spencer deliberately made sure he paused for a moment before each Androsian, met their unflinching gaze, and gave a nod of respect and acknowledgement. Galen meanwhile watched approvingly.

'Perfectly done, Spencer' he whispered softly once they were finished, and at a tiny gesture the ranks broke and the trainees began to chat amongst themselves. Galen steered Spencer over the balustrade at the edge of the piazza.

'They liked you.' he said simply.

'What? How do you know?'

'I know. When you have spent as much time with them as I have, many things don't need to be said.'

Spencer felt a little relieved. This had been a test, and apparently he had passed somehow.

Later that evening Spencer, Aila and Zan returned to *The Infinity*, but now they were joined by Galen, Astren and Qarak. Galen had informed Spencer that their journey now lay with him, their Emperor, in his time of need and that it was the solemn duty of every Androsian to lend their support wherever and whenever they could.

Spencer, for his part, was pleased and very relieved to have them along. He found Galen's calm presence and obvious wisdom to be reassuring, and he had no doubt that Astren and Qarak's skills and combat prowess would be much needed in the trials to come.

The Infinity broke orbit and headed away from Androsep, pointing its sleek nose toward a distant sector that Galen informed them was little visited and would give them some time to formulate their plans.

13

Duranian Destruction:

Nine Zylaxxian battle cruisers appeared from phase-space at the heart of the Vanadium Cluster. The ships, dark, brooding and menacing formed into three attack waves and turned to head toward the Duranian outpost on the fourth moon of the second planet.

In the control room of the outpost, a defence station for the system, the ships were soon detected. Holoscreens showed the starlight glinting on their hulls and an alert tone sounded urgently throughout the base. The station commander, a young Duranian female, sent increasingly desperate transmissions demanding to know their intent, but there was no response.

Across the surface of the moon, pilots scrambled into defence fighters, and weapons emplacements swivelled to lock on to the advancing Zylaxxian warships.

Two of the three defence squadrons launched within less

than two minutes of the Zylaxxian detection. The small but highly manoeuvrable craft rocketing away from the surface at high-speed, their ion drive engines at maximum thrust, and their pilots communicating over their shipboard AI's as they formed into a line of defence.

But still the Zylaxxian ships came on.

At fifty thousand kilometres from the moon, the cruisers launched their own fighter craft, and the space between the adversaries rapidly closed. The Duranian commander sent a priority message to her homeworld, deeper within the cluster, and issued the instruction to activate the defence perimeter field around the moon, knowing that it would not hold for long against the onslaught of nine heavily armed battle cruisers.

At seven minutes past fourteen, local system time, the Zylaxxian and Duranian fighters joined in battle. The Duranian pilots were skilled and fought bravely, but the Zylaxxians, supported with high-energy fire from the cruisers, quickly cut them down at a rate of two to one. In the Duranian control room, the screams of vaporising pilots could be heard over the intercom, while the commander and her staff watched in horror.

The cruisers continued without pause, and at twenty thousand kilometres out, she ordered the moon's heavy weaponry to open fire. A Zylaxxian cruiser was hit and began to lose attitude control, engines flaring. The remaining eight ships then deployed a swarm of missiles that zeroed in on the Duranian ground defences. As the barrage approached, the cruisers opened up with heavy fire, sapping the defence perimeter shield until it began to collapse, monstrous holes appearing in the shimmering sphere through which hundreds of smart self-guiding missiles poured, zeroing in on the weapon emplacements below.

From the command control room on the surface, it looked like a firestorm was engulfing the moon. Plasma cannons were overwhelmed and reduced to charred and twisted wreckage, the domed buildings that housed hundreds of workers and other Duranians were swept away in the ferocity of the conflagration, their inhabitants erased from existence in just moments.

And still the Zylaxxian ships came on.

At ten thousand kilometres distance the cruisers formed into three attack waves and directed all their weaponry at the now defenceless base on the ravaged moon.

On the bridge of the lead cruiser, the Zylaxxian Fleet Captain gestured to the AI and Haxenaar's face appeared on a holoscreen floating in front of him. 'We have arrived your eminence. All defences have been rendered inoperable. What are your instructions?'

'Destroy the base and kill every living thing on that moon.' Haxenaar growled, his eyes as cold as his heart.

The Fleet Captain nodded once and signalled to his weapons operator.

The barrage was intense. The surface of the moon glowed as it melted from the ferocity of the attack and the trillions of mega-joules of energy rained down upon it.

The last thing the Duranian Commander saw was the Zylaxxian ships continuing their inexorable advance.

*

Aboard *The Infinity*, Galen's face was grave. 'Spencer, we have just received news of an attack in the Vanadium Cluster, about fifty light-years from here. A defence base on one of the outer moons of the Duranian collective has been obliterated by Zylaxxian forces.'

Spencer was taken by surprise but wondered why Galen was telling him this.

'Why? Why was it attacked?' He dreaded the answer when it came.

Galen looked into Spencer's confused face and spoke softly. 'They were searching for you, Spencer.'

Spencer felt his knees go weak and begin to buckle. Qarak was immediately by his side, a hand grabbed his elbow to provide support.

'How many?' Spencer whispered, barely able to listen.

'Six hundred and eighty-seven.'

Spencer felt like he was going to throw up. So many dead, and because of him!

As if sensing his thoughts, Astren spoke. 'It wasn't your fault. You didn't do this.' Her normally composed face softened a little.

Spencer felt tears forming at the corner of his eyes. 'But hundreds and hundreds dead, because of those bastards,' (he spat the words as the impotent rage surged within him), 'wanted me!'

14

The Infinity:

For the past two hours Spencer, Aila and Zan had roamed *The Infinity*, at Spencer's insistence. He had decided that he wanted to explore and get to know what was, still quite unbelievably, his spaceship. *His spaceship*. The absurdity of it was still ridiculous.

Aila informed him that *The Infinity* was in reality a rather old ship, but had been continually upgraded and refitted, with no expense spared, over several generations of Emperor. The ship itself was legendary, as it had carried not only Emperors and dignitaries, but taken part in search and rescue missions, provided aid to planets in need, and once even commanded a fleet against the Zylaxxians before the Orion Treaty was signed.

She was built in the construction yards of Cassiopeia, which, Aila explained, was one of the most distant stars observable from Earth with the naked eye. The design, was, at the time, quite revolutionary, and due to the continual improvements, she remained state of the art in terms of her onboard technology and capabilities. Even if, as Zan pointed out with obvious affection, she creaked a bit from time to time.

'*The Infinity* is approximately three hundred of your metres in length, and about fifty across at the widest point,' Aila told him. Spencer had been shown images of the exterior on screens, and he had to admit, she was a beautiful looking thing. Her hull was a very soft gold sheen, she had a gently raked nose, and her engine pods sat near flush with her smooth flank. Spencer decided that she was somehow a cross between a shark and an arrow, with her various contours all seamlessly flowing into one another to create a simply breathtaking profile from any angle.

Aila continued, 'So she's not particularly big by any standards.'

'But she is very capable,' added Zan, the pride in his voice apparent.

They arrived at a door, which slid silently upward to admit them to an exquisitely furnished and spacious study. Soft carpets underfoot made even the floor feel comfy, and there were bookshelves and display cabinets, housing what Spencer was sure were priceless artefacts from across the galaxy. To one end, before a large picture window that spanned from floor to ceiling, there was an expansive desk in gleaming gloss white. The chair behind it looked to be upholstered in sumptuous gold stitched suede.

'Can I?' Spencer gestured toward the chair. He had the sudden urge to sit down and spin around.

Zan was confused. 'Of course, these are your quarters, sir.'

'Seriously?'

'Of course they are, Spencer,' interrupted Bradlii impatiently. 'Where did you think you would be sleeping? A bunk bed or a hammock somewhere?'

Spencer grinned. 'If you come through here I'll show you your sleeping space,' Zan continued, and gestured toward another doorway.

Ushering Spencer through, he remained at a respectful distance. As soon as he crossed the threshold, Spencer felt his feet begin to lift off the deck. Slowly, and with no effort on his part, his body rotated until he was suspended in mid-air. It was an extraordinary sensation. He felt weightless but still supported at the same time. 'If you want to get down, just give the command.' The pilot instructed.

'Down?' Said Spencer, and his feet slowly lowered to the deck once more. 'I could get used to this!'

'You were being held in an ultra-harmonic field. It creates just the right amount of gentle pressure to move and position you in complete comfort.'

'Amazing!'

'Come on, there's more to see.' Aila and Zan steered a now smiling Spencer out into the corridor once more.

A few minutes later they were standing in a hangar bay in the belly of *The Infinity*. Two identical small but extremely sharp-nosed craft were berthed. 'You've already seen they take up to six passengers plus the pilot. They are fast, highly manoeuvrable, and they are armed with plasma guns and miniature muon launchers.'

'Moo, what?'

'Muon launchers. Smaller versions of the large Muon Launchers that are *The Infinity*'s primary offensive weapons.'

Bradlii stepped in. 'A muon is a heavy particle. The launcher accelerates and directs a super-dense pulse of these particles into a very focused point. It delivers an absolutely devastating punch. A single well-aimed shot can split an asteroid in half.'

'Or destroy a Zylaxxian battleship?' Spencer asked quickly.

'Well, possibly yes, but they are very well shielded, heavily armed, and you would have to get within close range.'

Spencer gazed at the small ships for a few moments. All present knew exactly what he was thinking.

'I'd like to learn to fly one.'

Zan looked dubious and Aila was silent for a moment. 'I'm not sure you should be taking that kind of risk. sir…' It was the first time she had addressed him so formally.

Spencer set his jaw and turned to face them both. 'Given the situation, I might need to know how to pilot one of these things to escape, or for any one of a hundred reasons. I am fed up with feeling like everything is happening to me and I can't do much about it. I want to fly one of these ships, and I want you both to teach me. Now.'

Aila and Zan exchanged glances, and Zan shrugged imperceptibly, then grinned.

'Well, you are the Emperor, and if the Emperor wants to learn to fly, then he shall be taught to fly.' Spencer nodded his approval.

'Good, I'm glad you see it my way. Let's get started.'

'Now?' Asked Aila, surprise evident in her voice.

'Yes, right now,' said Spencer, firmly.

15

Flying Lessons:

The small flight deck was beautifully built and softly lit. Two seats, side by side, one for the pilot and one for the co-pilot faced a smooth console that wrapped around them. A clear glass window, using augmented reality to display information and allow for magnification and actual sight, cleverly combined, covered nearly one hundred and eighty degrees of vision. As Spencer settled into the pilot seat with Zan at his side, Aila took one of the seats behind them. Zan gestured, and the craft quietly came to life. The words 'Good morning Emperor' appeared in the centre of the canopy window, before fading to be replaced by what Spencer took to be some kind of navigational data array.

The surface of the console in front of him rippled and then extruded two controls that looked a lot like the joysticks pilots of aircraft on Earth would use. Spencer stared at them for a moment. 'Would you prefer a different control interface?' Zan, getting comfortable in the seat next to him asked.

'No, no, these will do just fine.'

'The left stick is velocity, forward to increase, back to slow, left and right open the lateral thrusters for more extreme manoeuvres. The right stick is essentially your directional control. It's pretty intuitive actually.'

Spencer took hold of the twin controls. They felt slightly malleable and he realised they were adapting to fit his hands.

Zan continued. 'The onboard AI takes care of much of the background systems, and will respond to your voice. For example, you can tell it to prepare for launch, or open cargo bay doors, or divert power to lateral thrusters, or whatever you want within reason.'

'Okay, got it.'

'There is quite a bit more to understanding the ship's systems sir, but if you are ready, then I guess we can get going. *The Infinity* has entered into orbit around a small planetoid in the Carsaria system, and sensors show no other ships within a couple of light-years. I will be right here to help and to step in if there is any danger.'

Spencer sighed, but Aila spoke up. 'This is now your ship, Spencer, but it is still our job to protect your safety.'

Spencer nodded. He did understand, even if their care occasionally felt a little suffocating. Then a thought occurred to him, 'Does this ship have a name?'

'No, it is designated Lander B, but I guess if you would like to give it a name that would be fine.'

Spencer thought for a moment. 'Then I'll name it Vengeance.' He saw the glances that Zan and Aila exchanged, but he didn't care. 'I think I'd like to introduce this little ship to Haxenaar.'

Zan didn't look happy at all, but dutifully said, 'Very well, Lander B, redesignate to name Vengeance.'

'Redesignation confirmed. Ship call sign is now Vengeance.' The onboard AI responded calmly.

'Prepare for departure,' Zan commanded, and the hangar wall before them dissolved, the illumination in the bay dimmed, and small points of light appeared in the floor providing tracks toward the boundless expanse of space. Spencer felt an almost imperceptible jolt as the Vengeance retracted its legs and the ship floated free. He grasped the controls, careful not to move them. 'Ease the left stick forward, gently!' Zan instructed, but Spencer had underestimated the sensitivity and the small craft suddenly sprang forward, accelerating hard as it left the hangar of *The Infinity*.

'Whoa!' Spencer exclaimed in exhilaration. Within moments they entered free space and his slightly heavy right hand caused their ship to pitch down hard. Zan moved to take control, but Spencer waved him off, pulling back more gently on the control column and the nose came up smoothly.

'Velocity 800 kilometres per second,' said Aila.

'Is that fast?' Asked Spencer.

'Fortunately not,' responded the usually taciturn Synth tartly.

'Then we'd better do something about that. How fast can this thing go?'

'It is capable of reaching 90% of lightspeed, nearly as fast as *The Infinity*, and more than plenty to hop around most solar systems. But be aware, the faster you go, the less reaction time you have if you need to manoeuvre. The AI will help you stay out of trouble, but you are the pilot and need to use that control carefully'

Spencer laughed gently. 'Yes, Mum.'

'What was that?'

'Nothing, just my little joke. Okay, let's see what this thing can do. Vengeance, find me an asteroid or two.'

'There is a small asteroid field ten parsecs from here at bearing 030 mark 651,' said the ship. A section of the canopy zoomed to show hundreds of light grey rocks, spread out over a few million kilometres.

'Set course,' Commanded Spencer.

'Course set.'

Spencer eased the left stick forward and a bar appeared in front of him at the base of the glass, rapidly growing in length as their speed increased.

'I suggest keeping to around point two five of lightspeed or less, and we'll be there in a minute,' advised Zan.

Within moments the asteroid field became visible to the naked eye, and the augmented zoom vanished to be replaced by what appeared to be targeting sights moving between the asteroids. Seconds later a large rock began to fill their view.

Spencer felt he was getting a feel for the little ship, and without hesitation banked to the left, slowed and pulled them round the asteroid in a neatly executed loop.

Zan was impressed. 'That was good, you are definitely getting a feel for this, sir!'

'It's like StarPilot, a game I used to play years ago,' responded Spencer, who was beginning to enjoy himself for the first time in a while. Using a combination of the controls he braked, then spun the ship on its axis, re-pointing the nose toward another smaller asteroid a little way off.

'Now, how do I shoot one of these things?'

'Activate weapons systems,' said Zan.

'Weapons active and online,' responded the AI.

'Targeting systems active.'

'Online.'

A targeting box appeared in red before Spencer.

'The AI can lock on to multiple targets simultaneously if you wish, or you can aim and shoot manually.'

'Oh, I'd like to do this myself.'

'Very well, centre the target, wait for the box to turn amber, then hit the button on the top of the right stick for the Muon Launcher, left for plasma guns. The launcher takes a few moments to charge and you can't fire continually for more than a couple of seconds.'

Spencer's lip curled into a savage grin that didn't go unnoticed by his companions. He visualised the sneering face of Haxenaar and pressed the plasma fire control. Blue beams of rippling energy raced out to the surface of the asteroid, strafing it and causing dust and debris to fly off into space. Again he pressed, and larger chunks began to break away.

'Activate muon launcher.'

'Launcher active and charging...' And then a few seconds later, 'Muon Launcher ready to fire.'

Spencer lined up on the asteroid again, the targeting box flicked to amber, and graphics zoomed in to frame the rock. A data readout displayed dimensions and mass, it was the size of an aircraft carrier on Earth and weighed about as much as a small mountain.

Spencer pressed the right button.

Pulses of green energy shot out from the launchers, converging on the space rock, instantly splitting it in half, and then into smaller fragments.

'Holy crap!' he exclaimed and Aila simulated a disapproving cough.

After two seconds the pulses ceased, and where there was once an asteroid weighing in at more than a million tons, there was now only fragments, rapidly spiralling away from each other.

'Whoa! Wow! That was intense!' Spencer was exultant.

'Spencer, these are powerful weapons. You can imagine the effect such a barrage would have on a colony or another ship.'

'Believe me, I can, and I'm counting on it.' Another worried frown passed over Zan's features.

'Okay, let's do some proper flying now,' said Zan, breaking the awkward silence that had fallen over them. Spencer grinned, now much happier than he had been in a good while. The destruction of the asteroid had felt like a sudden release of the tension he had been feeling for so long now.

They spent the next hour swooping, spinning, soaring and rolling around the asteroid field, then ventured further out toward a small planetoid and its surrounding three moons. Spencer whooped with delight, and even Zan and Aila seemed to be enjoying themselves after a while.

Later that evening, unbeknown to Spencer; Zan, Aila and Galen met in Zan's quarters for a private conversation.

'He is young, and he's had a lot to take in. He feels responsible for what happened to the Duranian outpost.

Anyone would struggle not to feel hatred toward Haxenaar after that.' Galen spoke quietly. 'But I also think he's a good person. He cares about the lives of others, and that is the most important quality in any Emperor of the Galaxy.'

'But does he have wisdom and judgment?' Aila voiced the concerns they all felt, especially following Spencer's behaviour earlier. 'He named the ship Vengeance!'

'And he was clearly imagining that asteroid to be a Zylaxxian ship when he blew it to pieces,' Zan said, unhappily.

Galen sighed. 'He does have a warrior within him, and I'm afraid that may be an absolute necessity given what we know he must face. It is our solemn duty to ensure he doesn't lose himself to anger and hatred, and becomes an Emperor of peace, not war.'

'Yes, but still, it may be that first he must fight a war.' Aila said quietly.

The three looked at each other in unspoken agreement.

16

Amy Alone:

At the suggestion of his companions, and because he desperately needed to experience some normality, Spencer returned home to a point just a few minutes after he last left.

His bedroom was unchanged of course, although it appeared that mum had been in and made his bed and picked up some clothing from the floordrobe (a family joke) and put it over the back of his gaming chair.

Spencer settled in for a couple of hours of gaming distraction. The latest update of BattleBlast was intense, and for just a little while, Spencer's focus was on beating Alfie Clarke, one of his gaming buddies, and maxing out his score.

But after a while, Spencer's mind began to wander back to the massacre at the Duranian outpost. Faceless victims of the Zylaxxian cruelty accused him of bringing death down upon them.

'Spencer, Spencer!' The voice became more insistent, snapping him out of his gaming-induced reverie.

'Spencer, I have a video call for you.' Bradlii informed him. 'It's Amy.'

'Amy, hi! Oh, it's so good to see you!'

Amy looked a little amused, 'But we saw each other earlier…'

'Well, yes, but I am always just so pleased to see you.' This whole time displacement thing was extremely confusing. Amy considered this for a moment and decided she was happy with that.

'So, you fancy meeting up tomorrow? We could go for a walk down by the canal?'

Spencer liked the sound of that very much. Very much indeed.

'Sure, what time?'

Amy started to speak, but the image of her face froze. 'Bradlii, what's happening?'

'The phone carrier signal appears to be being interrupted, Spencer, I am not sure why.'

The picture of Amy mid-word crumbled into digital dust and was replaced by a dark silhouette.

The figure turned toward the camera and stepped forward, the hideous features suddenly all too familiar.

'Hello Spencer, remember me?' The deep guttural tones of Haxenaar's voice sent a deep chill throughout Spencer.

'How could I forget? You killed those Duranians, and…'

'And I'm never going to rest until I find you and kill you, Spencer, and your family, and anyone who means anything to you.'

Spencer felt physically sick. The cold malevolence of

Haxenaar was beyond anything he had ever experienced.

But then his nausea began to give way to something else. Rage. Spencer felt fury building within him.

'Not if I find you first, Haxenaar, and call me Emperor you snivelling piece of crap.'

Haxenaar's red eyes seemed to widen, then narrow in pure hatred.

'Then I look forward to killing you myself, Spencer. I promise it will be long and slow and exceptionally painful.'

The transmission ended and within moments Spencer opened the wormhole and jumped back to *The Infinity*.

*

The three figures emerged through the glowing rip in space-time, black armour and cowls obscuring their forms. Moonlight bathed the street in a pale glow, and the streetlamps cast their orange sheen over the parked cars. Lights behind curtains flickered, as the inhabitants watched whatever was their choice of television programming.

Upstairs, bedroom windows betrayed late-night gaming.

The three figures spoke in low, guttural tones. One of them, perhaps the leader, consulted a small phone-like device that appeared to be giving directions.

Presently they stopped in front of a nondescript terraced house, with a faded No. 37 on the gatepost.

Inside, tucked up in bed, Amy Heartly flicked up a picture of Spencer on her Smartphone and gave it a little kiss before settling down to sleep.

In the living room, Amy's mother was settled in on the sofa, a cup of cocoa in one hand and a reality show on the

TV in the corner. She sighed as she relaxed, looking forward to her precious hour of downtime before she made tracks to bed.

It was the dog, a small cockapoo who heard it first. A scratching noise from the front door. Scarcely had Amy's mum had time to register than the door was opened, and a dark figure stepped through from the hallway. She opened her mouth to scream, but there was a flash and she slumped back into the sofa, the cocoa mug falling from her hand to spill its contents on the rug beneath. The dog yapped in distress before another flash silenced it.

The figure stepped over the prone creature and quickly scanned Amy's mother to confirm she was fully incapacitated. Indifferent that she was unconscious rather than dead, the figure nodded to the other two compatriots who turned and started up the stairs.

*

The room was very dark, but in the gloom, she could just about make out that it had form and structure. She wasn't cold, but the bench she was lying on was hard and unyielding. The total silence was very unsettling, and as Amy regained full consciousness she began to search her mind for any clue as to how she had got here, and where on earth she was.

There were none. She had absolutely no idea at all how she had got from her bed, to wherever she now was. Amy was not a girl prone to panic, but of course, she had heard stories of people, women, girls, being kidnapped, held against their will, and of unspeakable things that had happened to them.

She was scared, and fear wasn't a particularly familiar

emotion for her. Willing herself to stand up, she put one foot in front of another and forced herself to walk toward what she could just about make out to be some kind of door, odd in its semi-hexagonal shape though.

Summoning her courage, she banged her fist hard on the cold steel.

'Hey! Let me out! Let me out!'

She listened but heard no response.

Again she beat her fists on the door. 'I don't know who you are, but I want to get out of here, now!' She kicked the door hard, repeatedly so that it clanged dully.

Now there was a slight sound. To Amy, her senses heightened by her situation, perhaps it sounded like footsteps approaching. She shrank back from the door as the sounds paused outside. For several seconds there was nothing, and then the door slid aside to reveal a silhouette, backlit by a cold white haze. There was a flash, and Amy slumped to the floor.

17

Meeting:

Spencer paced the spacious meeting room onboard *The Infinity*. Windows along one side gave a spectacular view of a nebula, and a clear ceiling allowed visitors to contemplate the grandeur of the universe. Neither of which held much interest for him. He was both furious and very frightened.

Aila stood quietly to one side, while Galen, Zan and Qarak sat at the long conference table regarding him gravely.

Galen spoke first, his quiet but authoritative voice helping to bring some semblance of calm to the fraught atmosphere within the room. 'What exactly did he say Spencer?'

'That he would not rest until he had killed me, my family and everyone I hold dear to me.'

'I see. That is, unfortunately, a Zylaxxian custom, and I have little doubt he means it.'

'Well, thanks for that! Because I was beginning to think he might be kidding!' Spencer rounded on the old man, anger flashing in his eyes.

Galen didn't shrink, he merely held the palm of his hand up in a conciliatory gesture. Spencer immediately apologised.

'No need to apologise, Spencer, we are all on your side here. Always remember that. And we do understand how appallingly difficult this is for you. Please do sit down.'

Spencer pulled out a chair and slumped into it, his head in his hands. He felt like sobbing, but something stopped him. Aila quietly placed a cup of something hot and sweet next to him that she had obtained from one of the wall-mounted dispensers and Spencer took a sip. He had no idea what it was, but it tasted good and he needed something to remind him he was human.

Galen spoke carefully, his voice measured. 'Spencer, you must realise by now that you have become a pawn, an extremely important pawn, but a pawn nonetheless in a major galactic power struggle.'

Spencer nodded. This was hardly comforting though.

'The power of the Galactic Emperor stems not from military might, but from what that person symbolises. For aeons the Emperor or Empress has been a mirror that shows the rest of us what it means to be selfless, to lead by example, and to unite rather than divide. And all of these attributes are dangerous to the Zylaxxians because they must seek to divide if they are to conquer.'

As Galen spoke, Spencer began to understand, really understand, for the first time just what his role was and should be in all this. For days now, since he had first been whisked to Eloim III and met Volaria, he had felt simply carried by events. He had no sense of what he should actually be doing, what his purpose was, and how he might be instrumental in shaping events across the entire expanse of the galaxy.

'So my job here is to remind people, species, across the galaxy of what should be, not what the Zylaxxians want?'

'Exactly, and to lead them forward together, not back to the darkness that Haxenaar and his hordes represent.'

Finally, the confusion began to clear. Spencer realised that he, and he alone would need to be the example of the common values that united developed civilisations, and he would need to take a stand against Haxenaar and all that he stood for.

'Bloody hell. Bloody, bloody hell.'

Galen looked at him kindly. 'It's a lot to ask, Spencer, I know, we all know. But I also know this: there is something about you that makes me hopeful, that makes me believe you can do it.'

Spencer gazed at him, eyes wide. Despite the fraught circumstances, that might have been one of the most astonishing things anyone had ever said to him.

Zan, Aila, Astren and Qarak lifted their eyes to meet his. Astren spoke, 'We all think that, Spencer. You *are* the Emperor of the Galaxy, and even if you were chosen at random, somehow the galaxy ensured the right choice was made.'

Suddenly Bradlii interrupted. 'I am receiving a QEComms message from the Zylaxxian Executive.'

Spencer had already learned that QEComms was an acronym, standing for Quantum Entanglement

Communications. It was a technology developed thousands of years previously, that made use of the strange effect that two particles of matter entangled on the quantum level would reverberate in precise unison, no matter how vast the distance they might be apart. This reverberation could be manipulated to send communications and data across the galaxy.

Spencer looked to his companions, their faces were as shocked as his own. Galen nodded grimly.

Spencer took a deep breath and stood, taking a moment to steady himself. 'Bradlii, show us.'

A holoscreen materialised in front of them, and the graphics 'Incoming Communication' along with the Crest of the Zylaxxian Executive appeared and then faded to reveal the glowering face of Haxenaar. 'Spencer Edwards of Earth', he spat, the contempt in his guttural voice unmistakable, 'you and I have unfinished business that I am impatient to conclude. You will meet me at the coordinates contained in the datastream that accompanies this message.

'Just to incentivise you further, I will be accompanied by a delightful guest.' The image switched to show what was obviously some kind of holding cell. A figure was sitting in a corner and slowly lifted its head toward the camera. With absolute horror Spencer recognised Amy.

Spencer felt his legs begin to buckle, and he reached out toward the long conference table to steady himself. 'No!' he whispered.

Aila was there, as always, gently taking him by the elbow to steady him. 'This is pre-recorded, so he can't see you, Spencer.'

The horrible vision continued, 'Spencer Edwards, you have a standard galactic day to find your way here. If you don't, the next message I will send will be of me personally cutting this young girl into more parts than you can count.'

'Communication ended,' said Bradlii, quietly.

Spencer put his head in his hands. Tears welled in his eyes, and then he lifted his head. Something else was taking him over though. It was burning anger and determination. He knew with absolute certainty that Haxenaar would kill Amy regardless once she had served her purpose.

'We need a rescue plan. I'm going to get her.'

'That is extremely dangerous, Spencer,' Bradlii cautioned, 'Haxenaar wants you, Amy is simply the bait.'

'That's what I'm counting on Bradlii.'

Over the next hour, Spencer outlined his idea, and reluctantly his compatriots agreed it had a slim chance of working, although Spencer had to insist that he take full part in the mission, as the first duty of his colleagues was to his safety. Bradlii identified an extraordinary species that might be able to assist and Galen listened quietly, occasionally interjecting an observation or suggestion. When the meeting finally disbanded to allow the group some time for rest and food, he remained in the conference room making some QEComms calls.

*

Amy was standing in the centre of her cell when the door opened. As soon as she had heard the heavy footsteps approaching, she had willed herself to get to her feet. She was determined she wasn't going to cower in the corner regardless of who her captors might be, or what their plans were for her. Of course, she was scared, but she was damned sure she was going to do her best not to show it. She bunched her fists at her side and stood squarely to face the door.

The creature that entered was like nothing Amy had ever seen. Tall, of massive proportions and covered from head to toe in what looked like some kind of body armour. The huge head, with what appeared to be mechanical additions, was outlined against the light of the corridor outside.

'Come. Now.' Amy froze. 'Come. Now.' The apparition repeated. Amy shook her head. There was another bright flash and Amy crumpled to the floor.

*

She opened her eyes, groggy at first, and then her focus returned. She was held between two of these creatures, and was in some kind of gigantic dome, with an entire side open to the… Oh my god! Those were stars. Where the hell was she?

Some distance away another enormous figure was standing, gazing out into the blackness. It turned and strode toward her, stopping about two metres in front of where she stood.

'You are the one called Amy, yes?' a similarly accented, yet even deeper voice rasped. She nodded, her mouth dry.

'Good. That is good.'

It was then that Amy found her voice. 'Who the hell are you? Are you some kind of pervert? Why am I here? You are going to be in big trouble. You take me home right now, you dickhead.'

The figure started. 'I am Haxenaar, Grand Leader of the Zylaxxian Executive.'

'Never heard of you. Is this some stupid Cosplay crap? I want to go home right now, and if you don't take me you'll be sorry. You think you're a big man kidnapping young girls, bringing them here to, where the hell are we anyway? I'm going to make sure you get into a heap of trouble you absolute tosser.'

Haxenaar regarded her carefully. She was little more than half his height, and he could probably snap her in half with one of his great gloved hands, yet she glared up at him with furious defiance, and, it would seem to the Zylaxxian, surprisingly little fear. Haxenaar was accustomed to those brought before him begging for their lives while crying and wailing or less satisfyingly accepting their grim fate with resigned stoicism. He wasn't acquainted with teenage girls from Earth and was somewhat taken aback by her ferocious attack.

But Amy wasn't finished and was resolved not to be cowed. 'You've got issues mate. What is this, some kind of theme park ride? Is that where I am, some freakshow's private funfair? You wait till I post about this, everyone will know what total losers you are, you and your mates.'

Haxenaar drew himself up to his full height, but still she wasn't intimidated. 'Enough!' He bellowed.

'No, I'll say when it's enough you scumbag. I'm not done. I'm gonna kick you in the nuts if you have any.' Amy struggled in vain to break free and Haxenaar, despite himself, took a step backwards.

'Coward!' she yelled. The guards held her tight, but Haxenaar had had his fill. 'Take her away,' he hissed, and the guards dragged her backwards, Amy continuing to hurl insults at him until she was mercifully out of earshot.

18

The Crystalline Belt:

The Infinity re-entered normal space-time approximately half a million kilometres from the Proteus Field. 'Just look at it!' said Astren quietly. Qarak, Aila, Spencer and Galen stood gazing out of the expansive control room screen at an incredible sight that no human had ever seen before.

'We are receiving incoming messages from the warning buoys, patching it through.' Zan flicked at a holo-control in front of him.

'This is an automated warning system. The Proteus Field is recognised as a protected and hazardous environment for all space-travelling species. You are forbidden entry under treaty 37823.9 of the Algeron Accord. Please turn around and retreat from this area.' The message then began to repeat.

'Are we completely sure we have to do this?' said Zan, '*The Infinity* is not immune to the Proteus Field, and there is a reason no ship has ventured in here for thousands of years.'

'We have no choice Zan,' said Galen gently. 'It is by the Emperor's command, and it is necessary.'

Zan took a deep breath, 'Very well, approaching the outer perimeter of the field in five… four… three…'

The sheer scale of the asteroid field was almost beyond the ability of a human being, or any being for that matter, to process. It was the staggering beauty that belied such deadly danger that was most difficult to comprehend, for the asteroids of the Proteus Field were not only gargantuan but were almost entirely crystalline. And, to Spencer's astonishment, they glowed.

'This is life, Spencer,' Aila spoke quietly, 'But it is very different from any you will have encountered.' Spencer nodded silently, he was struggling to find any words to describe what he was seeing. Bradlii hadn't been exaggerating when he had referred to the species as "extraordinary".

As the enormous crystals slowly wandered through space, the intensity of their glow seemed to wax and wane according to their proximity to others of their kind. Some shone predominantly with colours from the blue end of the spectrum, others from the red, and still others with an almost endless variation of shades in between. Occasionally, energy seemed to arc in highly mobile yet delicate filaments between them.

'They communicate in a variety of ways, both physical and others more akin to telepathy,' noted Galen.

In between the giants, there were many smaller crystals, some appearing to move independently, others in small patterns,… *what did they look like?* Spencer recognised the patterns movement. Yes, that's it! Like shoals of small slow-moving fish.

'Those are the offspring, some of them barely a million years old I should think,' said Galen. 'Although they have no doubt registered our presence, the Galactic Database suggests they will be largely indifferent to us, as we barely register as a life-form to them. They may, however, be much more interested in our ship's power grid, as they draw their energy from the environment, including the dark matter that surrounds us all.'

'Okay, so they don't care much for us, but perhaps we can offer something they do care about and use it to persuade them to help.' Spencer said.

'How much more appealing might an enormous Zylaxxian battlecruiser be?' Asked Zan.

'A lot, I should think' said Qarak with a wry smile. 'Provided we can find a way to persuade some of these Proteans, or whatever they are called, to come along for the ride.'

'Bradlii, you're the one with access to pretty much all the knowledge in the Galaxy' Spencer challenged.

'Well, yes, I suppose I am, what would you like to know?' The AI responded.

'How do we communicate with them?'

'There isn't much known, even in the ancient records. It is clear that thousands of years ago early spacefarers encountered the field, and that it led to the destruction of a number of starships. As a result, a cordon was set up around their space, effectively to quarantine it, and so that the inhabitants be left undisturbed for their benefit and the wellbeing and safety of everyone else. Data suggests that the Ixenarians may have managed to initiate some kind of communication with them, but the details are extremely vague.'

'The Ixenarians!' Galen exclaimed. Spencer and the others turned to him sharply.

'Who are the Ixenarians?'

'One of the most ancient of races, very little is known about them other than they were once a powerful and advanced civilisation. Legend has it they retreated to the outermost regions of the galaxy several millennia ago, to live lives dedicated to the pursuit of science and the arts. They were, or indeed are if they still exist, an isolationist race. Certainly, no-one has had any direct contact with a living Ixenarian for centuries.'

'That is most interesting,' said Bradlii, 'Because I am detecting an energy signature, deep within the Protean Field that, according to the limited information I have available, has all the hallmarks of an Ixenarian negative ion drive.'

Spencer came to a decision. 'We don't have a lot of time. Zan, take us in, slowly.'

The Infinity's engine nacelles glowed a faint blue as Zan gently increased thrust. In less than a minute, alarms began to sound, but with a gesture, the pilot shut them off. With almost minimal momentum, the ship crossed the quarantine boundary, and the occupants on the command bridge held their collective breaths.

There was a soft bump that seemed to come from above. They all turned their gaze toward the ceiling. 'One has passed through our energy shields and latched on, whispered Zan, and with a wave of his hand the ceiling became transparent to show a small crystal boulder, glowing a soft purple, attached to the outer hull of the ship. 'Here comes another one…' and within moments another slightly larger crystal bumped into *The Infinity* and with a bright flash seemed to almost fuse itself to the ship.

'Energy banks are beginning to drain,' Zan intoned. 'I'm transferring reserve power to back up storage capacitors. That should buy us some time before...'

'Before?' Spencer asked sharply.

'Before we are dead in space, and they begin to disassemble, or rather digest the ship atom by atom.'

*

'I think it's some kind of probe, possibly a sentry, fully automated and very, very old. Length is approximately thirty-two point three metres along the axis.' Zan was running scans of the dodecahedron-shaped object that now lay ten kilometres off the starboard bow of *The Infinity*. 'It is still very much operational though and has actively scanned us.'

'Can we open communications with it?' asked Astren.

'I'm trying, but not getting a response other than an automated multi-lingual message warning us to vacate the area immediately.'

'We need to get aboard!' said Spencer decisively.

'There is a hatch, on the lower portion of the probe, probably for maintenance access. Penetrating sensors show there is a breathable atmosphere inside.'

'Then Astren, Aila and Qarak, you're with me. How do we do it?' Spencer asked.

Aila spoke, 'Spencer, you should remain here. Your safety is our first priority.'

Spencer felt his frustration begin to rise. 'Right, listen up everyone. You too, Zan. You keep telling me how important I am, well okay, I'll go along with you on that for the moment, but there is no way I'm going to be the kind of Emperor who sits back and lets everyone else take the risks. If you want me to lead, then I'll bloody well try to lead. And you all need to know that means that I am going to take some chances sometimes, and you'd all better get used to that.' Spencer flushed, he wasn't used to venting in this way.

'That bastard Haxenaar has my girlfriend, and I am going to do whatever it takes to get her back and destroy him and his plans in the process. Now you are either with me or well…' He faltered, his anger subsiding, 'Or you're not. But I *am* going to do this.'

He looked around at the stunned faces of his fellow crewmates, but then Astren began to smile.

'And this is why the Universe chose you to be Emperor of the Galaxy, Spencer,' said Galen quietly. 'We are all with you, come what may.'

The others nodded slowly, then more vigorously. Even Qarak grinned, and then slapped him on the shoulder before, with a horrified look as if he realised he had crossed a line, he stepped back and mumbled 'Sorry sire!'.

Spencer was delighted though. He slapped Qarak on the shoulder right back and beamed at them all. Suddenly his mood had brightened. They were at last going to do something. 'Alright, now that's sorted, let's get to work. So, how do we get over there?'

19

Communication and Escape:

The four of them stood facing the airlock door. Zan had carefully moved *The Infinity* to within five hundred metres of the Ixenarian probe.

Aila placed a simple clear helmet over Spencer's head, and his smartsuit then seemed to stretch to meet and seal with it. 'Fitting complete and airtight,' said the suit, in its most businesslike tone.

'Now we put this on your back,' Aila took what looked like a small plastic rucksack from a nearby locker, and held it in place, again Spencer was aware of his suit moving and flexing. 'Connection complete.'

'One more thing,' said Aila, and passed to each member of the team what was instantly recognisable as a small pistol.

'Spencer, this is a plasma pistol. Please don't use it unless absolutely necessary. Just press it to your hip and your suit will hold it in place. Bradlii will ensure the safety is on unless, well, something happens and you have to use it. Bradlii, can you interface with the gun?'

'Already done.'

'Okay, well, when we step out of the airlock we will be floating in free space, Spencer. Your smartsuit and Bradlii will do most of the work, but you will need to point yourself at your target and push your hands out in front of you.' She demonstrated. Spencer began to chuckle.

'Like Superman, you mean?'

Aila looked nonplussed. 'I have no idea who you are referring to, Spencer.'

Bradlii chimed in, 'Earth comic book hero from the 1930s, very popular.'

'Yes, alright, like Superman Spencer. We will be alongside you if you get into difficulty.'

Spencer took a deep breath. 'Okay, I'm ready. Let's do this!'

At a gesture from Astren, the airlock door dematerialised, and Spencer felt a sudden change in pressure. It wasn't uncomfortable, just unexpected and only lasted a second or two until his suit adjusted. An augmented reality display activated inside his helmet showing distance to target along with what appeared to be a flight path and various other data that meant little to Spencer, and then the voice of Bradlii came through clearly. 'All suit systems are ready and online, Spencer.'

'You sound like you're inside my head, Bradlii!'

'I am, in a fashion. My voice is being transmitted directly to the cochlear nerve in your inner ear. It means that if necessary, I can ensure you hear me, but no one else does. But for this situation, it just makes communication easier.'

Spencer wasn't exactly sure how he felt about that, but now was not the time to ponder on it. 'Now step forward and give yourself a gentle push off from the lip.' Astren and Aila were right alongside him, Qarak immediately behind.

Taking a deep breath, Spencer did as they instructed. 'Whoo! Whoa!'

The sensation was like nothing else Spencer had ever felt, he was "flying", well, at least gently floating, he tried to turn, but of course, his feet had no purchase on anything and for a second he began to flail. Then he felt the firm grasp of Aila on his right upper arm, and that of Astren on his left.

'Okay, I'm okay.'

'It is a little disorientating at first, so just give it a moment.' Astren advised.

Spencer's breathing slowed, and he began to feel much calmer. It wasn't an unpleasant sensation, just a very peculiar one.

'Now lean forward, smoothly, and push your hands out in front of you.'

Spencer did as he was instructed and became aware of a gentle but firm push in his back from the manoeuvring pack placed there. He looked to his left and grinned at Astren, who gave a rare smile back.

'This is good! I'm getting the hang of this!'

Astren gently let go, as did Aila, and Spencer was flying on his own. He looked around, and the sight that met his eyes was truly awe-inspiring as colossal crystals hove into view, suspended against the intense blackness of space. Slowly the hatch on the Ixenarian probe became larger, and when the augmented reality in his helmet registered a hundred metres to the target, Astren suddenly swooped ahead, performing a perfectly executed pirouette and somersault before landing delicately on her feet immediately below the hatch. Due to the angle, and of course, there being no actual up or down in space, she was now perpendicular to Spencer who was on his final approach. Instinctively he pulled his hands back and swung his feet downward. It wasn't elegant, but he did land and then drop to one knee before straightening up and turning to watch Aila and Qarak also touch down gently onto the probe's hull.

'Not bad, Spencer!' Astren nodded appreciatively, 'For your first time in free space.'

'Bradlii, are you able to interface with the hatch controls?' Spencer heard Aila say through his comms link.

'I'm trying, but at the moment I am locked out by various algorithmic security protocols.' The AI responded.

'Five minutes of oxygen remaining,' said the suit.

If we don't get access in the next sixty seconds we will have to return to the ship, although I can remain of course. Synths don't need oxygen,' Aila explained for the benefit of Spencer, who nodded his understanding. 'Bradlii, are you detecting any immediate threats or security countermeasures of concern from within the probe?'

'I am not, but I think it prudent to assume there are some.'

'Agreed, everyone please move away ten metres,' instructed Aila.

Spencer was about to protest, but Astren and Qarak quickly pulled him backwards with them as Aila examined the seals around the edge of the hatch before suddenly jabbing her fingers, like blades into the tiny gaps. Without making a sound her artificial muscles, evidently considerably stronger than those of an organic, started to take the strain and slowly the hatch began to give way.

Stepping through, Spencer felt as if he was entering an entirely alien space. The chamber was spherical, at least initially, and then as Aila pulled the hatch closed, it began to stretch and change form until it became a short tunnel with a glowing portal at the far end. 'Pressure equalized,' said his suit, and then 'Breathable atmosphere confirmed.' As the suit AI spoke the words, Spencer felt the return of weight, and he and his companions floated slowly down to what was now the floor. Their clear helmets then retracted into themselves forming a collar, and Spencer took his first lungful of air. It was a little musty, but not unpleasant.

Zan's voice came over the communications channel. 'There are now nine crystals attached, and the energy drain is becoming critical. Anything you guys can do over there to help now would be a good time to do it.'

'Don't move!' shouted Aila, holding her hand aloft in warning. 'I am detecting movement approaching from multiple vectors.' Spencer froze, and as he did so, three machines, shaped rather like mechanical birds of prey, emerged from the darkness and surrounded them. One emitted a tone and then something that sounded to Spencer like static.

Bradlii said, 'We are being challenged and asked to identify ourselves.'

'You can understand them?' asked Spencer, perhaps needlessly.

'Yes, it is an old machine dialect dating back many

thousands of years, but the meaning is clear. They are armed and their weapons are charged.'

'Tell them we mean no harm, and that we seek only their wisdom and help.'

Bradlii emitted a short burst of wavering tones interspersed with static.' There was a pause, and then, 'They are repeating their question – who are we?'

Spencer drew himself up to his full height and said, with as much confidence as he could muster, 'I am Spencer Edwards, Emperor of the Galaxy.'

There was another pause, and the devices seemed to be conferring, and then the first one spoke. 'Identity confirmed. Welcome, Emperor Spencer.'

Some thirty minutes later they returned to *The Infinity*, and Spencer used his portable wormhole initiator to return home for a few hours while the rest of the crew continued to work on the rescue plan he had put in motion.

*

'Spencer, have you finished your homework yet?' Mum called up the stairs.

'Yes, don't worry, nearly done.' Spencer had spent the first half an hour trying to persuade Bradlii to help him out with some algebra, but the AI had flatly refused, quoting various logical and moral justifications for his intransigence. Spencer had considered attempting to order him to be more compliant, but something had held him back from doing so. Reluctantly, Spencer had realised it was his conscience, and that, damn it, Bradlii was annoyingly in the right.

So for the next twenty minutes, Spencer had struggled

to concentrate but persevered, and then eventually politely asked Bradlii to take a look at his work.

'You are mostly correct, Spencer. Well done.'

Patronising jumped up mobile phone, thought Spencer to himself, but bit his lip and instead said, 'Thank you Bradlii, you did the right thing.'

'I know.' So unbearably smug.

After an hour of BattleBlast in an attempt to take his mind off Amy, tea was a rather subdued affair. Mum tried her best to be cheery and put on her brave face as she always did, but Hassan had received his redundancy notice that day and had just a few weeks before he would leave his job. He forced a smile, 'Don't worry Spencer, something will come along.' Mum put her hand on his stepdad's broad shoulder, 'It will love, you're too good a catch to be job hunting for long.'

Little Mo had gurgled a bit and thrown some spaghetti on the floor as he often liked to do. Spencer idly wondered why mum persisted in giving him foods that had such a potential for making a mess, but truthfully he was just pleased to have a few hours of normality with his family.

Later that evening, after everyone else had gone to sleep, Spencer was awoken by Bradlii's voice in his ear. 'I'm afraid we have to return, Spencer.' Rubbing the sleep from his eyes, Spencer and Bradlii jumped back to *The Infinity*, now more than eight thousand light-years away from Spencer's bedroom.

20

The Rescue:

Haxenaar's flagship glinted in the light of the nearby star, its awe-inspiring gloss black hulk festooned with needle-sharp antenna and weaponry. Nearby, three Zylaxxian cruisers stood sentry, their formation carefully arranged to protect their leader from all possible angles of potential attack.

As a result of Zan's skilful piloting, *The Infinity* had re-entered space-time less than a hundred thousand kilometres from the coordinates embedded in the transmission Haxenaar had sent a standard galactic day previously.

'Incoming communication,' Zan turned to Spencer who nodded. The face of Haxenaar appeared on a floating holoscreen, a cruel smile playing at his mouth as he gloated in his victory. 'Welcome Spencer Edwards of pitiful Earth. I am gratified that you have found the courage to face the inevitable. Prepare to transfer to my vessel immediately.'

As he spoke, the hangar bay doors on *The Infinity* dematerialised and the two Landers launched. One heading directly toward Haxenaar's battleship, the other immediately veering off toward the heavily-armed behemoth. Within moments, it began releasing scores of small crystalline boulders that immediately began to latch on to the huge Zylaxxian craft.

The exultant face of Haxenaar turned to surprise and then fury. 'And now you will die!'

As negotiated with the Ixenarian probe's AI acting as an intermediary, the Proteans immediately began to feast on the Zylaxxian's ship's high-capacity energy grid, and the image of Haxenaar began to break up.

'So far, so good,' muttered Zan. 'Now for the hard part.'

Along with the two Landers, *The Infinity* had launched a third ship. Coated in a substance composed of carbon nanotubes that absorbed more than 99% of the light that hit it, it was rendered near invisible to the naked eye. Following just metres behind the *Vengeance* Lander, it was all but undetectable for the short distance to the Zylaxxian flagship.

The *Vengeance* approached the illuminated docking port, but at the last second veered off, returning to *The Infinity* and leaving the port open for the stealth craft to latch on to.

Onboard the stealth ship, the real Spencer was waiting, the holographic image of him on the control deck of *The Infinity* having served its purpose, and with him were twenty of Galen's hand-picked Androsians, in lightweight battle armour, all carefully checking and rechecking their personal arsenals of unique weaponry.

The Infinity opened fire on the first of the Zylaxxian cruisers with her twin heavy muon launchers. At such close range, the impact was spectacular. Caught entirely by surprise, the Zylaxxian ship split in two and then exploded violently.

Spencer and his squad of chidwas felt the floor shake as they poured through the open docking port and into the dark interior of the giant vessel. Within seconds they confronted two Zylaxxians, but they were immediately cut down by two Androsians who threw razor-sharp glowing three-pointed stars.

The squad moved almost as if coordinated by telepathy. Whenever Zylaxxians were encountered, Androsians quickly eliminated them, never even seeming to break stride. A core of five chidwas kept Spencer shielded and running while their team members continued to clear a path as they headed deeper into the ship.

In his vast dome, several decks above, Haxenaar stood in front of a holoscreen and roared with rage. 'Bring that Earth girl to me.' Four of his elite guards immediately departed to do his bidding.

The Androsians and Spencer had entered a dimly lit corridor where handheld sensors indicated a door. Two chidwas crouched and fitted small explosives to the frame, before retreating and detonating them. The door crumpled, and with a hard kick fell inward. The two entered, then signalled for Spencer and the other three to step through.

There was a cry of pain, and inside one, Androsian was clutching his knee where it was clear the occupant had kicked him. It was then that Amy looked up and saw Spencer.

'Spencer? Spencer! Oh my God!' To Spencer's delight, she flew at him and grabbed him into a tight hug. 'What? How? I don't understand! How are you here?'

Spencer held her for a moment, then gently disengaged from her arms. 'I will explain everything, but right now we need to get you off this ship and to safety.'

'Ship? What do you mean ship? Are we at sea?' Amy's confusion was clear.

'Not exactly Amy, but come on, we have to get moving, and fast.'

Taking her hand, Spencer led her back through the ruined doorway and out into a plasma firefight. The chidwas immediately activated interlocking personal shields, and formed a barrier between the advancing Zylaxxians and their precious charges. The onslaught was fierce, and the shields glowed with the heat of the energy they were dissipating but the Androsians pressed on, heading back toward the docking port where their stealth ship waited.

Aboard Haxenaar's flagship, the power was failing as the Proteans drained the life from the enormous ship. Lights flickered, screens failed and the glow from the great engines faded into nothingness. Haxenaar strode from the command dome, unsheathing his hideous blade as he did so. The death of Spencer was now the only thought on his mind.

As Spencer, Amy and their entourage rounded a corner, now just fifty metres from the docking port, they were joined by the other chidwas, who now provided a moving circle of defence around Spencer and Amy, with those at the rear firing backwards down the corridor at the Zylaxxians in pursuit. Thirty metres... twenty metres... the docking port hove into view.

'Spencer Edwards of Earth!' The roar from behind them was riven with fury. Spencer looked over his shoulder to see the terrifying form of Haxenaar, blade drawn, pounding down the corridor perhaps thirty metres to their rear.

Spencer, Amy and the chidwas threw themselves through the open hatchway and into the stealth ship.

'I will kill you, Spencer Edwards, I will kill you and your friends.' A sonic grenade from one of the chidwas stopped him perhaps just ten paces from the hatchway where Spencer stood.

Their eyes met, but this time, Spencer didn't feel abject terror, in fact, he actually smiled at the enormous Zylaxxian, 'Perhaps you will Haxenaar, but not today.'

The door materialised, as black as the rest of the craft, and the docking latches disengaged. The last thing they saw on a holoscreen was Haxenaar standing at the port, his great head thrown back as he howled in fury.

Zan pitched *The Infinity* over, and Galen transmitted a signal. The Proteans on the hull of the Zylaxxian battleship began to disengage. 'Holford Clamp activated,' said Zan calmly as they flew over the young crystals, scooping them up in the device's electromagnetic field and drawing them into one of the cargo bays.

A holoscreen appeared, and Qarak, at the controls of the stealth ship, his face a little flushed from his exertions, said, 'Matching heading and speed now.'

'Speed and heading matched,' confirmed Zan, 'Hangar bay open,' and then seconds later, with jubilation in his voice, 'We've got them! Multi-drive engaging.'

The Infinity released four homing mines in its wake, which immediately began tracking toward the still pursuing cruiser before space stretched and snapped as *The Infinity* vanished.

*

Spencer, Amy, Aila and Astren stood looking out of the conference room windows. Amy was quiet, which in itself was a rarity, but Spencer held her hand and hadn't let go since they had escaped from the Zylaxxian so intent on killing them.

'So we are on an actual spaceship, right?' Amy said softly, her eyes shining.

'Yep. An actual spaceship, Amy.'

'And how are you here, Spencer? Why are you here?'

Spencer looked uncomfortable. 'I, uh, um, there's something you need to know about me, Amy.'

For a moment she looked nonplussed, then she frowned and nodded at Astren. 'Is it about her?'

'Oh no, nothing like that!' Spencer smiled, and then on impulse kissed her. 'Amy, er, I'm not quite sure how to say this, but well here goes, I'm, er, I'm the Emperor of the Galaxy.'

Amy stared at him and then began to laugh. 'You! You're the Emperor of the Galaxy? I've never heard such a load of crap in my life!'

Spencer said nothing but just held her gaze. Aila spoke, 'It's true Amy, Spencer is the Emperor of the Galaxy, and he has risked his life to rescue you from a ruthless and deadly tyrant who wants to depose him and take his place.'

Amy's mouth dropped open. She looked like she was struggling to speak. 'I know Amy, it's a lot to take in isn't it?' Spencer said gently.

Amy took a deep breath, 'So you are saying my boyfriend is the Emperor of the Galaxy, right?' She looked around and Aila and Astren both nodded.

Amy thought for a moment, evidently processing this. Then she cocked her head to one side in a way that Spencer found most endearing, 'That's pretty cool!'.

21

Home for a Moment:

Spencer and Amy stepped out of the wormhole and into Spencer's rather untidy bedroom. Spencer was immediately somewhat embarrassed. This wasn't quite how he had hoped Amy would first see his bedroom, especially with his pants on the floor. Shamefacedly he kicked them under his bed and turned to Amy. 'Okay?'

'I think so, that was quite an experience... it felt like…'

'Like falling for a moment, right?'

'Yes, a bit like a roller-coaster, but I'm alright now.'

'Right, now we need to get you out and home without my mum, or Hassan spotting you.'

'You're not ashamed of me are you, Spencer?' said Amy a little playfully.

'You know that's not true, but I don't want to explain how you came to be in my bedroom without them knowing if you get my drift.'

Amy nodded. 'Okay, so how do we get me out of here?'

'Spencer? Is that you?' Mum's voice rang up the stairs.

'Yes mum, it's me.'

'I didn't hear you come in!'

'Sorry, I just needed to get something sorted, I'll be down in a moment.'

Spencer turned to Amy and raised his finger to his lips.

'Damn, this isn't going to be easy...' There were the sounds of footsteps on the stairs. Spencer looked panicked, 'Quick, under my bed!'

Amy grimaced but didn't hesitate, dropping nimbly to the floor and rolling sideways until she was concealed.

The door opened, 'Spencer, there you are! Is everything alright?'

'Yes, mum, totally! Why wouldn't it be?'

'Well we haven't seen a lot of you these past few days, and you do look rather tired sweetie.'

'No, I'm good, thanks, mum. Just busy with school work, you know how it is.'

Mum smiled and frowned at the same time. In a way she alone somehow seemed to manage. 'This room desperately needs a tidy, Spencer! I don't mind doing your washing, but I'm not picking it all up off the floor for you. You're not a prince and I'm not a servant.' Mum chided.

'No, no, sorry, I will sort it.'

Mum reached down to pick up a pair of joggers on the floor right by his bed. Spencer held his breath.

'Just put them in your wash bag, okay?'

'I will, I promise.'

'Alright then, tea in half an hour, and I'm doing something extra nice for Hassan to cheer him up.'

As soon as Mum left, Spencer gave Amy the all-clear.

'Phew, that was a bit too close.'

'Yes, and I spent more time under your bed than I would like, it's not a nice place, Spencer! I was down there with several pairs of your underpants.'

Spencer felt his face turn crimson. 'I'm so sorry Amy, I'm going to sort that just in case we ever have to do this again, I promise.'

Luckily, it was at that point that Mum called up to say she was just popping to the corner store to get some mango chutney and would Spencer watch Mo for a few minutes? So after waiting a moment, Amy was able to slip out after Spencer arranged for them to meet again later that evening for a return to *The Infinity*.

In the meantime, it was nice to tuck into a plate of Mum's special Chicken Madras and play a little with Mo.

22

Andromeda:

The enormous Zylaxxian fleet had been assembling in orbit around the blue hypergiant star Eta Carinae for more than the past year. This enormous star, nearly two hundred times the size of Earth's sun, and burning four times hotter, radiated simply staggering amounts of energy into the surrounding space. The Zylaxxian fleet, parked in a geosynchronous orbit more than forty AU out, was bathed in the hot blue light of this nuclear fusion-powered monster.

In between the cruisers and larger destroyers floated gargantuan constructions that looked much like angular spiderwebs, stretching out hundreds of thousands of kilometres in every direction.

To any observer, their purpose would be hard to fathom, but to an engineer, they would be sinister in the extreme. These were immense energy collectors, dormant at the moment, but designed to harness a single gigantic burst of energy and channel it for a split second before being completely obliterated in the process.

In between the myriad ships scurried small supply and maintenance craft and drones, endlessly attending to the needs of their masters, as the grid inexorably grew little by little.

*

The door chimed and then dematerialised to admit Galen and Aila. Spencer and Amy had been enjoying a little peace and quiet over a few snacks helpfully supplied by the dispenser in his quarters. The Parathean Mingle-chips had been a particular revelation, quite like crisps but with an epic crunch and flavours that seemed to evolve in your mouth to mimic an entire feast, while the Denosian Doozberries were simply spectacular, beautiful little balloons of juice that exploded with a tangy pop.

Spencer sighed and waved his visitors to the comfortable couches that surrounded the table where the mountain of delicacies resided. 'I have a feeling you aren't bringing me good news,' he said resignedly. Amy glanced at him, she felt likewise.

'I'm sorry Spencer, no, I'm not.' Galen's usually impassive features betrayed real concern. 'I've received word that a Zylaxxian fleet, comprised of many hundreds of ships, has been sighted assembling in orbit of a blue giant some five thousand light-years away.'

'Okay, so what is it you think they are doing?' The news was alarming enough in itself, but Spencer sensed there was worse to come.

'Intelligence suggests this is a fleet with a very specific purpose. There are constructions in place that appear to be for the purpose of energy harvesting and transmission.'

Spencer thought back to the warning from Volaria when they had first met.

He closed his eyes. 'Andromeda!' he said quietly.

Galen nodded gravely. 'That is our assessment too.'

Spencer stood silently, gazing out of the enormous viewing portal that dominated this area of his luxurious quarters, while Galen quickly explained to Amy his fears. She listened attentively and asked one or two pointed questions. When Galen had finished she slid from her couch and joined Spencer at his side.

'Heavy stuff, Spencer, these Zylaxxians are properly dangerous aren't they?'

Spencer nodded glumly. Two chidwas had succumbed to terrible injuries. He sighed and turned back to the virtual window.

'Just look at it, Amy. It's so huge, so vast, there's room enough for everybody a million times over. So why does there have to be conflict, why…' He paused, exasperated, 'Why all… this?'

Amy understood. 'Some people just can't help it, Spencer, they seem to want to control and hurt others. It's what they do.'

Spencer shook his head thoughtfully, then straightened. 'You're right Amy, but not on my watch. Someone's got to stop them, and I guess that someone is me. Or rather us. Are you in?'

Amy reached for his hand and gave him a little smile.

'Who's asking? The Emperor of the Galaxy or the slightly

geeky guy I love?'

At that moment, despite everything, Spencer felt as if his heart might burst. 'Me, Amy, the guy who loves you too, more than anything.'

'In that case, how could I refuse? The other bloke I might have turned down.'

23

Training and The Spear of Rigel:

Spencer and Amy arrived at the door to *The Infinity's* fitness centre. Amy was now replete in her own Smartsuit, which Spencer found extremely appealing. Amy had initially appeared a little embarrassed, but as soon as the suit had begun its fitting and adjusting routine her eyes had widened, and then she had smiled with delight. 'Just so long as Lisa Catchpole or Mehak Patel doesn't see me in this, I'll be fine.' Lisa was, of course, Amy's nemesis back on Earth, but Spencer reassured her that she looked great (and she really did, he thought to himself), her long glossy black hair tumbling down over the shoulders of her dark blue smartsuit.

'You don't look too bad yourself ,Spencer,' Amy grinned back and elbowed him in the ribs. Spencer, who was naturally pretty shy about such matters flushed hotly, but was secretly delighted.

'If you two have finished admiring each other, then it is time for training to commence.' Astren stood at the far side of a large brightly lit open room, with a firm matted floor. Around the sides were ledges and various climbing frames. It was not unlike a school gymnasium, Spencer thought to himself, only a lot posher.

'Spencer, place me on the floor, and I will record this,' instructed Bradlii, and as Spencer did so, a holoimage appeared of a middle-aged blue-skinned man in what looked suspiciously like a judo suit. The image turned to Spencer and Amy, 'It's me, Bradlii. I thought this projection might be useful. Spencer, in here you are not the Emperor of the Galaxy, you are a student. Do you understand?'

'Okay…' Spencer was beginning to feel some mounting trepidation.

Without warning, Astren launched herself into a rapid tumbling routine, complete with twists and kicks that saw her cross the floor in less than two seconds. Before Spencer could react, her foot, held aloft in a perfectly executed kick, was just millimetres from his face. After a momentary pause, Astren lightly tapped him on the tip of his nose with her toes before slowly, and with perfect precision, lowering her leg to the ground so that she stood just a couple of paces in front of him.

Spencer gulped, and Amy hooted with delight. 'Wow! Astren, that was incredible! Do it again!'

Qarak spoke, 'Astren can do that because she has trained for many years, and has mastered and honed her reflexes to the point that she has complete control over her body. You don't have the luxury of that time, so with Bradlii's help we are going to programme your smartsuits to, well, speed up the process.'

Aila chimed in, 'That doesn't mean they can do it all for you though. You will have to initiate the movements, speed up your reactions, and,' Aila looked at Spencer in a way that he felt was a bit too pointed, 'get considerably fitter', as she handed them both gloves that once pulled on seemed to fuse with their sleeves. 'The gloves will work with your suits, and protect your hands from… excessive damage.'

The Bradlii-image spoke next. 'Spencer, strike Astren.'

'What?'

'Strike her, now.' The AI instructed.

'I'm not going to hit Astren.' Spencer said flatly.

'Don't worry, you won't.' Qarak said and broke into a rare smile.

Spencer was starting to become a little irritated. They all just seemed a bit too smug for his liking. He knew his reflexes were actually pretty good because BattleBlast wasn't for wimps after all. Trying not to give any warning signals he suddenly struck out, but Astren instantly moved aside, turning, and catching his fist while yanking it downwards so that he had no choice but to drop to his knees.

'Ow! Astren, that bloody hurt!' It properly did, and Spencer felt his cheeks sting from the humiliation. He tapped his badge for a self-e-scan and it responded with 'Minor trauma to the flexor carpi radialis.' Spencer looked accusingly at Astren.

'Then get up and do better,' was her rather cold response.

Spencer shuffled to his feet and stood before her again. This time he swung with his left, but Astren simply ducked and then kicked him sharply on his knee.

'Astren! For God's sake!'

'Do you think the Zylaxxians will be so forgiving,

Spencer?' The Bradlii-image said softly. 'Because they will not, and you definitely won't get a second chance. Now, Amy, you try.'

Amy set her jaw, she looked absolutely determined and squared up to Qarak. 'Alright big boy, let's see what you've got.'

She dropped to the ground, leg sweeping outward and nearly catching Qarak by surprise. He hopped backwards and smiled his approval.

'Amy, how did you do that?' Spencer was agape.

'Five years of karate, Spencer. Didn't I mention that?'

'No, you blinking well didn't! Great! My girlfriend's a ninja and better at fighting than me.' Spencer rolled his eyes and Amy blew him a kiss.

'Right, now I want you both to follow the moves Astren and Qarak make, and your suits are going to attempt to acclimatise to your musculature and kinaesthetic abilities,' the Bradlii-image instructed.

'What? How are they going to do that?' Spencer's curiosity was immediately piqued.

'Your suits are state of the art and made from smart fibres interlaced with carbon nanotubes. Each and every fibre can be individually controlled, and act together to enhance muscle performance and resilience. Sensors are linking their onboard nano-computers to the motor control centres in your brains so that they can react as you think. In essence, these suits can not only protect you but make you stronger and faster.'

'You're joking, Bradlii!'

'I am not joking, and I find your suggestion that I am slightly offensive.' The Bradlii-image retorted, a disapproving expression clouding his blue holographically-generated face. 'I am now linked with your suits and so will be able to monitor progress and assist with their acclimatisation to your physiognomy.'

'Learning mode active,' said the suits in unison.

For the next few minutes, Spencer and Amy took part in what felt like a faintly ridiculous aerobics workout. It was clear to Spencer that Amy was in considerably better shape than he was, as she barely broke a sweat whereas he felt himself getting frequently short of breath. Perhaps, he conceded to himself, the hours sitting in his gaming chair hadn't been time quite so well spent after all.

'Learning mode complete. Combat mode accessible and online,' said both Spencer and Amy's suits together. A shimmering ripple seemed to run across the surface of both their suits and to Spencer, it felt as if there was a slight flexing of the material.

Aila appeared and handed them both hydrating pouches. Spencer gratefully glugged his, while Amy took a few deep sips. She did look very focused, Spencer thought to himself, and he was suddenly intensely proud of her. That's my girlfriend! And she's a super-cool badass!

'Ready?' Astren asked. Spencer and Amy nodded. 'Then let's fight!'

Suddenly Spencer felt as if his suit came alive and he leapt and span in mid-air before landing at Astren's feet and striking out. This time he didn't miss, and she blocked him. He struck again, moving forward, his fists moving under his control, but far faster than he could have possibly imagined. To his left, Amy had landed a kick on Qarak and was now back-flipping out of reach of his retort.

Astren spun, delivering a full round-house kick, but somehow Spencer jumped into the air over her head, perhaps more than two metres from the mat, and executed a somersault. He felt the suit move his legs and align them for a perfect landing that neither jarred nor left him off balance.

'This is incredible everyone! Did you just see that?' Spencer was almost giddy with excitement. 'Amy, did you see what I just did?'

Amy performed a single-handed back flip with pivot and landed next to him. Her eyes were flashing, and she was clearly loving this as much as he was. 'Holy crap Spencer, this is amazing! Let's go again!'

And for the next hour, Spencer and Amy whirled and spun, performing superhuman feats of acrobatics, and developing fighting skills that would have easily handed them victory in any Earthly kung-fu competition.

*

A little later, above the conference table, a hologram of a strange-looking device rotated slowly. It was roughly cylindrical, tapering to a sharp point, and covered with tiny lights, some of them blinking on and off.

'What on earth is it?' Spencer asked Galen, who was sitting quietly, gazing at it.

To the surprise of all present, it was Astren who spoke, her voice hushed as if she were contemplating a most sacred object.

'Everyone in the Galaxy knows what that is.' Well, apart from me, Spencer thought to himself. 'It's the Spear of Rigel,' Astren continued in awestruck tones.

'Okay, you are going to have to explain it to me better than that.' Spencer was less than impressed.

Galen took over, 'The Spear of Rigel is named for the star Rigel, a blue supergiant that is the brightest and hottest star in the constellation you know as Orion. Where it came from, nobody knows for certain. It was found in orbit many millennia ago and has been lost for nearly as many years. In the short time it was in possession of the forerunner of the Galactic Council, the Imperial Galactic Government as it was known, it was studied intensively. Ancient records show that the scientists of the time believed they had discovered its nature.'

Now Spencer was becoming intrigued, and he could see Amy was too. She asked, 'Okay, I don't know much about this physics stuff, but it's clear you guys think this is something pretty special. So what is it?'

Galen lifted his head. 'It's death for billions of beings, or at least in the wrong hands it could be.'

Bradlii interjected, 'It is believed that the Spear of Rigel is an extremely advanced piece of technology. The mystery surrounding it began immediately upon its discovery, as it was far beyond the capabilities of the science at that time, and,' the AI seemed to pause a moment for dramatic effect, 'If it is what it is believed to be, it remains so.'

Spencer was now genuinely fascinated, 'So you are telling me that this Spear thing if it still exists, is still much more sophisticated than your technology even today?'

'That is correct, and we have information that the Zylaxxians are sending out probes and expeditions with the specific purpose of trying to locate this device if it still exists.'

'So I'll ask again, what is it?'

Galen looked Spencer directly in the eye, 'It is believed to be a fusion inhibitor.'

'A what?'

'All stars are massive fusion reactions. Hydrogen atoms are fused together under extreme pressure, and in doing so stupendous energies are released. This energy is what makes stars burn and shine.'

'Okay, I'm with you so far…'

'It is a star killer. The Spear of Rigel, if fired into a star, can stop all fusion taking place, almost instantaneously. In essence, it kills the star.'

Spencer felt his throat turn dry. 'So you are telling me, that this thing has the power to turn off a star, permanently? My God! That would destroy an entire solar system in one go.' He paused and then thought he might throw up as the full horror of what he was hearing suddenly hit him like a plasma bolt. 'Earth's sun! Oh hell no!'

24

Horus Prime:

The Infinity swept into the small planetary system and on toward the third of four gas giants, their broiling surfaces each a different colour, effervescing against the intense blackness of deep space. As the ship approached, it slowed and moved into orbit around the giant that glowed a beautiful deep crimson. It was a breathtaking sight, and Spencer, Amy, Aila, Zan, Galen, Astren, Qarak and the rest of the Androsians stood silently, their heads slightly bowed.

At a nod from Galen, Spencer spoke. 'Friends, we come together to give thanks to Elan Persikaner and Janna Antinori who gave their lives for a cause that was right and noble, but one that causes me great sorrow, because it was for me, and those I hold most dear, that they died.' Spencer felt as if his voice might break, but he stiffened his resolve and swallowed hard. He would not do the deceased Androsians the discourtesy of weeping over their loss, at least not here and now.

'It is a mark of their faith and discipline that they made the supreme sacrifice for what they knew in their hearts to be virtuous and just. We will always remember them, and we will honour their memories by ensuring that we do not rest until the enemies of peace are vanquished, and harmony is brought to the Galaxy once more.'

The Androsians stepped back one pace, lifted their heads, and exclaimed in unison, 'They are the best of us and will walk beside us evermore.'

Spencer concluded, 'I, Spencer Edwards the First, Emperor of the Galaxy and all dominions within it, command that their names be entered in the hallowed Scroll of Honour, whereby they and their deeds will be known for all eternity and to the end of time.'

At this point, two bright points of light emerged from the side of *The Infinity* and sped off to become rapidly engulfed in the crimson fire of the nearby planet.

Amy squeezed his hand. 'That was beautiful Spencer,' she whispered.

'Thanks, Galen did give me a hand with the words,' Spencer smiled wanly and sighed. 'I'll never forget what they did for me, and for us and that they helped me get you back, Amy.' Despite his every effort, he sniffed and a tear rolled down his cheek. Amy gently brushed it away.

'Ready to break orbit', Bradlii, who had connected to the shipboard AI announced. Spencer stood straight and then turned to his fellow travellers. 'Right, where are we heading now, Aila?'

'Horus Prime.'

Zan gave a small grin, 'Oh, you have no idea what's in store for you, but I'm pretty sure you are going to like it!'

Spencer and the others laughed, releasing the tension they all felt as the moment for sadness was passing. No matter what lay ahead, Spencer had a sudden and absolute conviction that they could overcome it together.

'Okay, Horus Prime it is, and it had better be good!'

*

For more than a hundred thousand years, Horus Prime had been a galaxy-wide byword for excess. It was a playground, a holiday destination, a place of occasional debauchery, and the home to the Horovian race, whose entire economy was built upon pleasure and gratification.

In more recent times it had cleaned up its image, and developed attractions that would prove to be suitable for even the more reserved and prudish races, but it certainly retained some of its history of a place where anything went, and no questions, well at least not too many, would be asked.

Horus Prime itself was, in essence, a theme park resort the size of a planet, and each of the eight orbiting moons had a distinct identity and recreational specialism, be that gambling, gaming, music, sensational foods and wines, sports, combat, and even some of the more base pleasures of the flesh. Amy looked less than impressed when that one was read out and Spencer summoned up his most disapproving look and made sure she saw that he directed it at a smirking Zan.

The crew of *The Infinity* needed provisions, and Galen had also determined that an acquaintance of his, from many years ago, was somewhere on the planet, although efforts to reach Traz Blixt had so far proven unsuccessful. 'I expect she goes by a different name now,' said the sage, 'She was always a bit of a character but loyal to the Empress. Put simply, she's a purveyor of information of the most difficult to obtain variety. She may have some clue as to the location of the Spear, or at least know someone who may be able to help us in our quest.'

Galen had advised that it would be much safer for all if they went incognito. As he explained, 'Since the death of Volaria, the Zylaxxians have been busy cementing their hold over the Galactic Council, and they undoubtedly have paid agents and operatives everywhere looking for us, and for you in particular, Spencer.'

Spencer didn't need persuading and readily donned casual garments over his smartsuit that gave him the appearance of a tourist on holiday, or at least according to Galen and Aila it did.

*

With *The Infinity* remaining far out of local scanner range hidden behind a small uninhabited moonlet, Spencer, Amy, Astren, Aila and Galen took the second Lander and headed down toward the main landing port of the Northern Hemisphere of Horus Prime. Qarak remained behind to support Zan if they ran into any difficulty, and, as Galen pointed out, too large a group would gain unwelcome attention.

The port itself was, Spencer soon realised, so enormous it was visible almost from space. As they approached the planet, the traffic lanes of craft shuttling to and from the orbital docking berths became increasingly congested.

'Blimey, this is a busy place!' Spencer voiced the thoughts the others also shared.

'It is one of the most active destinations in the Galaxy ,Spencer,' Galen advised. 'There will be members of almost every sentient space-faring species either planetside or on one of the pleasure moons at any given time. It is, for want of a better description, a teeming hive of excess.'

It was difficult to detect whether Galen, who certainly gave the appearance of living a simple almost monastic life, disapproved or not. Spencer raised an eyebrow inquisitively, and Galen, in a rare moment of openness gave a small smile. 'I have lived a long life filled with many chapters, Spencer.'

Spencer gave a little knowing grin and nodded. Galen was perhaps the most inscrutable of all his companions, so the moment carried a certain significance, or maybe perhaps enlightenment. Regardless, he rather appreciated Galen sharing a little moment with him.

As they touched down after being guided expertly in by Horus Space Traffic Control, the door to the Lander dematerialised and a warm, scented breeze immediately filled the cabin. 'That smell is from the Lapisbeutilia Flower that grows almost everywhere here. Some say it gently stimulates the pleasure centres of the brain in most species and lowers inhibitions. It is thought it may be one of the reasons why Horus Prime became such a popular destination so many centuries ago.'

'You sound like an automated travel guide, Bradlii!' said Amy, good-naturedly. 'Happy to be of service!' responded the AI, equally pleasantly.

'Tell me this flower doesn't affect you, Bradlii?' Spencer said in surprise.

'Of course not, but I do respond to the endorphins I detect and monitor in your bodies, and right now I am detecting slightly elevated levels of oxytocin, serotonin and dopamine in you all at significantly varying quantities, with the exception of Aila, obviously.'

'Okay, well, whatever it is, I do feel good' said Spencer, jumping, from the Lander without using the steps that had materialised from the doorway.

A few minutes later the group were riding a terrapod rapid transit bubble at high speed as the automated capsule sped toward a sprawling complex that the onboard AI had identified as a gigantic commercial retail centre. As they rode, various holoscreens appeared displaying the wares of different shops, life-changing beauty treatments (have a complete skin replacement), thrill-seekers extreme experiences (Strato-surfing in the upper atmosphere), and every possible type of dining experience, many of which Spencer felt utterly no compunction to try.

Galen had departed separately to try and track down his mysterious contact, and Spencer and Amy told Astren and Aila that they were under strict orders to enjoy themselves as well as arrange provisions for the ship. Aila looked a little confused, whereas Astren's face made clear her general disapproval of anything so frivolous as time-wasting fun and entertainment.

The pod glided to a smooth stop and one side of it retracted upwards over the top of the other, so that the band of four could step onto an arrival platform. There were yet more moving advertisements, and as Amy stepped forward a holographic salesperson appeared directly in front of her. 'Hi there! Have you ever considered a full body wax and depilation treatment?' Amy was nonplussed, then raised her eyebrows at Astren who waved the holofigure away in exasperation, muttering to herself about how much she despised such a place as this.

However, Spencer had already stopped in front of a screen that seemed to be showing a zero-G eating and entertaining facility, and, much to his delight, something that looked exactly like a massively stacked burger. 'We have got to go here!' he turned to his friends. 'Look, the tables and chairs float, and the food flies to your table on self-propelled plates!' Amy couldn't help but smile at his infectious enthusiasm.

'And there's a show!' he continued, his voice rising. 'Some kind of acrobatics and pyrotechnics thing that looks pretty spectacular!'

'C'mon, let's have some fun! You too, Astren. That's an order!'

Aila spoke dubiously. 'Well, if that is your wish, but we should secure the supplies and provisions we need first.' Spencer sighed but relented. 'Okay, we'll do that before anything else, but then we take a bit of time to enjoy ourselves, agreed?'

'Agreed.' Aila said resignedly.

'If we must.' Astren grunted but didn't offer any further opposition. Perhaps the Lapisbeutilia scent was even working on her, Spencer wondered to himself.

25

Traz Blixt:

Spencer and his small entourage spent the next couple of hours visiting various provisioners. Horus Prime was, he thought, without a doubt a uniquely extraordinary place. There were retailers of every kind and purveyors of truly remarkable wares from the four corners of the Galaxy. More than once Aila had to gently remind both him and Amy that they weren't there to window shop, as the two of them stared in wonder at a display of ancient artefacts from a long lost civilisation or a lavishly spectacular outfit from a high-end tailor.

And of course, there were restaurants, food stalls, snack stops and dispensers selling anything from what was broadly recognisable as confectionery through to more exotic dishes that smelled sensational, or, on occasion, absolutely vile. Spencer noted that nutritional tastes obviously varied widely amongst the myriad species present.

To all intents and purposes, the commerce centre where they found themselves reminded Spencer of a mega-shopping mall like those found on Earth, but the scale was beyond anything he had ever experienced. Places of entertainment were mixed cheek by jowl with every possible kind of shop you could imagine, and then hundreds more you couldn't.

But what was perhaps most remarkable was that according to Bradlii, this was just one of the many tourist centres on the planet, and not even one of the largest.

Aila and Astren were rarely distracted by the shops or their offerings though, but instead continually scanned the crowds, checking for any hint that they might have been recognised or were being followed.

Astren did not look happy. 'Too many people,' she muttered more than once to Aila within earshot of Spencer, who found himself becoming increasingly irritated.

'Look, Astren, even if we are spotted, nobody is going to try anything here. It's too public.'

Astren pursed her lips and seemed far from convinced. Aila said, 'We can't be too sure of that, Spencer, and we are doing whatever we can to keep you and Amy out of harm's way.'

'Okay, I get that, and please don't think I don't appreciate it, but come on, we just need a little bit of a break here,' he smiled sympathetically.

'We all deserve a bit of downtime.'

Aila spoke again, 'I've just received a message from Galen, he has located Traz Blixt and is en-route to us with her from the neighbouring continent. They should be here in about an hour. We have also concluded our re-provisioning orders for *The Infinity*, and the supplies are now being delivered and loaded aboard by an automated shuttletruck.'

'So we've got an hour to kill?' Spencer asked, brightly.

'That is technically correct.'

'Food then! Let's find something really good.'

Ten minutes later the four were seated in a small taverna-style eatery that was, Spencer and Amy agreed, very cosy. It was also clearly popular, as almost all of the tables were full, and waiters and waitresses scurried about delivering all kinds of dishes that did look genuinely appetizing. Spencer was famished, and so it would appear was Amy, who ordered enough for two, but was apparently intent on polishing it off herself. Spencer smiled admiringly, and thought to himself, not for the first time, just how cool she was.

Spencer was just about to tuck into his mountainous plate when Aila blocked his hand. Then, without asking, she took a small morsel and placed it in her mouth, chewing a few times. Spencer was nonplussed.

'I've never seen you eat anything, Aila!'

'24.8% gluten-based compounds, 31.4% complex proteins, 42.7% vegetable organics, and the remainder refined carbohydrates with trace spices and seasoning. It is safe to eat,' she replied.

They all looked at her in bemusement. 'But what do you think of it, Aila?' Amy asked.

Aila paused as if analysing the contents of her mouth further.

'Yes, it is very nice.'

They all laughed and Spencer grinned broadly. 'I am delighted to hear it, Aila, here, try something else. The Synth looked a little unsure, but then relented, 'Oh, if you insist!'

'I do Aila, I do insist!' Spencer chuckled, and for the next half an hour the companions chatted and laughed and joked in a way that could almost pass as normality for any group of friends enjoying lunch together. Even Astren smiled more than once, despite herself.

*

The comms from Galen had instructed them to meet him and a companion in a recreational zone, just a five-minute terrapod ride from where Spencer and his entourage had been enjoying their lunches. As the capsule whisked them through beautifully tended parkland, Spencer gained the strong impression that Horus was a wealthy world. Sculptures, some tens of metres high, stood amongst the trees, and an intricate network of what looked like bicycle paths on Earth met and converged to provide picturesque and gently undulating routes for the myriad of different species who were out enjoying the clear sunlight. Some sat astride machines that hovered a metre or so above the ground, seemingly propelling themselves by thrusting up and down on pads connected to pistons, while still others were mounted on domesticated animals that while bearing little resemblance to horses, seemed to behave in a not dissimilar fashion.

Their pod slowed, then stopped at a small platform, and Astren quickly ushered them out. Galen and another figure were seated on an intricately carved bench perhaps twenty paces away under the branches of a tree, its perfect dome of leaves a deep and luscious purple and red.

Galen rose as they approached, as did his companion.

'Emperor, this is Traz Blixt, Traz, may I present Emperor

Spencer Edwards the 1st.' Not for the first time, Spencer felt both foolish and fraudulent.

Traz's clear green eyes met his for a moment, and then she bowed her head. 'Emperor, it is indeed a great honour to meet you.'

Spencer did his best to smile modestly. She was of medium height, with skin that was deep gold and exceptionally lustrous. Her hair was cut quite short, and she wore a simple flight suit that had evidently seen some years of use. Her high cheekbones framed a sharply pointed face that was almost impossible to age. Spencer was aware that Galen had known her a long time, so assumed that she was probably considerably older than she looked, and then he reminded himself that he had little frame of reference for judging the ages of different species that were, ultimately, entirely alien to him anyhow.

'Traz, Galen, let's sit down. This is a lovely spot for a chat,' Spencer suggested.

'Traz does indeed have some information that may prove valuable to us, Spencer…' Galen nodded at Traz who cleared her throat and began.

'Emperor, Galen tells me that you come from a planet that has not yet joined the Galactic Council?' Spencer nodded. 'And that you are now in open conflict with the Zylaxxians, and seek the Spear of Rigel in order to prevent it from falling into their hands, and, well, an ensuing catastrophe?'

Again, Spencer nodded.

'The Spear certainly exists, although I am not convinced it is exactly what many believe it to be.'

Spencer was puzzled. 'Galen said it was a, what was

it? Yes, a fusion inhibitor, and that it could stop stars from burning.'

'It may be able to do that, but there are some of us who think it can do a great deal more.' For the next twenty minutes, Spencer and his companions listened intently as Traz told them a story that was so incredible it was hard to believe.

'The Spear was indeed discovered many millennia ago, floating in orbit around the star you know as Rigel. The ship that discovered it was a research vessel from a nearby system, and at first they believed it to be some kind of weapon, and it can certainly be used as such, but there are those whose research over the countless years since has led them to conclude that aggression is not it's true purpose.' Spencer raised an inquisitive eyebrow.

'I'm not a scientist Emperor, and to be honest, I don't know much about the actual device, but it has been suggested that it can disrupt spacetime, and cause a range of effects that in the wrong hands would prove cataclysmic for the Galaxy, but equally could, if deployed for the right reasons, save it.'

This was making little sense to Spencer, but he was determined to hear everything Traz had to say.

She continued, 'The Dark Aeons fell upon the galaxy, with wars that killed trillions of sentient beings across countless civilisations, and the Spear disappeared. Slowly it became more myth than fact. Despite this, scientists knew that it had existed because they had the detailed scans and research papers of the vessel that found it and the highly-advanced race they hailed from. They recognised it was a device of incalculable power and for these reasons, it is almost certain that the device still exists, but has been kept hidden for thousands of years. Just as those ancient scientists realised, if it was taken and used by those committed to violence it could prove disastrous for us all.'

'Do you know which species it was that found the Spear?' Spencer almost sensed the answer before it came.

'Yes, it was the Ixenarians.'

'And then they retreated to somewhere in the outer edge of the Galaxy soon after?'

Galen glanced sharply at Spencer, clearly impressed. 'Yes, it is reasonable to assume that the two events are related.'

'So we need to find the Ixenarians before the Zylaxxians do, and make sure that the Spear, or whatever it is, doesn't fall into their hands because if it does, it could mean the end of Earth and my home solar system as a best-case scenario, or pretty much the entire Galaxy if we want to be especially pessimistic.' Spencer looked around at their group. They were all shaken, Amy especially.

'Yes, that's about the sum of it, Spencer.' Galen said quietly. 'You, or rather we, will have to face Haxenaar and defeat him one way or another. It is inevitable.'

'One more thing Emperor,' Traz's voice was urgent. 'The Ixenarians only found it, they didn't construct it. Someone else did.'

'And you are going to tell me who?'

Traz took a deep breath, 'There is good reason to believe the Spear did not originate in our Galaxy.'

'Well, where did it come from then?'

She looked Spencer directly in the eye, 'Andromeda.'

26

Vari-G Hyperball:

Vari-G Hyperball is a galaxy-wide phenomenon. Ever since the game's invention, some centuries past, its growth in popularity has been little short of spectacular. Every year, more and more teams from diverse worlds across the immensity of the cosmos, fielded teams in their regional competitive leagues in the hope that one might make it through to the grand final and lift the trophy of "Galactic Vari-G Hyperball Champions." Several species had come to dominate, so it usually ended up as a race between them, but such was the popularity that most schools and communities now had their own Hyperball Arenas. The appetite for watching games seemed almost unlimited across all the worlds of the Galactic Council and some who were not yet joined but already affiliated. The very best players became hyperstars, their names known and their prowess studied and analysed in trillions of homes on millions of planets.

The game is, in essence, quite simple, Bradlii explained to Spencer and Amy. Two teams of four players compete to take possession of a glowing sphere and plant it in the opposition's scoretube. 'Not unlike basketball on Earth, except without the bouncing.' Spencer suggested as they stood outside the entrance to the arena, brightly lit with advertising and infomatics.

'Well, not quite,' Bradlii continued. 'The arena is a large oblong box with rounded edges and corners. The floor, walls and ceiling are all identical and completely smooth, with projected and changing markings denoting various scoring zones.'

'With you so far,' Spencer nodded, and Amy also indicated she fully understood.

'And then,' the AI resumed, 'the gravity during the game is varied at random, or in patterns, and there are gravitational eddies, streams and tunnels that experienced players can use to their advantage. At the beginning of each ten minute quarter, the arena is flooded with charged graviton particles, which will illuminate and fluoresce all the gravitational anomalies present for that game. Part of the skill is being able to quickly identify, assess and predict the patterns, and the other part is in being able to react and re-orientate yourself instantly to the changes in gravitational strength. One moment a player might find themselves floating in mid-air, the next, they are running upside down on the ceiling and then zooming in a high-speed arc toward the opponent's score tube. It's a very fast game, and not for the faint-hearted, or so I'm led to believe.'

'Wow! That sounds incredible!' Spencer's eyes were wide. 'We have got to try this!'

Standing next to him, Amy giggled her agreement, while Aila and Astren looked dubious.

Aila spoke, 'The game is very physical and potentially high-impact Spencer, so injuries are not uncommon. Your suits will help protect you, but they don't make you invulnerable.'

'And keeping you safe is our first priority.' Astren added unnecessarily, clearly uneasy.

'Okay you guys, I get that, and I know you are doing your jobs, but I really feel I need this. There have to be some benefits to being the Emperor. Human beings need fun in their lives otherwise they don't function well after a time.'

Astren rolled her eyes at that, and Aila did a good approximation of pursing her lips in the way that an irked parent might to an errant child.

'Very well, I will inform Galen to wait for us at the spaceport, but if you are injured, I will stop the game,' said the Synth, in a tone that brooked no argument.

'Agreed.' Spencer and Amy nodded together, their eyes sparkling.

*

The arena was, Spencer guessed, about fifty metres in length, thirty wide and thirty in height. He stood near his team's scoretube, staring hard at the Synth team supplied by the facility who stood implacably in a diamond formation at their end.

With a rather affected show of disappointment, Spencer had accepted the advice of Aila and consented to the difficulty level being set to the lowest.

'Game commencing in ten, nine, eight...' The disembodied voice intoned, 'three, two, one... Commence play.'

Suddenly the arena lit up with green, blue, orange and various other hues as it was bathed in charged gravitons that revealed an incredible vista of swirling eddies glowing like whirlpools, while streams of green and blue gravity waves flowed through, under and over each other, filling the void space, and tumbling waterfalls of oranges and reds poured particles from on high down to the floor.

Spencer and Amy gasped. Nothing either of them had seen on Earth came even remotely close to this incredible spectacle. It was like being inside an all-encompassing light show where light itself created an impossible playground. At the sound of a klaxon, a glowing ball was fired into the centre of the arena and every player launched themselves toward it.

Spencer began sprinting forward before diving into a stream of purple particles gushing about five feet from the floor. Instantly he was swept along, his feet leaving the floor and his body leaning forward as if he was on a fantastical glowing waterslide.

A Synth rocketed past, riding a gravity stream running in the opposite direction, and Spencer perceived Amy, somehow ahead, fast closing in on the glowing ball as she flew first toward the ceiling and crested the top of a particle fall, before pitching over and swooping toward the floor and her target. She grabbed it, then shouted to Spencer over the helmet intercom, 'To you!' before throwing it into a spiralling orange graviton whirlpool that whipped it around and then on toward Spencer.

He threw himself forward and reached for the ball, somehow connecting it with his glove whereupon it seemed to stick.

A Synth was closing on his position fast, surfing a tide of blue sparkles. Spencer looked, identified Astren, and then spotted a red current that was heading toward her. He threw the ball, timing it well, and it sped off toward the Androsian who performed a deft backward flip in mid-air, caught it, and hurled it into the opposing team's scoretube.

The klaxon sounded. 'Team One Scores!' Game resetting. Play!' The ball reappeared, this time almost next to a Synth who caught it, then leapt into an updraft of green gravitons, soaring skyward before turning and throwing to a fellow team member, but out of nowhere, Aila shot past, intercepting the ball and then spinning over to cross into a gushing torrent of pink particles that took her to within a few metres of the scoretube. She didn't miss. 'Team one scores! Game resetting…'

'Hang on,' Spencer shouted. Let's up the difficulty rating a bit.'

'Spencer,' Astren called over the intercom, 'next levels are full contact.'

'Okay, fine with me. Let's do it.'

'Game level increased. Resetting. Play!'

Now it was serious, thought Spencer to himself, and then, 'this is simply the most incredible thing I've ever done!'

27

Fight To The Death:

The klaxon sounded once again, but this time the Synth team formed up and marched in unison through a doorway that materialised in the wall behind their scoretube. Almost immediately four other players emerged and quickly spread out. Spencer assumed they were the more advanced opponents, and turned to grin at his teammates at precisely the same time as a plasma blast whistled past his head, impacting on the back wall in a shower of sparks and static.

Then everything happened fast. Aila and Astren launched themselves forward, Aila grabbing Spencer, while Astren caught Amy mid-air. Plasma blasts were now ricocheting around the arena, many of them being deflected by the variable gravity as the four shadowy figures advanced rapidly toward Spencer and his team. As Spencer felt himself propelled sideways, out of a line of fire, he saw one of the blasts deflect around a graviton stream and hit one of the assailants in the leg. The figure immediately dropped to his knees, but still the other three came forward, stepping into a beam of light that momentarily illuminated their heavy features.

'Zylaxxians!' Spencer shouted in warning.

'Yes, I've seen them.' Astren's voice was a growl inside his helmet.

And then Spencer caught Amy out of the side of his eye. Her face was set hard. 'Let's take them, Spencer!' Their eyes locked and Spencer nodded, there was little choice, either they fought back or they would be cut down in moments.

'Astren, Aila, Amy, fight! That is an order! Smartsuits to combat mode.'

All four turned as one, and rushed forward, catching the Zylaxxians by surprise. A shot hit Aila, who froze as blue energy rippled across her body, and Spencer landed a kick directly at the lead Zylaxxian, contacting directly with his armoured chest plate. The assailant was knocked off his feet, landing heavily and for a moment stunned.

Amy struck the second while Astren somersaulted into a graviton stream that rapidly propelled her toward the third Zylaxxian, knocking him to the ground.

The fourth Zylaxxian, let loose a hail of plasma bursts that seemed to electrify the air around them. Spencer threw himself down a graviton wave, and the current swept him out of the blast path and into a side wall. His boots immediately gained a hold, and he ran horizontally for half the length of the chamber before throwing himself into a purple stream that cascaded back down toward the floor and the Zylaxxians who, having gathered their wits were now reforming into the assassination squad that they most definitely were.

Spencer reached the lead Zylaxxian, and kicked out at his shin, buckling his knee inwards. The Zylaxxian howled in agony, his red eyes burning with fury. He lashed out, catching Spencer on his cheekbone, and for a moment Spencer's world exploded in pain, but the adrenalin surge was powerful and Spencer quickly blocked the next lunge and smashed his foot into the Zylaxxian's groin.

Spencer glanced around, Aila was still struggling to move, but Astren was in action perhaps ten metres away, her long hair flowing as she wheeled and turned, delivering blow after blow to her deadly adversary who, powerful though he was, lacked her speed and agility. He pulled a lethal-looking blade from a holster on his hip and lunged forward toward the Androsian who neatly sidestepped, caught his wrist and with a deft wrench shook the knife free, caught it in her other hand and rammed it into the space beneath his ribcage. The Zylaxxian gasped and collapsed as his life ended, but it was at that moment that Astren saw Spencer's adversary reach for a fallen plasma rifle, and stagger to his feet.

Spencer didn't see the Zylaxxian raise the rifle and take aim. Astren sprinted toward her Emperor and flung herself at Spencer, grabbing him in a flying tackle. She saw his eyes widen in surprise at precisely the moment the blast, aimed for Spencer, hit her from behind. At such short range, it blew a hole clean through her lower back and out through her midriff.

'No!' Spencer bellowed in fury, grabbing the plasma rifle from the hands of her killer, and using the butt to knock the Zylaxxian off-balance before flipping the rifle and firing multiple shots that ripped chunks of burning flesh out of the heavily-armoured assassin.

Astren was still standing, her face a mixture of shock and surprise as she looked down to see the extent of her injuries. Slowly, she brought her chin up and tried to smile at Spencer, before sinking to her knees and pitching forward.

Aila was there at his side. 'Get Astren out of here, now!' Spencer ordered, his heart racing. Without hesitating, the Synth picked up the fallen Androsian and, cradling her across her arms, ran toward the wall where the emergency exit materialised. Spencer grabbed Amy as the remaining two Zylaxxians were beginning to struggle to their feet once more, and the pair of them dashed after her, their smart suits enabling them to cover ground far quicker than any Olympic sprinter.

Bursting through the doorway into a twilight crowded with pleasure seekers, Spencer and his group caused immediate gasps and shouts as they pushed themselves through the noisy throng, Aila carrying the prone figure of Astren, Spencer and Amy taking the lead bellowing, 'Out of the way, please, coming through!' The bustling hordes parted, and there were a few screams as some of the denizens saw the extent of Astren's injuries and the bruised and bloodied faces of the two earthlings.

More shouts erupted from behind them, and Spencer turned to see the imposing figures of two Zylaxxians, shoving their way through the morass, hurling men, women and children aside and holding their plasma rifles aloft.

Suddenly there was a shouted command from ahead, 'Halt! Stop right there and do not move!' A Horovian, clearly a police officer with several other similarly suited law enforcers behind her, was barring their way. She had drawn a plasma pistol and was taking direct aim at their group.

Spencer and Amy stopped, raising their hands in submission. Aila, still carrying Astren bumped into them from behind.

'Halt. Any sudden movements will be interpreted as a threat and we will respond with force.'

Spencer glanced over his shoulder. The Zylaxxians were still fighting their way through and were now just moments behind. It was clear that local police or not, their intent was deadly.

Spencer turned to the officer, 'Please, you have to let us through. Those Zylaxxians are going to kill us, whether you are here or not.'

The officer looked over Spencer's shoulder and saw the advancing Zylaxxians, but clearly, she was determined to deal with one threat at a time. 'Down on the ground. Now!'

Amy pleaded with her. 'We can't, we have to get our friend to safety.'

'Down, now, I won't ask again!' The tip of the pistol glowed as the officer released the safety catch.

It was Aila who then addressed her, 'Sergeant, you have to let us pass, now. Please, scan this individual to confirm his identification.' She indicated toward Spencer.

The officer frowned, and then unclipped a device from her belt, raised it and pointed it at Spencer. It beeped, and the police officer's jaw dropped in amazement. The profound shock was apparent on her face, and she looked at Aila, who nodded confirmation, then back to Spencer, who also nodded. For a moment the officer struggled with her confusion, and then her training took over.

She straightened up, saluted and said, 'Sir, we stand ready to assist.'

'Thanks, please protect us and stop those Zylaxxians!'

The officer spoke into her mouthpiece and within seconds her squad had formed a protective ring around Spencer and his friends. Other police officers were already hurrying through the crowd, and drones swooped in from above, flashing warning lights and instructing the crowds to disperse.

Spencer and his group were already moving again, this time toward what he could see was an airborne ambulance descending from the sky toward a nearby open plaza, as a protective line of law enforcement officers created a barrier, blocking the Zylaxxians from any further advance. Moments later a fierce plasma firefight erupted, now fifty metres or more behind the hurrying Spencer and Amy, and Aila with her precious charge was moving rapidly ahead toward the waiting paramedics.

As soon as they had boarded, the Airbulance lifted off vertically. Spencer looked down on a vicious exchange of plasma blasts, but it was already clear that the Zylaxxians, although prepared to fight to the death, were on the verge of being overwhelmed. One fell, and then the second was obscured from view by a hail of flashes, now rendered silent due to their increasing altitude.

Spencer turned to Aila. 'How's Astren doing?'

Aila spoke matter of factly. 'She's dead, Spencer.'

28

Space Combat is not a Video Game:

Spencer felt like he had been punched in the stomach and was about to throw up.

'Oh God no!' Tears welled and Amy reached across from the seat next to him to grab his hand.

Aila spoke quietly, 'Astren died soon after she was hit by the plasma shot, but I injected her with a stabilising agent that will slow cellular degeneration for a couple of hours. That means that there is a very small chance that if we can get her back to *The Infinity*, MediBay, Galen and I may be able to use your ship's advanced facilities to repair and then reanimate her. But I must warn you, Spencer, her injuries are extremely severe. I rate her chances of surviving this at less than ten per cent.'

Spencer was resolute. 'She's strong, Aila, very strong. If anyone can get through this, it's her.'

Amy leaned over, 'Wouldn't we be better off getting her to a hospital on Horus?'

'Too risky, Zylaxxians are clearly in this system and they are looking for you. Besides, the MediCentre onboard *The Infinity* contains some of the most advanced medical technologies in the Galaxy.' Aila returned.

'Really? How come?' Spencer asked quickly.

'Because it is designed to save your life if needed.'

Spencer was silent for a moment as he reflected on this. It was not easy to confront your own mortality when you were only fourteen. 'Okay, that's good then, because I want you to use every damn thing we've got to save her.'

*

After a rapid transfer to an armoured shuttle, they were flown directly to orbit, with an armed escort of several Horan police interceptors flying alongside. In less than an hour, they had made rendezvous with *The Infinity*.

Astren had by now been transferred to a floating stretcher and was easily and quickly manoeuvred through the corridors to the Medibay. The stretcher was then docked with a securing clamp and integrated into an extensive suite of scanners, robotic surgical equipment, and monitoring screens.

Above her inert body appeared a holographic representation of her prone figure, and data began to flow onto screens surrounding the bed. Spencer realised that he didn't need to be a doctor to see that there was no heartbeat, no pulse, and very little brain activity.

Galen looked grave as he manipulated streams of holodata. 'The damage is, for want of a better expression, catastrophic. The effects of a full-charge plasma bolt at zero range are absolutely devastating. Almost all of her internal organs on this side of her torso are either extensively damaged, or completely missing.' He summoned up more data. 'The stabilising agent is delaying cellular death, but will only hold for perhaps another twenty minutes. I can't administer any more, as Aila has already pumped her full of the maximum dose.'

Spencer understood the situation was extremely grim, and nothing Galen had said so far gave any cause for hope.

'Okay, but we can't do nothing Galen, we have to try,' he pleaded.

Galen spoke gently, 'I know this is hard Spencer, but even if we attempt to repair her, the chances of anything like a full recovery are very small. She could be crippled for life and in permanent pain.' He looked at Spencer closely. 'You know how proud she is, how dedicated she is. She gave her life to save her Emperor. What Androsian would want for more? Perhaps you should let her go…?'

Now the tears came and there was nothing Spencer could do to hold them back. He looked at Amy, but she was already staring directly at him. She gave an almost imperceptible shake of her head, but to Spencer her meaning was clear. For not the first time he felt the enormous weight of responsibility fall upon his shoulders. He was only alive because other Androsians had died to keep him that way and he bloody well wasn't going to add another name to the Scroll of Honour without a fight.

'No, Galen, damn it. I'm not giving up on her yet. If anyone can pull through this, it is Astren. If we have any chance of saving her, we are going to try it.' He straightened up. 'Do it, now, whatever it takes.'

Galen took a deep breath and then nodded. 'Yes Emperor, we will do our best.' He gestured toward a robotic arm that responded by stretching out. A nozzle on its end rotated and then moved down into the gaping hole in Astren's torso. Immediately a fine spray of sparkling silver dust emanated from it and began to settle into the wound. Within moments, the dust began moving, and it seemed to Spencer that it was organised and somehow intelligent, like an army of ants, but on an infinitely smaller scale. The dust twinkled, shimmered and flexed as it began its work.

'What on earth is that?' he asked.

'That is the most advanced medical technology in existence, Spencer.' Galen spoke with a sense of pride. 'What you are seeing is more than a billion artificial life forms, all working in harmony at the cellular level to sample her tissue, synthesise it, and rebuild her organs a cell at a time.'

'Incredible!' Spencer watched in total fascination.

'On your Earth, some of your scientists have been proposing the possibility of what they call nanotechnology for some years now. Well, this is like that, but the result of several thousand years of research and advances. Every single one of those billion devices is in contact with the ship's medical AI as well as each other. Every single action is controlled, and referenced back to the full bio-scans we hold for Astren.'

'How long before we know if it has worked?' Amy asked, voicing Spencer's own thoughts.

'Several hours at least, and then we have to attempt to reanimate her. That means, in essence, we will try and reboot all her vital functions and her brain activity. Spencer, Amy, I must warn you that this is where even we reach the limits of technology. Even if the nano-swarm have managed to accurately and completely reconstruct her body, we won't know if what comes back is Astren as we knew her until we restart all her physical and mental activities and functions.'

*

The ship's alarm sounded, jolting Spencer from his reverie as he gazed out of the expansive virtual window of his quarters. Amy sat quietly on one of the sumptuous couches, attempting to watch some entertainment streams on a small tablet-like device to pass the time.

What now? Did this never stop? 'Come on Amy, we have to get to the Command Bridge.' Amy jumped to her feet, gave a sigh, rolled her eyes, and then sped out the door with Spencer in close pursuit. The moving floorway in the corridor outside the Emperor's Quarters, working in tandem with their smartsuits, enabled them to cover the hundred metres to their destination in only a matter of seconds.

'Zan, what's happening?' Spencer shouted, his voice urgent.

The pilot didn't look up from the displays in front and around him,

'We are tracking two inbound vessels, approaching at high velocity. We have accelerated, but they are on an intercept course and will catch up with us in less than two minutes. Energy signature scans suggest they are...'

Spencer interrupted. 'Don't tell me, let me guess. Zylaxxian?'

Zan simply nodded. 'Okay', Spencer continued, 'We

must make sure Galen and Aila aren't disturbed. Zan, is there an asteroid or debris field nearby?'

'Scanners show one about a minute off our port bow,' Zan confirmed, and then added, 'I'm with you sir, let's make it more difficult for them to get a target lock.'

Despite the impending danger of their newest predicament, Spencer felt strangely calm and focused. There was something vaguely familiar about all this... yes! This was very similar to a BattleBlast mission, and if there was one thing he was genuinely good at, it was that game.

'Coming up on the asteroid field in five... four... Zylaxxian cruisers still closing, now thirty seconds out...' Zan deftly looped *The Infinity* into a wide arc that quickly closed the gap between them and a large space rock, before turning the ship on its tail and coming to a complete stop with the surface of the asteroid just fifty metres behind them.

'Qarak, Amy, can you take the muon launchers and lateral plasma emitters? I'll grab the forward plasma cannons.' Spencer instinctively felt like he knew what he had to do.

Amy and Qarak quickly threw themselves into the chairs that erupted from the floor, holoscreens immediately appearing before them displaying targeting data and weapons status.

'Incoming hostiles actively scanning,' the ship's AI announced.

'Bradlii, can you interface with the ship?' Spencer asked.
'Done.'

'Okay everyone, in a moment they are going to figure out that we are hiding, and then they are going to start shooting asteroids to try and flush us out.' Spencer warned his compatriots, and Zan nodded.

'When that happens, I want to use the Holford Clamp to try and hold our asteroid together. Bradlii, do you think we can do that?'

'I've never tried to make such a calculation. Stand by, the ship's AI is attempting to calculate mass and I will corroborate it with the energy specifications of our electromagnetic clamp… calculations are complete. I estimate that we will be able to maintain the structural integrity of our asteroid for approximately thirty-seven point five two six seconds.'

Spencer grinned savagely. 'Approximately?'

'Well, I have taken a bit of a guess on the last thousandths. But Spencer, the asteroid will essentially be charged with so much energy that when we release, it will detonate with extreme destructive force.'

'That's exactly what I am counting on, Bradlii.'

'But won't we be destroyed in the explosion too, Spencer?' Amy looked worried.

'That's the tricky bit,' Spencer conceded. 'We need to be moving away from it at the time we release the clamp, hopefully having nudged it toward the Zylaxxian's.'

Zan was impressed. 'I've never even heard of any strategy like this! It is a long shot, but…'

'We need long shots!' Spencer finished his sentence for him. 'Now activate the clamp, maximum power.'

'Clamp active, and power threshold set to 100%,' The ship's AI intoned calmly.

'Go higher', Spencer instructed.

'Warning, threshold exceeded. Clamp now at 110%, 112%, 115%…'

'Here come the Zylaxxians, they've detected us. The asteroid is blocking a direct assault but they are firing,' Zan said urgently.

Plumes of energy erupted from the other side of the asteroid, and *The Infinity* shook as shock waves radiated outward from their million-ton rock.

'Clamp holding at 124%.'

'Zan, set the engines to full, but hold for me. Get ready…'

The Infinity shook again, hard. 'Hull pressure increasing,' the AI informed them, needlessly.

'How close do we think they are to the asteroid now?' Spencer called.

Zan studied his screens. 'Best guess is approximately eighty kilometres, based on localised gravimetric disturbances.'

'That'll have to do. Qarak, Amy, are you ready?'

They nodded.

'Zan, engines to full now.'

The next few seconds felt longer but as Bradlii would later confirm, time neither slowed down or stood still. *The Infinity* rocketed away from the asteroid, and within three seconds was at the limit of the Holford Clamp's range.

'Clamp failing,' the ship's AI announced, and then, on the enormous v-screen in front showed them a reverse angle view as the asteroid, now charged with billions of gigajoules of energy flashed once, and then detonated violently. For an instant, two Zylaxxian warships were visible before they were obscured as the expanding debris cloud engulfed them. The closer of the two ships was ripped apart by enormous chunks of rock that sliced through the hull in multiple places, but the other ship further back was less damaged and still operational.

' Lead ship destroyed. Second ship damaged, but firing.'

A heavy blast rocked *The Infinity*. 'Aft shielding depleted.'

'Zan, loop us around and aim us directly at the second ship to reduce our target area. Qarak, ready with the muon launchers, I need a direct hit front on. Amy, we'll then bank past so you can hit him with everything you've got.' Spencer knew they had just one chance to win.

The Infinity pulled up, engines at full burn, and rolled over hard. For a moment the onboard gravity struggled to match the high-speed manoeuvring, and all present felt the effects of an increase in g-forces followed by a sudden plummet as they crested the loop.

The Infinity swooped down on the Zylaxxian warship which fired again, and as their range rapidly closed, Qarak returned fire as Spencer also opened up with the forward plasma cannons. Two of the Zylaxxian's plasma blasts missed, passing just metres to the starboard, but the third was a direct hit and *The Infinity* shuddered. Less than a second later, the muon pulse hit the Zylaxxian front on, smashing the forward section to smithereens before *The Infinity* banked, passing by the flank of the stricken ship as Amy let loose with the plasma emitters and ripped through the now listing enemy, raking the hull from stem to stern and then detonating the engines.

The Zylaxxian ship exploded completely. Fragments of its hull slammed hard into *The Infinity* as it accelerated away into the darkness.

The Infinity's AI spoke. 'Pressure hull breach on decks two to four, we are venting atmosphere. Internal communications systems are down. Drones dispatched to repair.'

Spencer closed his eyes momentarily, then said with dread in his voice, 'The Medicentre is on deck three!'

29

Resurrection:

Spencer, Amy and Qarak raced down the corridor and through into the Medicentre. It had taken the repair drones more than an hour, but they had already temporarily patched the holes, using what Spencer would later learn was a poly-alloy, in essence, an intelligent metal that could be manipulated on the atomic level to create an airtight seal.

Aila and Galen were bending over the inert form of Astren, still prone on the medical couch. Graphics hovered in the space above them, and Spencer immediately realised that something had changed. Where previously there had been no sign of life, now there was… something.

'How is she?' Spencer asked urgently.

'Well, we had to use a pocket of nano-air to mitigate against the effects of the high-speed manoeuvres, but she is responding to treatment. It's quite remarkable to tell the truth, the nanoswarm has nearly completed the reconstruction of her damaged or missing organs, and is beginning to test them.' Galen spoke quietly, but there was evident pride in his voice.

'Test them, how?' Amy asked.

'Once an organ or repair is complete, the swarm remain in situ and use the electrical charges they collectively generate to locally activate the new tissue. Think of it as a bit like component testing.'

'Incredible!' Spencer leaned over the body of his friend and gasped as he realised that the once gaping hole in her torso was now almost fully closed. Inside the small remaining aperture, he could see the swarm still at work, emitting tiny flashes of energy as it activated nerves, checked blood vessels and arteries, and continued to rebuild Astren's tissue a cell at a time.

Qarak stood motionless by the door and Spencer realised how hard this must be for him, given his relationship with Astren. 'Qarak,' he said gently, 'Come here.'

The big Androsian hesitated for a moment, and then joined them. His usually taciturn face betrayed his concern, and even, as Amy suggested to Spencer later, his love. His mouth moved, and Spencer could hear some words, spoken softly and reverently, although he struggled to understand them. Qarak looked up after a moment and saw the question in his eyes.

'It is an ancient Androsian prayer, Emperor, I felt it was appropriate.' He gently rested his hand on Astren's shoulder.

Amy placed her hand on top of his. 'It was very, very appropriate, Qarak.'

The five stood silently for some minutes, watching as the nanoswarm finally closed the remaining wound. Galen explained that the swarm would now remain inside her body for the rest of her life, endlessly monitoring, modifying and repairing with a single purpose – to keep her body functioning.

Aila manipulated some data in the holoscreen above the biobed.

'According to the swarm's diagnostics, all her systems are nominal. In theory, we could now attempt to reanimate her now.'

All eyes turned to Spencer, but he shook his head. 'Qarak, I think you should be the one to make this call.'

Qarak dipped his head in acknowledgement, then stood up straight and saluted. 'Go ahead. Do what you must.'

Spencer reached for Amy's hand and felt it close tightly around his. Please work. 'Come on Astren! You can do this!' He whispered to himself.

Aila gestured toward a holocontrol and the medical AI's voice filled the room. 'Full analysis complete. Biological reactivation commencing in five, four, three...' Amy's grip tightened.

'Two... one.'

Astren's body gave a start, then convulsed for a moment. She gasped and her eyes opened wide. Her arms and legs were restrained by padded hoops, and for several seconds she struggled against them. Qarak moved toward her but Galen gently put out a hand to stop him.

Astren's eyes closed, and for a moment Spencer thought she was lost, but then she began breathing, irregularly at first, but within a minute or so more evenly. Her eyes opened once more and focused on the concerned face of Qarak, a look of surprising tenderness softening his usually hard features.

She raised her head and her mouth moved, trying to form words, and then she spoke in a hoarse whisper. 'Qarak! The Emperor, is he…'

'Right here Astren, thanks to you.' Spencer stepped forward to Qarak's side so that she might see him.

Astren smiled weakly and her head slumped back onto the pillow, but the smile remained on her lips.

'She will be exhausted for days, Spencer', Galen interjected quietly. 'You'll just have to give her time. We don't yet know how complete her mental recovery will be, even though the indications are her physiology is progressing surprisingly well.'

Spencer looked at Amy, and then at Astren. 'Thank you, Galen and Aila. I think Amy and I need to visit home and have a little rest also. I suggest you do likewise.'

'I would like to remain by her side' Qarak said firmly.

'Of course you would,' said Amy knowingly. 'Come on Spencer, let's give them some time.'

30

Home for Tea:

Spencer spent a much needed quiet evening at home. After smuggling Amy out the front door, her blowing him a kiss as she headed off to spend some time with her family, he flopped on his bed and stared at the ceiling.

Time was becoming increasingly confusing and disorientating. Just a few days, weeks, months ago his biggest worries had been his homework, BattleBlast rating, and whether Amy Heartly would ever have any interest in him. Now, he felt the weight of the Galaxy bearing down on him, and it felt suffocating. Although Volaria had explained that time was relative and that the remarkable wormhole technology essentially acted as a shortcut through spacetime, it was, Spencer reflected, not something a human brain was easily able to process.

He and Amy had lived weeks aboard *The Infinity* now, and experienced events that no human being had ever even imagined. But meanwhile, back on Earth things had been proceeding pretty much as normal. His family, completely unaware of his extraordinary double life, carried on with the humdrum challenges of living on Earth in the twenty-first century. Mum always trying to balance working, looking after Mo and keeping things running, and Hassan, now at home pitching in and doing all he could to support everyone while searching for a new job.

The big man was always cheerful, but Spencer could see the worry in his kind eyes. These were unsettling times on Planet Earth, as the pandemic had changed people and society in ways that were not yet fully understood. Many large companies had not returned to operating as they had before the virus struck, and jobs in some sectors were becoming more and more scarce.

Spencer felt intensely frustrated that he was expected to somehow lead the Galaxy against a dangerous, violent and aggressive Zylaxxian foe, yet was powerless to help his own family in their time of need. It was just so bloody unfair!

'Bradlii, if you are as smart as you claim to be…'

'Yes, I can confirm I am as smart as I claim to be.' The Galaxy's smuggest AI responded without a shred of modesty.

'Right, well then you need to help me to help my family. I am risking my life for everyone, and right here, right now my mum, my brother and my step-dad are in trouble. Yet you tell me I am powerless to help?'

Bradlii was silent, but Spencer was getting increasingly angry. 'Hassan needs a job. He isn't looking for charity or free handouts. He's always worked damned hard. But I can see that he and mum are worried that they are going to have no money soon, and I am struggling to concentrate on saving the Galaxy while I am also worrying about how my family are going to pay their bills.'

'Oh, it's money that you are primarily concerned about?' Bradlii asked, and Spencer detected a note of surprise in his synthesised voice.

'Well, yes, of course. Everyone needs money to live, and my family doesn't need lots, but they do need to be able to feed us, clothe us, and pay the rent.'

'I understand, Spencer. Well, have you considered paying for such requirements from your salary?'

Spencer stopped. 'What did you just say?'

'Have you considered using some funds from your salary?'

'What salary?'

'All Emperors, and indeed public servants receive a modest salary. I presumed you would know this.'

'No Bradlii, I didn't bloody well know that. Are you serious?' Spencer felt like throwing the supercilious AI at the wall, he was so irritated.

'Of course. You are entitled to receive your salary in any form or currency you nominate. For example, you could choose to be paid in grain, or minerals, or as one Emperor did a thousand years ago, ice comets because his homeworld was riven by drought.'

'Okay, so just to be absolutely clear, I am actually being paid to be Emperor?'

'Yes, but of course being Emperor is far more than just a job, it is the supreme honour that the galaxy has to bestow on any being,' Bradlii said grandly.

'Yes, yes, I get that. But alright, I need to know how much am I being paid.'

'Well, it isn't easy to answer that directly, because due to Earth not yet being a member of the Galactic Council, there isn't any formal currency exchange mechanism in place.'

'Can you make an estimate?'

'I can, but I don't like guessing, as you know.'

'Just bloody tell me, Bradlii!'

'Okay, well, I'm converting the sum through various mediums and taking into account supply and demand of a range of commodities considered desirable on the majority of inhabited worlds. Also, your stipend is usually paid periodically in a way that roughly corresponds with a month on Earth...'

Spencer gritted his teeth in frustration.

'Calculation complete. I do have an approximate figure for you, Spencer, but I want to stress there is some possible margin for error.'

'How much, Bradlii?'

'You are paid approximately one hundred and forty-eight thousand six hundred and fifty-two pounds and thirty-three pence. With a margin of error of five-point two per cent.'

Spencer's jaw dropped open. 'Per year?'

'Per month.'

Spencer's mouth moved, but words weren't coming. And then he began to laugh.

'As I said, it is a modest salary, Spencer, and more of a token gesture for the responsibility your position bears.'

'Modest! Modest Bradlii? I'm stinking rich!'

'Well, wealth is relative, but I have just accessed various data streams from your primitive Internet and yes, it would appear that by Earth standards your salary is at a substantial level.'

'This is incredible, Bradlii. Just incredible.' Spencer's euphoria suddenly abated. 'But I can't just give it to Hassan or my mum because there would be no way of explaining it. I need to think about this.'

'You could consider making some kind of investment, perhaps in a small business that could provide employment and an income stream for your family?' Suggested the AI.

Spencer brightened a little. 'Keep talking Bradlii…' he instructed.

'It rather goes against my ethical code to engage in subterfuge, but I assess that the circumstances are extraordinary and it is also my duty to do all I can to look after your wellbeing, Spencer. It is clear to me that providing security for your family is integral to that role.'

'Yes, yes, it totally is!' Spencer nodded vigorously.

'In that case, can you identify a form of employment that Hassan would not only enjoy but also excel in? If you are to purchase a business opportunity it needs to be viable and one where we can keep your involvement and identity hidden, in the interests of making this arrangement work.'

Spencer thought carefully. Hassan was a capable and hard-working man, but also a proud one. He wouldn't accept charity, and neither would mum for that matter. What had he always had an interest in? His old job, the one he had been made redundant from, was insurance, but that was complicated and, Spencer suspected, even with his now considerable financial means, not one he could easily buy into.

And then it suddenly dawned on him. Hassan had worked in car insurance, and he had a love of cars. Even more than that, he knew a lot about them.

'Bradlii, I've got an excellent idea!'

31

Bullies Get Theirs

Spencer and Amy walked home together, taking their favourite route down by the canal. School had not been great for either of them. Amy had found some of her friends, and their petty interpersonal rivalries and gossip rather tiresome, and Spencer had been pushed around by Wayne Billingsthorpe, a large and unimaginative bully who had decided that today Spencer would be an easy target.

'It all seems pretty ridiculous doesn't it, Spencer?' Amy summed up their feelings very precisely. 'I mean, we've seen and done stuff that is beyond incredible. You're the Emperor of the Galaxy for heaven's sake, and here we are back in school, having to deal with all kinds of stupid crap. I could kick Wayne's arse for you if you like though?' She flashed him an impish smile. 'Well, only after you've kicked it first of course!'

Spencer allowed himself a small grin and sighed. 'Believe me, Amy, nothing would have given me greater pleasure than to show that moron up in front of all his pathetic mates, but I have to try and be better than that.'

Amy nodded, and then stopped and pulled him close.

'You are my hero, Spencer, you know that?' He was amazed to see she wasn't joking. Spencer nearly choked and then mumbled, 'I'm no hero Amy. I haven't got a clue what I'm doing in any of this.'

But Amy was having none of it. 'Yes you do, and although you might not realise it, you've earned the respect of Astren, Aila, Galen, Zan and even Qarak. They trust you to do the right thing, and not just because you are Emperor, but because you are just you.'

Her arms encircled his waist and she pulled him nearer, stepping up on tiptoe to kiss him. Spencer felt his heart melt again, as it always did when Amy was near.

'Thank you, Amy, I needed that. I love you, you know.'

She nodded. 'Right back at ya, Emperor!'

'Oi, bender!'

Spencer and Amy separated from their embrace, and with horror realised their path was now blocked by Wayne and two of his henchmen. They turned, to see two more about ten yards behind them, preventing a retreat. All were standing with their arms folded, contempt on their bullish, and, Spencer thought to himself, rather spotty faces. One had his phone out and was obviously recording, presumably with the intention of uploading the encounter later to social media.

'We're just trying to go home, Wayne. That's all. We aren't looking for trouble.' Spencer knew his words, spoken as calmly as he could manage, carried little weight. For some reason known only to himself, Wayne had decided that Spencer was going to get a pasting.

Wayne ignored him and spoke to Amy. 'You need to run along Amy, because your boyfriend is about to get a slapping, and you don't want to get in the way.'

'They're not exactly the Zylaxxians, are they?' Spencer whispered to her.

'No Wayne, I think I'll stay. And I strongly recommend you and your little friends walk away now before you get hurt.' Spencer recognised the look on Amy's face, she was furious, but also resolute.

Wayne and his gang started laughing. 'Who's going to hurt us? You? Him?' Wayne pointed at Spencer. 'He's a nobody! You could do a lot better Amy, 'cos you're actually quite fit.'

'And you are a total tosser, Wayne, so like I said, get out of our way before you get yourself into something you can't handle.' Amy's voice was quietly authoritative.

Wayne's crude features hardened. 'Oh, really, little girl?' He stepped forward. Spencer spoke, with calm assuredness. 'If you come any nearer Wayne, you are going in the canal.'

Wayne paused, clearly unable to believe what he had just heard. He stared hard at Spencer and then Amy. 'You're a couple of losers, from loser families. I heard your stepdad lost his job. He's probably a loser like you too.'

Amy and Spencer caught each other's eyes and exchanged resigned sighs. They were ready.

'I'm warning you, Wayne, take your little gang and leave, right now.' Amy said evenly, and both she and Spencer felt their smartsuits tense under their school uniforms, the onboard AI's detecting their increased adrenalin and responding by switching to combat mode.

The attack came quickly, but clumsily. Wayne launched himself at Spencer, swinging a hard punch. Amy intercepted, catching his big fist in her own delicate hand, then twisting and pulling down and around, forcing Wayne to his knees with a yelp of surprise and pain. She released him. 'Had enough?'

'Just getting started,' Wayne growled with an oath. 'Get 'em lads!'

The next few seconds were a blur. Spencer wheeled around and landed a kick on his nearest assailant, dropping him gasping to the muddy path. Amy swept Wayne's legs from under him, landing him onto his back, directly into a rather deep puddle. Another came at them both, punching wildly, and Spencer blocked, then twisted his arm up behind his shoulders before planting his foot firmly in the small of his back and sending him sprawling.

Spencer and Amy formed up, standing in identical martial-arts-style poses. Please stay down, Spencer thought to himself, but he knew Wayne now had his blood up and wasn't going to let this humiliation pass.

'Screw you and this little cow, Spencer!' He staggered to his feet, swaying, his eyes blazing with fury. 'I'm gonna make you both pay for this.'

Spencer and Amy were implacable. 'Final warning, Wayne. Stay down.' Spencer was surprised at how controlled his voice was.

But he didn't stay down. He launched himself at Amy, who neatly side-stepped his ungainly assault. Spencer blocked a wide punch, and then using Wayne's not inconsiderable momentum, caught his arm, twisted his own body down and under the much larger thug, and then threw him over his shoulder, directly into the fetid waters of the canal.

With an enormous splash, their would-be assailant pancaked into the freezing water, but within seconds was at the surface, floundering as he tried to stand up. Spencer and Amy both knew that canals are generally only about a metre deep so he wasn't in serious danger of drowning, but Wayne swore and coughed, clearly having swallowed a good deal of the murky water. He struggled to his feet and tried to wade to the bank. 'My shoe's stuck, damn you,' and then 'it's come off!' he wailed.

There was a groan behind them, and Spencer and Amy turned to see their other foes also getting shakily to their feet, rubbing bruised limbs and wearing cowed expressions. The cameraman was still filming, but at Spencer's stern admonishment he sheepishly lowered his phone.

Wayne reached the bank, and by now he looked close to tears. Spencer felt a pang of guilt and stepped forward to offer him a hand getting out, but Wayne was clearly in no mood to be gracious. 'Get stuffed!'

'If that's the way you want it, Wayne, then so be it. But listen,' Spencer leaned down and spoke quietly, 'If you ever so much as look at Amy or me again in a way we don't like, this will seem like a nice little chat down by the canal. Next time we'll do the same and worse to you in front of the whole school. Do you understand me?'

Wayne looked into his eyes, and at that moment his bravado deserted him. He sniffed and then nodded in submission.

Amy turned to the rest of his gang, and with an icy stare froze them to the spot.

'Boo!' She stepped toward them and they turned and

fled, leaving Amy and Spencer to carry on their way, hand in hand, chuckling as they went.

32

Balairen IV:

Balairen IV is a remote arboreal world, orbiting a medium-size star at a comfortable distance that over billions of years had allowed an immense ecosystem to evolve and cover the entire land surface of the planet.

Plant life had developed to an astonishing level and become the dominant life form of the planet, whereas animal life remained primitive and relatively sparse. Viewed from space, as *The Infinity* completed her jump, Spencer and Amy marvelled at the deep green of the planet where the clouds parted to allow them to see the surface.

There were some settlements where a variety of small colonies of beings had established themselves, mostly living from the land, and enjoying the relative solitude of one of the quietest corners of the Galaxy.

For this reason, and others, Balairen IV had for many centuries been a location for one of several Galactic Council retreats – spacious and sumptuously appointed facilities that were at the disposal of the current Emperor for recreational purposes or sometimes for discreet meetings and conferences.

Galen had been firm. Astren needed time to recuperate. Her recovery had been impressive, and it was clear that despite appalling odds, her strength of will had carried her through the reanimation procedure and the astonishing repair work of the nano-swarm. But, he pointed out, she was a long way from being ready for active service, and the quiet relative safety and seclusion of Balairen would be an ideal place for her to convalesce.

However, despite appearances, security around the planet was substantial. The entire outer perimeter of the system was monitored by a sophisticated sensor net, and the Emperor's Palace, located in the temperate northern hemisphere next to a broad lake, was not only staffed but also home to a detachment of the Council Guard who were permanently stationed there, ready to provide a defensive capability should it ever be required.

After some discussion, it was agreed that they would stop briefly to replenish supplies before resuming their quest and enable the well-equipped maintenance facility to complete repairs and service *The Infinity*. Privately, Galen had suggested to Spencer that they should then leave Astren in the care of the small but very capable medical team for her rehabilitation treatment to continue. 'She won't like it, or want to agree, Spencer, so you may need to order her to remain.' The old man had confided earnestly. But Spencer didn't need convincing. Having got her back from the dead he wasn't prepared to take any chances with Astren's recovery.

The Infinity didn't enter orbit, but instead, Zan plotted a direct course to the large landing pad within the perimeter of the palace. As the heat of entry dissipated, Spencer and Amy, who were watching from the command bridge, gasped at the sight. Vast blue lakes twinkled in the sunlight, their shores and the land beyond crammed with a seemingly never-ending and impenetrable carpet of intense green. As they descended, the enormity of the forests and the trees themselves became evident. 'Some of these trees grow to hundreds of metres in height,' Bradlii informed them. 'The biosphere here is one of the most biggest and most established in the entire Galaxy, and as a result, the air is heavily oxygenated, so you will feel invigorated and it will aid Astren in her recovery.'

The Infinity levelled out and flew at low level toward their destination. Spencer was spellbound, it was like looking at a world that was largely untouched by development, and as a result, had thrived in a way that ecologists back on Earth could never imagine. There were flocks of birds that occasionally appeared on the scanners, riding thermals generated by the topography, and mountain ranges and rivers passed by in a continual and spectacular vista.

Presently, their ship slowed, and then, as a large walled compound hove into view, Zan brought them to a hover, before gently lowering *The Infinity* with an imperceptible bump as her hydraulic legs extended and absorbed the impact of landing.

'All engines stop and shut down primary and secondary propulsion systems.' The pilot instructed the ship's AI. Then he turned and smiled, 'Welcome to Balairen IV Emperor. Your Guard of Honour awaits.'

Spencer's heart sank a little. He still couldn't get used to the attention and, well, the deference that he would so often receive. "Impostor Syndrome" he had heard it was called – the continual nagging doubt that you really shouldn't be in the role you are in. It was only a matter of time before he was found out.

He had confided these feelings to Galen more than once, but the sage, while a little sympathetic, was resolute. 'Get used to it Spencer, it isn't all about you, it's about what you now represent. The hopes and dreams of countless trillions are invested in the Emperor of the Galaxy.'

If that had been meant to provide some kind of reassurance or to make it easier, it definitely hadn't, and Spencer wondered if he would ever feel remotely comfortable in the role that fate had thrust upon him.

'Ready to disembark,' said Aila, and with a sigh, Spencer made his way to the ceremonial exit of the ship. The long ramp to the landing pad's surface was already extended, and in the clear air, he could see what looked like at least a hundred troops lined up either side of an intensely purple carpet that led all the way to an astonishingly grand entrance to what he assumed was the Emperor's Palace.

Amy stood beside him and squeezed his hand. 'Galen tells me our quarters are beautiful, and the food here is amazing, and your private swimming pool has to be seen to be believed.'

'I'm going to have to ask Galen how he knows all this because I'm pretty sure he isn't always straight with me,' Spencer muttered, and then took a deep breath. 'Okay, let's do this.'

He forced a smile and began to walk down the ramp.

As their party reached the bottom, the troops snapped to attention and a woman, identified as a commanding officer, stepped forward and saluted.

'Emperor, we are humbled by your presence. May I present your guard of honour, ready for your inspection?'

Spencer groaned inwardly. This kind of thing just felt so awkward, but he remembered Galen's advice and knew that he owed these people due respect, for they had dedicated their lives to the position he now found himself in.

With Amy at his side, Spencer did his best to conduct a detailed inspection of the assembled men, women and other genders and species. He tried his hardest to appear authoritative, and conjure up a serious but appreciative and kindly demeanour. By the time they reached the steps to the imposing palace, he felt his face might crack, but he turned, and spoke in the loudest and clearest voice he could muster.

'I would like to thank you for your welcome, and my respects to you all. You are a credit to yourselves, your commanding officers, and to the Galaxy.'

Galen, who was standing behind him leaned forward and whispered,'Nicely done Emperor. You're getting the hang of this!'

As they turned, Spencer heard the order for dismissal, and then something else. A rhythmic stamping of feet. He froze and then turned slowly. 'They're applauding you, Spencer,' Aila said softly. 'They have faith in you, as do we.'

Spencer felt like he might choke, but instead stood and for some reason, he could never quite explain in the years that followed, took a small bow.

33

Respite:

To call the Emperor's quarters sumptuous would be an understatement of an order of magnitude akin to saying that Haxenaar had mild anger management issues, thought Spencer to himself, as they entered through a luminescent glass archway.

The walls, polished smooth from a pure white stone sparkled with crystal inclusions as they soared toward an arched roof perhaps thirty metres above. Incredible objet d'art were displayed on plinths and columns throughout the network of chambers, and uniformed assistants stood ready to, well, assist, Spencer assumed, with any request he might have.

Amy was grinning from ear to ear. 'Whoa! This is something else eh, babe?' Spencer grimaced, thinking of his bedroom back on earth and wishing he could spend a few nights there, but Amy's good humour was not going to be spoiled.

'Hey, look at this!' To one side of the master chamber was a large bathing pool, with a waterfall cascading over an enormous natural cluster of quartz type crystals, many of them larger than a person. The water was a deep blue and shimmered in the soft light that radiated from sources unseen.

'Oh boy, I could do with a good soak! And there's room in this for twenty, let alone two!' Amy gushed.

Spencer felt his face turn hot. He hated that he blushed so easily. Amy spotted his awkwardness and laughed, 'Don't worry, I won't embarrass you!' And without even waiting for him to respond she began to peel off her smart-suit down to her underwear, 'Come on Spencer, last one in is a wussie!'

Spencer hesitated, but then said, 'What the heck, the water does look good.' He rapidly pulled off his suit, making sure his boxers remained firmly in place and threw himself into the pool with a laugh.

The temperature was simply perfect, not too hot and not too cold. Later he would learn that an AI had already adjusted it to the optimum for his body temperature, but right now it just felt wonderful.

Amy splashed about happily and then threw some water in his face. Spencer retaliated and for a few minutes, the two of them forgot everything and just enjoyed themselves.

After their games had subsided, Amy swam over to Spencer and placed her arms around his neck. 'You know what I want right now?'

Spencer felt his face turn crimson, and he stammered, 'Er, no, I'm not sure I do Amy, what do you want?'

She cocked her head to one side and winked. 'I'd really, really love a Yumburger!'

Spencer let out a sigh of relief and then laughed. 'You know what Amy? I'd love a Yumburger too!'

One of the assistants, who had been standing quietly some distance away, advanced. 'Your eminence requires some sustenance?'

'If you mean would I like some food, then you're spot on, we would love something to eat if it isn't too much trouble?'

'If your eminence could describe what you desire, we will do our utmost to provide it.'

Amy needed no further encouragements, and quickly reeled off a surprisingly accurate description of a double Yumburger, with fries and a shake. 'And some ketchup and mayo,' Spencer added.

Less than twenty minutes later Spencer and Amy had been joined by the rest of their crewmates, and with a small fanfare, a catering team of three arrived and began setting out a table with beautiful dishes of fruits, cakes, salads, plates of things Spencer didn't recognise, and then with evident pride, two platters containing what looked astonishingly like Yumburgers with French fries before Spencer and Amy.

Amy didn't wait and took a huge bite. Her eyes went wide, and through her enormous mouthful spluttered, 'This is incredible! It's like a Yumburger, but even better!'

Spencer took a bite of his own, and then, 'Oh, wow!' as the burger melted in his mouth. He looked up to see the concerned faces of the caterers, clearly anxious to learn if they had satisfied his request. Spencer swallowed, and smiled at them, 'Superb! Better than that, absolutely delicious! Thank you!'

'Galen, Zan, Qarak, Astren, you have got to try one of these!' Galen looked doubtful and reached for a fruit. 'C'mon, this is an Earth delicacy, and I so want you to enjoy one.'

*

Two thousand six hundred and forty-eight light-years away, Haxenaar stood in the centre of the communications dome of his flagship. The holoprojections of his fleet and battle group commanders gazed down deferentially on him as he issued his commands.

'Despite the best efforts of our spies, we have not yet been able to locate the impostor and his collaborators with precision, but we have narrowed the search down to this sector.' At his gesture a holoimage of several star systems appeared in the centre of the dome, rotating as various planets and their moons were highlighted for the benefit of those watching.

'Intelligence suggests it is likely that he is hiding out on one of several neutral planets, and three have fortified compounds that make them potential refuges for his gang.' The planets in question illuminated as he spoke – Jincis VIII, Tornia, and then Balairen IV.

'An orbital attack similar to our recent victory at Duranian is unlikely to guarantee success, as any of these installations will have secure bunkers buried deep underground. Therefore our best option is a full-scale ground assault, where we can ensure that every potential threat is eliminated.'

The commanders nodded slowly in unison. One

asked, 'Do we have any data on the nature of the defensive capability of these compounds?'

Haxenaar paused, and then with a snarl responded, 'It does not matter. We will destroy them with overwhelming force, and then we will send a QE holocom of the execution of Spencer Edwards and his friends to the Galaxy so that every sentient being understands the price of resisting our will'.

The commanders enthusiastically murmured their approval, and one, his large mouth contorted into a dripping wound in his hideous face, barked, 'Your brilliance and leadership will bring us total victory my liege. We pledge our lives to your righteous cause.' His compatriots threw their heads back and uttered guttural howls of agreement.

Haxenaar was pleased. His hold over his forces was, at least for the moment, unquestioned. But he also knew that failure to find and kill his nemesis would lead to questions over his authority and lay the ground for a future coup. Zylaxxian leaders fought to achieve dominance, slaying any who stood in their way, but their hold on power lasted only so long as they won victories. It had always been thus.

34

Bioshock:

The two days that the crew had spent on Balairen had been restful, and Spencer had been delighted by reports that Astren's recovery was exceeding expectations, but there was still considerable uncertainty as to whether she would regain full physical functionality in due course. Of her mental acuity though, there was no doubt. On several occasions, she had favoured Spencer with one of her most withering looks, although this time he found that he rather welcomed them.

On the second evening, Spencer had requested to spend some time with her alone, and they strolled contentedly along one of the many beautiful terraces that surrounded the palace and overlooked the never-ending forests of this most tranquil of worlds.

'May I speak freely sir?' Astren had paused and leaned against a carved stone balustrade, her hands resting on its banister as she gazed out across the treetops.

'Of course Astren, anything.'

'You should have let me die, Spencer.' Astren spoke without anger but in earnest. 'My role, my purpose in life is to protect you. I had done that, and the cost was my life. It was a price I was more than willing to pay.'

Spencer nodded that he understood. 'But I wasn't. The price was far too high for me.'

'You cannot protect us all Spencer, we are at war and people will die. You have to be prepared to accept that, because if you aren't, then you will not be able to make the hard decisions when the time comes. And if you can't, all may be lost.'

Spencer was silent for a moment, and then turned to Astren. 'I know that, and I know there may come a time when I have to order people to lay down their lives in the quest for galactic peace, but I will never be comfortable with that. If I can save a single soul, then I will do all that I can to do so.' Astren gazed at him thoughtfully, but said nothing.

'I never asked to be Emperor, Astren, and God knows I am sure there are many who could do a far better job than me, but I know this; every life is precious, and I will mourn for each and every one that is lost, but,' and at this, his voice took on a steely edge, 'I will also ensure that the enemies of peace are defeated and held to account for their barbaric crimes. On that, you have my word.'

Now Astren looked Spencer directly in the eye as if she were weighing the strength of his resolve. It was a determination that she recognised, and an attribute she admired. 'I believe you sir, and I will gladly die once again for you if that is necessary,' she said, and for a brief moment Spencer thought he detected a small grin threatening to break her taciturn features, but she recovered herself and gave a little nod instead. If this was an attempt at humour, Spencer thought it was a poor one, but then Astren gave what was the closest approximation of a smile Spencer had ever seen from her. Delighted, he smiled broadly back, and then on impulse embraced her. 'I'm just so damned glad you didn't die, Astren!'

Awkwardly, she returned the hug and then stepped back. 'You truly are the Emperor of the Galaxy, Spencer, and I am honoured to fight at your side.'

And then suddenly there was a flash on the horizon, and then another, and another. Spencer and Astren turned to look. 'A storm?' Spencer asked, but before his companion could respond there were shouts and the sound of feet running. Within moments they were surrounded by armed guards, and being hustled back into the palace and then seconds later into a zero-g elevator to hurtle down into a bunker deep beneath the mountainside they had been enjoying just a minute before.

'What the hell is going on?' Spencer demanded of a senior officer who rushed to attend to them as they stepped off the pad.

'Zylaxxian shock troops are landing twenty kilometres to the west, sir. Multiple units with mechanised all-terrain assault vehicles and heavy weaponry.'

Spencer and Astren were ushered into a command centre, where glowing holoscreens showed countless smooth cylinders penetrating the atmosphere, before slowing and touching down on a series of neighbouring hilltops. Out of each cylinder stepped a single fully armed Zylaxxian trooper, and it was clear that there were already perhaps a thousand or more forming up into squads, each equipped with rapid armoured vehicles that looked not unlike a trilobite from Earth's prehistoric past.

'Where are Amy and the rest?' Spencer shouted to the officers present.

'They will be here momentarily, sir', and at that, a door opened and Amy, Zan, Galen, Aila and Qarak burst through. Zan was clearly shaken. 'This is not good, not good at all sir. *The Infinity* is still not fully repaired and her systems haven't yet been tested.'

'Defence forces are mobilising,' an AI intoned. Spencer grabbed the arm of a nearby officer. 'How long can we hold them off?'

'Hours perhaps, but no longer than that. We are well equipped, but there are simply too many of them. Sensors show five Zylaxxian battlecruisers in orbit, and based upon what we know about their carrying capacity, we estimate there could be as many as eight thousand Zylaxxian combat troops in the process of landing. We have a little over a thousand trained council guards here, and although we are well emplaced, we will be overwhelmed before long.'

'Then we need to attack now, while they are still landing and preparing for their assault.' Astren spoke quietly, but clearly. The room paused, and eyes turned to her.

'She's right,' Spencer agreed. 'While they are landing they are more vulnerable. We need to launch a pre-emptive strike now and try to do as much damage before they begin advancing. What can we hit them with?'

Another officer stood up from his console. 'Sir, we have plasma cannons, but they are currently just beyond the horizon so we cannot hit them directly. They know that of course, which is why they landed there.'

'What else?' Spencer demanded.

'We have a wing of intra-atmosphere single-seat attack craft, and four larger heavy lifters that can drop charges. We also have eight missile batteries and thermocharge launchers.'

Spencer met the individual gazes of each of his companions; they were looking to him for his command to send men, women and others into deadly battle.

The holoscreens above and around them showed images of Zylaxxian war machines blasting trees from their path as they began to move forward, huge swathes of ancient forest being incinerated in seconds by their purple and blue plasma cannons.

He took a deep breath. 'Do it. Launch an attack now, while we still can.'

The officers saluted, and an AI spoke. 'Pilots boarding, and launching. Missile batteries free and pivoting.'

From far above, through hundreds of metres of rock, came distant roars as the batteries opened up, their deadly hypersonic missiles leaving their launchers before detonating just seconds later in the air above the Zylaxxian landing sites. The hilltops momentarily disappeared in a bright haze of explosions, but as the glare subsided it was clear that although the strike had caused damage, the heavily armoured Zylaxxian's were barely pausing. Hundreds of hectares of forest and thousands of noble trees that had stood for a millennia were now ablaze as they cut through to press onward toward the palace beneath which the Emperor and his entourage sheltered.

Next, the small ground attack craft screamed in, firing their plasma cannons at the advancing Zylaxxian troop columns, but their barrages were being returned and several of the defenders erupted in fireballs as they were hit. One spiralling down into the dense undergrowth before an explosion marked the place where its brave pilot had met her end.

The heavy lifters, large and ungainly transporters swooped down, releasing hundreds of charges from their bellies that spread out in a carpet of white-hot plasma across the relentless Zylaxxian advance, but within moments two of them were shot out of the sky, a third was heavily damaged and forced to crash land into a nearby lake. Only the fourth survived to turn, now divested of its lethal cargo, and limp back toward the palace landing pads to re-arm.

Spencer stood transfixed before the largest holoscreen. 'It's like a scene from World War One,' he whispered in horror. It was true. The once beautiful and pristine forests now looked like hideous scars seared across several miles of landscape, the vegetation obliterated and burned away as the Zylaxxian hordes continued their relentless advance.

He cleared his throat and then spoke calmly. 'We cannot escape. Even if we could launch *The Infinity*, there are five Zylaxxian battlecruisers in orbit that will shoot us out of the sky. The Zylaxxians are here for me, and me alone. So as I see it, there are two options. Either I surrender, or…' He locked gaze with each of his friends in turn, 'I must die in battle. The Emperor cannot be captured by Haxenaar. That will be a victory I will deny him, no matter what.'

The bunker was silent for a moment, save for some gasps. Amy looked at him in horror, and tears sprang from her eyes,

'No Spencer, no way!' Spencer took her hand gently and gave her the bravest smile he could muster. 'Amy, I love you more than anything, but if the price of your life is my own, I will gladly give it. Besides, there is more than just you and me at stake here, we have the whole Galaxy to think about.'

'Sir, I'm getting some strange atmospheric readings.' One of the officers present looked up from his screens, and then his partner sitting to his left cut in. 'I'm registering intense gravimetric disturbances, localised in the area of the Zylaxxian advance.'

Spencer looked at Galen, but the old man raised his eyebrows and shook his head. 'Anyone? Any ideas what's going on?'

It was Bradlii who spoke. 'If I were to hypothesise, I would say the planet is responding to this attack, in a way similar to how a body might respond to the invasion of a virus.'

'Zylaxxian troops now four kilometres from the outer defence perimeter.' The AI intoned without emotion.

On the screens, the sky was darkening rapidly, and then there was a flash as a lightning bolt struck the ground just a few hundred metres from a Zylaxxian armoured assault vehicle. The ground shook, and rock dust fell on their heads, causing them to cough, the lighting dimmed momentarily before the emergency lighting cut in.

'What in Hades name was that?' Zan cried.

'Localised earthquake, the epicentre is directly below the Zylaxxian columns,' called out an incredulous officer.

And then all hell broke loose. The sky above the Zylaxxians began to flash with an intensity that hurt the eyes, as lightning strike after lightning strike lashed the

Zylaxxian brigades. Fissures opened in the ground as it shook continuously with repeating quakes and aftershocks.

Spencer and all in the bunker stood and watched in awe as Balairen IV unleashed its fury on those who had injured it.

Zylaxxian armoured vehicles were bursting into flames as they were struck repeatedly with millions of volts of electricity. Panic began to break out amongst the foot soldiers as jagged lightning bolts cut them down in their hundreds and flames began to spew from cracks in the ground.

'Seismic activity is off the scale, but remains constricted to the area around the invasion force.' Another officer reported, his voice shaking.

The images flashing across the holoscreens were nothing short of apocalyptic. Lava began to erupt from the fissures, raining molten death on the Zylaxxian forces who were now in total disarray.

'I've never seen anything like this in my life,' Galen gasped. 'It's incredible!'

Spencer watched, unable to tear his eyes away from the dreadful scene, and he became aware of an uncomfortable sensation. He was, in a most savage and primordial way, almost enjoying the spectacle.

The central holoscreen zoomed out, and a live feed from an orbiting satellite filled the room. Lightning was arcing up through the clouds and reaching out toward the Zylaxxian battle cruisers in geosynchronous orbit above the battlefield. The warships began to move away, perceiving the threat, but one was too late. A massive tendril of billions of volts grabbed it, flashing up and down its hull, and explosions followed as the cruiser began to list out of control, its bow dipping downward as it scraped and then began to enter the upper atmosphere.

Spencer and his companions watched transfixed as the mighty craft began to burn and break up, showering incandescent fragments across the stratosphere that instantly became shooting stars.

For more than twenty minutes the intense barrage continued to brutalise the helpless landing forces before finally, it abated. The images on the holoscreens were horrific. Burned corpses littered a wide area, scattered amid the smoking hulls of assault vehicles that had become macabre coffins for their inhabitants.

Lava had spread out, immolating all in its path, and the scorched earth bore testament to the massacre as a deep scar in an otherwise vista of glorious deep green.

The AI spoke, 'Life signs negligible, no movement detected.'

Nobody made a sound, it was as if words were an inadequate response to the carnage they had just witnessed, but then they turned their eyes toward the Emperor.

Spencer, his face impassive, said coldly, 'They had it coming to them.'

*

An hour or so later, orbital scans showed that the other four Zylaxxian cruisers had fled the system, and so Spencer and his compatriots seized the opportunity to depart, but not before he had issued Astren with a direct order to remain and continue her convalescence. Unhappy as she was, she was disciplined enough not to argue, and so, after a few moments alone with Qarak, *The Infinity*, mostly repaired but not fully tested, lifted off without her.

Galen, clearly shaken in a way that Spencer had never seen before, was already speculating. The scientist within him craved an explanation for what had occurred. 'My hypothesis, and it is purely speculative, is that the gigantic biomass of Balairen IV has, over countless millions of years, achieved some kind of collective consciousness. When the forests were attacked by the Zylaxxians that consciousness hit back in self-defence. It had identified that if not completely obliterated, the invaders would continue to inflict damage to the ecosphere, and so it destroyed them, utterly and completely.'

'So basically you are saying that the planet fought back as Bradlii suggested?' said Amy, her eyes wide.

'Yes, Amy, that is exactly what I am saying, extraordinary as it may seem. I simply have no other viable explanation.'

35

Threat:

Haxenaar's fury was boundless. The bisected corpses of several senior commanders lay scattered in the great dome of his flagship. The holoimages of other Zylaxxian high-commanders and members of the Executive gazed down impassively, but Haxenaar knew that privately they would now be having their doubts about his leadership, and beginning to consider who might take over as his successor. It was the Zylaxxian way and had always been so. A leader only remained as the leader for as long as he was victorious.

If that authority was eroded by failure, others waiting in the wings would become emboldened, and it would not be long before there was an open challenge. When that happened, Haxenaar would have no choice but to either destroy his would-be usurper or stand aside and be slain himself.

He had been personally briefed on the catastrophe of Balairen IV, and although he understood that the cataclysm visited upon his invasion forces was impossible to foresee or respond to militarily, his first priority had been to assert his dominance over his forces by a public display of retribution upon the hapless field commanders who had failed to capture Spencer Edwards of Earth.

And so the bodies of three loyal Zylaxxians now lay at his feet. They had met their end with composure and resolve, even though they had known that the failure was not theirs alone. Perhaps, Haxenaar thought to himself, there were already those who were readying themselves to lay the blame on him.

Their executions had been relayed across the Galaxy on QEComms, as a message to all those who might dare to oppose Zylaxxian might, along with holoimages of the Galactic Council members still being held in the Grand Hall and its grounds. A personal message from Haxenaar himself, threatening anyone who might aid his foe with diabolical retribution had ended the transmission.

Haxenaar paced, as he sometimes did when in deep thought, and then he turned and snarled at his attending lieutenants. 'I want full details of the system known as Sol, and in particular the planets designated tri-helio and quadra-helio. If Spencer Edwards is not ready to give himself up, then perhaps we need to give him no choice. He must choose between his own life and that of his pitiful home planet if it is to be permitted to exist and serve the Zylaxxian executive.'

36

Leads:

After departing Balairen IV, *The Infinity* had jumped into a sparsely populated region of the Galaxy, far from the inner systems and teeming galactic hub.

Long-range sensors were showing fewer stars and even fewer systems. They were now more than forty thousand light-years from Earth, and space itself had changed. As there were now many fewer stars to fill their vistas, other more distant galaxies were visible to the naked eye.

Spencer and Amy stood by one of the large virtual windows of his quarters. Both were silent and had been so for some time.

'It's incredible isn't it, Amy? We are now so far away from home, that the light that left stars here when Neanderthals and Woolly Mammoths roamed the Earth is only now detectable by astronomers back home. What would the scientists and our families think or say if they knew where we were now, and what we have seen?'

'I think they'd be pretty terrified to be honest, Spencer' said Amy earnestly. 'I mean we've had a glimpse at how incredible the Galaxy is, but also how violent, dangerous and deadly it can be.'

Spencer thought for a while on her words, and the realisation he had been resisting for some time, perhaps hoping not to have to confront, began to solidify into the inevitable. He had known that in the end they would have no choice but to fight Haxenaar in one final desperate battle.

'We have to destroy the Zylaxxians, Amy. Every last one of them.'

Amy reacted, but not in the way Spencer expected. She looked horrified.

'We can't do that! I mean we shouldn't do that, even if we could, Spencer, my God, listen to what you are saying!'

Spencer was immediately defensive. 'I know how it sounds, but what choice do we have? Haxenaar isn't going to give up until he has defeated us and taken the throne for himself, and then what will happen? Do you think he will just let us go? Do you think he won't threaten Earth? Bloody hell Amy, he could even destroy it. Everything gone, our friends, our families, our homes, our entire damned planet. The whole of human civilisation as if it had never existed!'

'But you are talking about genocide, Spencer. Exterminating an entire race, no matter what or who they are. That is wrong. You know it's wrong! How do we even know if all Zylaxxians think like Haxenaar? Perhaps there are some who are different! Would you kill all of them too?'

'If I must, yes!'

Amy was aghast. Spencer reached out toward her but

she roughly pushed him away. 'No boy I love would do such a thing, and I certainly won't be a part of massacring an entire species, Spencer!' She turned and fled from the room, leaving Spencer standing alone, shocked and struggling with his anger, and yes, perhaps even some shame.

*

Spencer saw little of Amy over the next day or so, as she was obviously avoiding him. And, to be honest, Spencer wasn't yet ready to speak with her. He was angry, but increasingly less so with her, and more and more with the situation he and his crewmates had been forced into. But most especially he raged against Haxenaar.

He spent most of his time reading and researching with Bradlii and the ship's onboard AI. He slept little, and by morning he had something he needed to discuss with the crew, who, upon his request, assembled in the extensive conference suite.

He attempted a smile at Amy, but she pointedly looked away, and that hurt a lot. Still, Spencer was more determined to lead now than ever, and he needed the help, support and belief of everyone in the room. First, though, he needed their agreement.

'Thanks for coming everyone. I've been doing a lot of thinking over the past day, and I've realised a few things. So before I start, I owe someone an apology.' He turned to Amy. 'You are right. We cannot set out to destroy an entire race indiscriminately. No matter how dangerous a foe Haxenaar is, we cannot hold all Zylaxxians responsible for his actions.

If we do that, we are no better than him.'

Amy's eyes met his, but she was clearly still wary. She had seen a side to Spencer that she didn't like one bit, and, now he had had time to think and reflect, he had discovered he didn't like it either.

'If I am to be Emperor, and bring peace to the Galaxy, I cannot do that by being even worse than those who have chosen to be our enemies. I have to lead by example, by being just and fair and, well, responsible. How could I possibly have any moral authority if I go down in history as the Emperor who committed genocide?' He looked directly at Amy, his face was apologetic.

Amy closed her eyes for a moment, and then when she opened them they were damp, but she smiled and nodded her relief to Spencer, who crossed the room, sat down next to her, and kissed her on the cheek.

'I'm so sorry, Amy, and you were right. I am better than that, but thank you for reminding me.'

Under the table, her hand sought his and gripped it tightly. 'I knew you were, but you had me worried there for a bit, she whispered.

Spencer gazed around the table, all those present were waiting on him.

'Okay, so this is what we are going to do. I've learned a lot, and an awful lot about the Zylaxxians and their history thanks to Bradlii and the ship's archive. Yes, their history is one of military conquest, but there is more to them than that. Like any sophisticated society, there are many factions within the Zylaxxian civilisation. Most are aggressively expansionist, but not all. There are Zylaxxians who are scientists, who are doctors, who are teachers, even some who are artists and poets.' He paused, but most of his companions looked confused, with the exception of Galen and Amy.

'So what I am saying is that Haxenaar rules by fear, but not all Zylaxxians necessarily think like him, or have the same aims. We need to talk to those who think and act more like us. We need to use the Zylaxxian militaristic system to work in our favour, and foment a coup against the existing leadership.'

Galen nodded slowly. 'I have heard of a Zylaxxian dissident leader named Vortrax, who leads a small but growing band of resistance fighters opposed to Haxenaar's plans for conquest and expansion. It may be possible to get word to him. I will see what I can do.'

37

Footie:

Spencer wasn't very good at football, but he enjoyed the game nonetheless. His team, Allerington Thunderclaps Under 15's were in their usual position in the league, that is to say, bumping along the bottom. Sometimes they changed places with the Bromsley Bazookas, but then the Bazookas usually had to play with ten or less players as one or more would frequently be either injured or in trouble with the Young Offenders Team, who weren't a football team at all, but an overstretched social service.

It was the first game of the season, and supposedly a "friendly" with South Camberley Tigers who were the undisputed league leaders, as they usually were, but, as Spencer reflected, a less pleasant team to play would be hard to find. All the players were hard as nails, seemingly well-coached in the art of the dirty tackle, and virtuosos at taking a dive and writhing around in fake agony.

Upon his return to Earth, in response to a plea from his team manager for 'Every lad to turn up and give these Tiger buggers a good thrashing' Spencer had made sure his kit was washed and ready. Amy had insisted on coming to support. She wore a woolly hat in the team colours and was ready to cheer him and his fellow players on. If they were going to be humiliated once again, it would at least be nice to see a friendly face on the touchline Spencer thought to himself.

And then Mum had said she was coming too and bringing Hassan. The big man beamed at everyone, including the surly-looking Tigers who glared back. Their parents weren't much better, scowling and sneering at Spencer's team as they warmed up. But Spencer was greatly distracted. He watched as Mum and Hassan, with Mo in his own little kit, positioned themselves directly next to Amy, and then, (oh the horror!) began to chat to her. Spencer couldn't make out anything being said, but within minutes there seemed to be plenty of laughter (presumably about him, he thought miserably), and they seemed to be getting on like a house on fire.

Naturally, Spencer wasn't wearing his smartsuit as that would have been far too obvious. He realised that he felt vaguely vulnerable without it, so used had he become to wearing it. Besides, as Bradlii had unhelpfully pointed out, the capabilities of the suit would have been much akin to cheating in a competitive game. Not for the first time, Spencer resented the AI's piousness and had sulked for a few minutes, but eventually acknowledged that Bradlii had a point. So the AI had been relegated to the pocket of Amy's jeans and told to stay quiet, although of course he had immediately ignored that and accessed Amy's inner ear so as to make himself heard.

After the initial surprise of hearing Bradlii inside her head, Amy seemed to have adjusted very quickly. On more than one occasion, Spencer had noted that Bradlii seemed to like Amy a good deal more than he liked Spencer. She liked to tease him at times, and despite having a galaxy-spanning intellect, Bradlii didn't seem to mind. In fact, he appeared to rather enjoy it.

Suddenly a thought flashed into Spencer's head, 'Did Bradlii fancy Amy? Did the most advanced AI on the planet have a crush on his girlfriend?' He immediately felt the hot pangs of jealousy, but then smiled to himself. Even if that was the case, it wasn't as if Bradlii could do anything about it... unless... oh, he projected himself as some kind of dashing hunk who Amy would find irresistible. Stop it, Spencer! Now you are being totally ridiculous! He slapped the thoughts down and resolved never to mention his insecurities to Amy, who would undoubtedly think he had gone mad.

Now concentrate on the game, you idiot!

Spencer usually played in defence, but this time the coach had told him to get busy in the midfield.

'Peeeep!' Kick off and the ball was coming straight toward him. Spencer stopped it, and began to run toward the Tiger's goal until, Ooof!, he was on the floor with the wind knocked out of him, the result of a heavy tackle from an enormous opposing team member. Damn, that hurt! He staggered to his feet, and caught sight of Amy who looked pleasantly concerned before mouthing, 'You okay?' He nodded, not feeling all that okay at all.

'That wasn't very nice was it?' Spencer's Mum said to

Amy as they stood side by side on the touchline. Hassan grunted his agreement,

'Not very sporting at all' He grumbled, his usually beaming smile slipping for a moment.

Amy nodded, 'That was probably a foul, but I think Spencer's alright.'

Spencer's mum squeezed Amy's arm. 'I know he's not very good at taking care of himself, but he honestly is a sweet boy.' Amy thought of just some of the experiences she and Spencer had shared the past few weeks and smiled inwardly at the recollection of him heroically charging down corridors to rescue her from the heart of Haxenaar's ship, and nodded. 'I think he'll be alright.'

The game continued and within five minutes The Tigers had scored following two fouls and a warning.

'They're a rough lot, aren't they?' Hassan ventured, and then 'Oh, another one.' As a particularly large striker brushed aside a Thunderclaps defender and walloped the ball into the back of their net.

It wasn't long before a Tiger received another warning, and then a particularly nasty foul left the Thunderclap's best striker, a lad called Geoff who Spencer was quite friendly with, writhing on the ground in agony.

Spencer watched Geoff as he rolled around, clearly in a great deal of pain, and out of the corner of his eye saw several Tigers smirking at each other. He immediately felt his blood begin to boil. Geoff was helped off the pitch and into the arms of his worried-looking mum. He was limping badly, desperately trying not to cry in front of the onlookers. Good for Geoff, Spencer thought, he's not going to give anyone the satisfaction.

The whistle blew and the game resumed, but it was clear

that the Tigers weren't going to change tactics, and despite the vigilance of the referee, there was no shortage of very heavy tackles and two more goals.

At half-time and four-nil down, Spencer's team were understandably disheartened. They were getting a drubbing and they knew it. Despite the entreaties of their coach to rise above the dirty tactics of their opposition, they were angry but becoming more and more resigned to their impending defeat.

Spencer grabbed a few seconds with Amy and his family. 'Such a shame, Spencer,' his mum said. 'They don't deserve to win. What a shocking example they are setting to their younger brothers and sisters.' Amy though was staring at Spencer hard, 'You go get 'em, Spencer, we know you can do it.' And she made sure he saw that she tapped the pocket where Bradlii was carefully stowed.

Spencer was nonplussed. He had no idea what Amy meant but guessed she had hatched some kind of plan with the normally self-righteous AI. He jogged back into position, warily watching the hard-faced freckled lad who was his marker.

Within moments, the ball was coming directly at him and Spencer ran toward it, catching it just beyond the halfway line. Immediately, three Tigers were closing in on him, so he looked around, and tried to pass to a teammate. No sooner had the ball left his foot, than it seemed to accelerate, rocketing past his incoming interceptors, arcing spectacularly as it curved downward and then, surely not, past the Tiger's keeper and into the top right corner of the goalmouth.

Spencer stood, his mouth agape, as the referee blew his

whistle and an enthusiastic round of applause and cheering broke out from the Thunderclap supporters.

The next two goals came in quick succession, one from Spencer, the other from teammate Samesh who looked absolutely flabbergasted.

The first, seemingly bending the laws of physics as the ball left his right foot and performed a mid-air swerve around a charging Tiger before walloping into the back of the net, and the second, a closer range header that ricocheted off two bewildered Tiger team members before dropping over the goal line while a furious keeper stood shouting and swearing in frustration.

As the game headed into the final minutes, the score stood at four goals each. Tiger players launched a desperate and dirty offensive, with two Thunderclaps going down hard. Spencer was now a marked man, and the Tigers swarmed around him, determined to block any chance he might have of scoring again, but in the closing seconds, a miss-kick sent the ball on a trajectory directly toward Spencer. He leapt, and as he took to the air, Spencer became aware of a force that seemed to grab him, turning him over and connecting his foot with the ball in what would later be described as the most remarkable back-flip kick any of those present had ever seen.

Spencer landed on his feet just as the ball blasted past the stunned Tiger goalie and the crowd erupted in cheers. He had no idea what had just happened, but out of the corner of his eye, he saw Amy beaming, and immediately knew she had something to do with it.

He also noticed that several of the spectators had their phones out, and vaguely wondered if they had filmed his winning performance. Somehow that was troubling.

*

Later, as he walked her home, he asked, 'Amy, what did you do?'

Amy feigned innocence. 'What do you mean?'

'The match Amy, I couldn't play like that, yet somehow I was better than Ronaldo. I'm not stupid.'

'I didn't do anything, Spencer, I promise!' She squeezed his hand, but he could see an impish smile playing at the corners of her lips.

'Okay, so what did Bradlii do?'

'I'm right here, Spencer,' the AI said petulantly from his pocket.

'Alright Spencer,' Amy said, 'I didn't like how that other team were playing, and I was worried you were going to get hurt. And besides, they needed to be taught a lesson.'

'Go on!' Spencer didn't know whether to be annoyed or to just hug her.

'So Bradlii did something clever with... what was it, Bradlii?'

'Focused ultra-harmonic fields.'

Spencer sighed. 'Bradlii, for the benefit of those of us who don't have a complete mastery of physics, what does that mean?'

'Put simply, (oh boy, he was patronising, Spencer thought for the thousandth time) it is possible to use highly targeted and focused sound waves at exceptionally intense levels to move and manipulate objects at a short distance. I merely modelled the entire pitch with the surrounding environment and used it to reflect and control several billion sonic beams simultaneously.'

'So you could control the ball, and even my movements using these sound waves?' Spencer was impressed despite himself.

'Well done Emperor, you are correct.' Spencer grimaced at the self-satisfaction copiously mixed with his inherently condescending tone.

'So how does that square with the lecture you gave me about how wearing my smartsuit would be cheating, huh?' For once, Spencer felt he had caught the self-satisfied AI out.

Bradlii was silent for a moment, and then, 'There are some rare instances when the greater good outweighs some minor infringements of the rules. After observing the unsavoury tactics of your opponents, I judged that this was one of those times. I stand by that decision. If it troubles you, you are of course at liberty to speak to the referee and explain your ethical concerns.'

Damn. He had no answer to that, so to save face Spence grudgingly conceded. 'Okay, well, just this once Bradlii, and only because Amy asked you to for the right reasons.'

'Oh, she didn't ask me to, she just said, 'Bradlii, do something!' so I did. And it worked brilliantly if I do say so myself.'

Spencer had heard enough. 'One more question Bradlii, how do I turn you off?'

Bradlii, perhaps sensing the tone, chose not to respond.

38

Gravity Well:

The Infinity was at her maximum velocity of over 99 per cent of the speed of light, and at this speed, the view through the unaugmented windows was very strange. Stars and planets appeared stretched and warped as the ship came close to outrunning their light. Fortunately, the shipboard AI compensated on the holoscreens, and Spencer gasped as they passed close by a small planetoid, before arcing round and heading toward a nebula.

Without warning the shipwide alarm sounded in the control bridge, and Zan threw his hands up in horror. 'No!' he exclaimed in a panic-stricken voice.

The ship suddenly decelerated hard, and in the split-second, before the artificial gravity compensated, Spencer, Qarak and Amy, were flung into the air and hurtled forward to collapse in a heap against a bulkhead. Only Zan, who was seated and Aila, whose lightning reflexes had stabilised her footing, remained in position.

Spencer's head hurt as he staggered to his feet. Amy was on her knees, clearly groggy, and Aila helped her up. Qarak was out cold, a trickle of blood from his temple, and Aila hurried over to begin first aid.

'What the hell?' Spencer was winded and grasped a handrail as he struggled not to be sick.

'We've been caught in a gravity well,' Zan responded. 'I didn't see it coming and the sensors detected it too late to avoid it.'

Spencer straightened up and checked on Amy who was now standing at his side. She was pale but signalled that she was okay.

'What is a gravity well?' Spencer felt sure he wasn't going to like the answer.

'It's a localised area of space that acts rather like a miniature black hole. Gravity here is in flux, but at the bottom of the well is a piece of superdense matter, possibly the heart of an extinct star, that is warping spacetime around it. If we are dragged in, we will be crushed.'

'So how do we get out?'

'We don't. We have crossed the threshold and our engines are at maximum just keeping us from slipping in. Even so, we are being dragged toward the well, and I calculate that in less than an hour, our hull will be unable to withstand the gravimetric forces and we will be crushed.'

'Bradlii, figure something out!' Spencer commanded.

'Not so, easy Spencer, I'm afraid we are at a point further in than any ship has been known to escape from.'

'Well, that's not acceptable. It's not all going to end here after all we've been through. I won't have it.'

'I need options,' Spencer commanded. 'Zan, scan the area, what do we have nearby?'

'Just multiple small asteroids, both inside and outside of the gravity well perimeter, and what appears to be the derelict hull of a freighter. Probably the crew abandoned it decades ago and managed to escape just in time. It's currently at the Lagrange point between the gravity well and the nearest planet.'

'Okay, so what if we could somehow anchor ourselves to that freighter, and maybe drag ourselves out?'

'That won't work,' Bradlii said quickly. 'We currently weigh far more than that ship due to the forces being exerted on us, so we would simply drag the freighter in with us.'

'Can we boost our engine power?'

'We are already at over 100%, and we're not even holding position. The engines won't be able to take more than an hour or so of this, but we'll be crushed before then anyhow,' Zen confirmed gloomily.

Despite their predicament, Spencer felt strangely calm. 'Alright, so somehow we need to increase our power massively in a very short space of time, and do so without destroying ourselves in the process.'

'That's it, in essence,' Bradlii confirmed.

Spencer thought for a moment, and then an idea began to form in his mind. 'Every action has an equal and opposite reaction.' he mused to himself.

'What was that?' Bradlii asked.

'Something I remember from a physics lesson,' Spencer answered.

'Newton's Third Law I think...' Go on Spencer!' Amy squeezed his arm.

'So if we could tether ourselves to that floating hulk, then attach some kind of booster to it and accelerate it toward the gravity well, we could pivot against it, using it as a counter weight, a pendulum, and with our engines on maximum thrust throw ourselves clear.' He paused and looked up to see his friends staring at him, hard.

'That's quite brilliant, sir' said Zan. Aila nodded.

'I'm sorry to pour cold water on this idea,' Bradlii interceded, 'but how would we get anything across to the freighter? We would be subject to the same forces currently being exerted on *The Infinity*… unless…' he paused, 'Speed. The only way to temporarily reduce the gravitational pull would be to use something small and very fast-moving. Spencer, I have an idea.'

Spencer rolled his eyes, but said graciously, 'Now would be a good time to hear it, Bradlii.'

'We use the *Vengeance* Lander, with every booster strapped to it we can find, and fire it out of the hanger bay toward the other ship. Attached to the Lander must be a carbon nanotube tether that is anchored to *The Infinity*. We have a number of those aboard that are long and very thin with an exceptionally high tensile strength. The *Vengeance* must then be landed onto the old freighter, with its engines on full burn to fuse it to the hull. Then finally a plasma charge can be detonated to throw the ship toward the gravity well, which, if it all works will cause us to be thrown in the opposite direction away from it.'

'And what happens to the pilot?' Spencer asked.

His friends turned their eyes downward, they were all thinking the same.

'Unfortunately they would have little chance of survival.

Even if they launched their escape pod at precisely the right moment, I would calculate their chances of being sufficiently clear of the explosion to be less than fourteen per cent.'

Qarak stood straight. 'I will pilot the Lander sir, it will be my honour.'

Spencer looked at the proud Androsian but shook his head. 'No Qarak, your bravery is beyond question but I need you to survive this along with the rest of us. There is only one person here who might have a long shot at making this work.' He turned and looked at Aila. 'Aila, I must ask you. Not because you are a Synth, or because I value your life any less than any one of ours, or mine, but because only you have the reaction times necessary to even stand a chance of pulling this off, and because only you could survive in space if the escape pod failed.'

Galen had joined them on the Bridge. 'He's right you know,' he said softly. Aila also nodded her agreement. 'That is the right call, sir, I will gladly undertake the mission.'

*

The next twenty minutes were a flurry of activity. The Lander was prepped, and under the direction of Qarak and Aila, maintenance drones scurried around fitting the nanotube tether and auxiliary booster packs.

Meanwhile, *The Infinity* strained against the gravity well with the shipboard AI reminding them every few minutes of the increasing stresses on the hull and engines. Spencer could distinctly hear the ship creaking and groaning, as the entire structure struggled to hold together under the relentless strain inflicted upon it.

'We are ready sir.' Aila stood to attention, her clear eyes fixed on Spencer, waiting for his command. He held out his hand and gently touched her on the shoulder. 'You can do this, Aila. I know you can.'

'I will try my best sir, and, well, if it all goes right I'll be holding my breath waiting for you.'

Spencer smiled, that was probably the closest he had heard Aila come to making a joke. Was it possible she was nervous? 'Count on it. You'll be back on board *The Infinity* soon.'

The Synth nodded and then turned to climb the short-stepped ladder that had extruded from the side of the Lander, before entering and seating herself in the pilot's chair. She gave a thumbs-up to Spencer, Amy and Qarak, and then a soft glow emanated from the base of the Lander as it lifted off the flight deck. Now Spencer and the others retreated to behind a blast door and watched on a holoscreen as Aila initialised the Lander's drive systems, and brought the auxiliary boosters they had fitted online.

The nanotube tether, affixed to the rear of the Lander appeared impossibly fragile to Spencer, and he marvelled that something so thin could have such extraordinary strength. Bradlii had informed him that the cable was capable of lifting more than twenty million metric tons so that according to his calculations, it should be sufficient to catapult *The Infinity* out of danger, but it was going to be a close-run thing.

Under normal circumstances, *The Infinity* had a mass of more than 750,000 tons, but with the intense gravity now gripping it, the AI estimated that mass had increased by a factor of more than twenty.

'Launch countdown set and initiated. Preparing for launch in five…four…three…'

The engines on the Lander rapidly built to maximum thrust and the holoscreen dimmed to protect their eyes, 'Two… one… zero.' All the auxiliary boosters and packs ignited simultaneously and the small craft accelerated so rapidly that in just a fraction of a second it was clear of the hangar door and hurtling across the void toward the deserted freighter.

The holoscreen switched to a view from the cockpit, and the friends could see Aila, exerting herself against the intense g-forces of the acceleration, begin to control the craft as it closed in on its ancient target. She pressed a button, and the Lander began to descend, releasing the burned-out boosters as they failed. Spencer watched in silence as the gravity well seized the spent rockets and grabbed them back, crushing them in moments.

The Lander made contact with the upper hull of the derelict, and immediately robotic arms extended tipped with grappling hooks so as to latch on. The engines beneath the tiny ship flared as they melted the outer hull, fusing the Lander to the metal plating.

'Tether holding, tensile stresses increasing.' Bradlii began relaying real-time updates as they raced toward the bridge.

Zan was at his station, his focus absolute. He was speaking to Aila. 'We are ready for you to deploy plasma charges.'

'Confirmed. Deploying charges.' Multiple canisters ejected from the Lander and formed into a small cluster a few hundred metres from the freighter. 'Stand by for detonation in ten seconds.' Already the gravity well was beginning to grab them.

The cameras inside the Lander cockpit showed Aila standing and stepping toward the rear of the craft. A panel opened, and she entered a small tubular escape pod.

'Ejecting now, and... detonation.'

The flash was an intense green and blue, and Spencer could not see if Aila's escape pod had cleared the explosion. He feared it had not. The ancient carcass of the freighter was hurled toward the gravity well, splintering as it tumbled end over end toward its doom.

'Tether holding, just, and brace!' Zan shouted as *The Infinity* lurched violently as the cable went taught. The holoscreens showed the ancient hull of the freighter crumbling and disintegrating as the gravity well crushed it in its intense grip. *The Infinity*, essentially now the counterweight, swung wildly and was thrown in the opposite direction, just as Newton's Third Law predicted, Spencer thought incredulously to himself, as he hung on to a handrail for dear life.

'Accelerating at two point five gees, three, four-point five, hold on everyone, six gees.' Spencer and his crew sank backwards into seats that extruded themselves from the floor, as the intense acceleration pressed down on them.

'Eight gees, if it goes to ten I will activate the nano-air.' Zan warned them. 'Approaching Lagrange point, now twenty thousand k's ahead.'

They all willed *The Infinity* to pass the Lagrange point, the place where they would be free of the intense forces of the gravity well. Come on! Come on! Spencer mouthed silently.

'Velocity falling off.'

'No!'

'We aren't going to make it,' Zan said resignedly. *The Infinity* was slowing rapidly, and they could all feel it. The central holoscreen was counting down the distance to safety, ten thousand kilometres, eight thousand… seven… but it was clear their speed was dropping off too quickly. Spencer closed his eyes for a second. So close.

The shipboard AI spoke. 'Single incoming contact, no identifying transponder. Size…' It paused, 'Size approximately five kilometres in length, no weaponry detected, bio-mechanical.'

Spencer turned his head to look at Galen, but the old man's eyes were wide.

The holoscreen zoomed out to show something almost incomprehensibly massive and dark silhouetted against the stars for just a fleeting moment. Spencer gasped and tried to speak. Then terrifying razor-sharp metallic talons extended and *The Infinity* rocked and pitched forward as it was grabbed, like a bird of prey might clutch a small rodent, and they were swept away, snatched from the grip of the gravity well, and out into deep space.

39

The Servant:

'I see two possibilities here,' Galen said to the group, now all assembled on the command bridge. 'Either we've been rescued, or we are going to be eaten. The two possibilities aren't mutually exclusive, we may have been rescued so that we can be eaten.'

In the minutes since their escape from the gravity well, they had been carried several hundred thousand kilometres and apparently entered into orbit around a small and rather nondescript planetoid further out in the system. Their saviour, or captor, it was not yet clear which was the more accurate description, seemed in no hurry to release them, but perhaps encouragingly, Spencer thought to himself, they were still in one piece.

Aila though was still unaccounted for. Although she could survive in the hard vacuum of space for some time, she was not indestructible, and besides, she was his friend and he wanted her back, safe and sound.

'Bradlii, what is this… thing that has got us?' Spencer asked.

'I'm afraid I have insufficient data to draw a definitive conclusion.'

'Well then, speculate Bradlii! Come on, you must have some kind of best guess, surely?'

'Once again Spencer, you ask me to do something I abhor, but under the circumstances, I will make the following observations, from which we may be able to draw some kind of conclusion. First, we are held in the grip of a part mechanical, part biological creature, massive in its scale. That narrows it down, as there are comparatively few species in any of the historical records of a size approaching this. Secondly, it is clear that this is a space-faring entity, and thus must be both resilient and sentient so that it might navigate the vast distances of the cosmos and be able to find sustenance and others of its kind.'

'Okay, Bradlii, all that makes sense, but can you speed it up a bit?'

'Very well' (not for the first time there was a touch of petulance to the AI's voice), 'My best 'guess' is that this is a Ratarian. There have been no documented encounters with them for more than ten millennia, and even then the records are, shall we say, a little unreliable.' Holoscreens displayed an array of images, including some that looked like drawings, of… 'It looks like some kind of massive metal hawk!' Amy exclaimed.

Spencer admitted that she was not wrong. 'Okay, the fact it hasn't eaten us yet has to be good, right?' He directed the question to Galen, who shrugged. 'Maybe it's just taking its time to savour the moment?' He said somewhat unhelpfully.

'Bradlii, tell me more,' Spencer commanded.

'Legend has it that the Ratarians are an ancient species from beyond the galactic outer rim. They were once plentiful, but over time their numbers dwindled, although the reason is unclear. They are sentient and highly intelligent, comprised of both machine and organic parts, but whether they have a civilisation in the way we would recognise it remains unknown, as does their method of propulsion, although ancient scientists speculated that they might have an ability to create eddies in space that they use to propel themselves along.'

'So can we communicate with it?'

'There are records of limited communications, but there is no data on their language. Apparently they were believed to be aligned with the Ixenarian civilisation.'

Spencer bit his lip. 'You might have led with that Bradlii, because that is probably the bit we needed to hear most!'

'Well, I didn't rank the information in order of importance, but if you wish, I can apply such a filter in the future.'

Spencer sighed in irritation. 'Alright, so figure out how we can communicate with it. We need to know its intentions, and maybe it can even lead us to the Ixenarians.'

'I can attempt a direct neuro-tech link, using the ship's sensor array to amplify the signal if you wish?'

'Then do it, now.'

'Link established, that was remarkably straightforward.'

Suddenly the control room was filled with a deep rumbling whisper that seemed to wash over them like a wave. 'I am here. Greetings Spencer Edwards of Earth, Emperor of the Galaxy.'

Spencer was shocked but recovered himself quickly. How was it possible that this incredible creature knew of him? 'Greetings to you, and my hand in friendship. I wish to thank you for your intervention and rescue, and would like to know the name of our saviour.' There was a pause. Galen nodded his approval, but Spencer wondered if the Ratarian was still considering whether to consume them.

'You are most welcome. I was simply doing my duty, as my ancestors would wish it. My name is Satyvrat and I bring you a message, Emperor.'

'I would be glad to hear it.'

'Very well. The Ixenarian High Council would like to extend its grace and solidarity to Emperor Spencer Edwards and invites him and his noble fellow travellers to join them on Ixenar, the home of galactic civilisation.'

Spencer turned to his friends, his eyes wide. 'Wow!' he mouthed, and they all returned his sentiment with their own expressions of surprise.

Spencer, Bradlii and Galen spent the next half an hour talking to Satyvrat but learned little more about the Ixenarian masters who had sent this remarkable lifeform to make contact for them. Indeed, it turned out that the Ratarian was not able to reveal the location of Ixenar directly but instead had been instructed to provide the crew of *The Infinity* with a starting point for their journey, where it was understood they would receive or discover a signpost to their next destination. It quickly became apparent that the Ixenarians took their privacy, or perhaps more probably security, very seriously indeed. Although Spencer found this frustrating, Galen and Bradlii admired the rationale behind it and persuaded Spencer of the wisdom of this approach. 'Spencer, we are being hunted by the Zylaxxians. The Ixenarians have to be absolutely sure that we will not compromise the safety of their homeworld by inadvertently revealing its location. We must comply with their wishes, even if it does take us more time.'

Much to everyone's relief, Aila was recovered safely. Zan had located her, floating in free space, her escape pod smashed into fragments near the Lagrange point where they had been thrown by the explosion. She had shut down most of her radiation-hardened systems, and so was in low-power mode when brought aboard the ship. Within twenty minutes she was fully operational once more, although Galen insisted she spent some time running self-diagnostics in the MediBay.

Spencer visited her to express his thanks and make sure she was genuinely well, as his decision to send her into danger had weighed heavily on his mind throughout. 'Aila, you have no idea how glad I am to see you!'

'And I am glad to see you, Emperor.'

Spencer regarded her carefully, a frown evident upon his face.

'You are troubled, sir?

'Yes, I am Aila. I want, no, I need you to know that I hated sending you into danger like that. What if something had happened, and you hadn't made it back?'

Aila nodded slowly. 'I cannot begin to comprehend the weight of responsibility that now rests on your shoulders Spencer, but I know this. You are a good person, and you made the right decision for the sake of everyone. I want you to know that if I had not survived, I would have ended my existence knowing that I had contributed to our cause. For me, that would be enough for my life to have had meaning and purpose, and I thank you for that.'

Spencer blinked back the tears. It wasn't the first time he had struggled to understand the loyalty that others seemed to have to him, and their astonishing level of belief in him. He stood awkwardly for a moment, and then reached out and laid his hand on Aila's shoulder. It was soft to the touch and warm, just like that of a human. She turned to meet his gaze, her unwavering clear blue eyes like crystal pools. 'You really are one of the most remarkable people I have ever met, Aila, from any world.'

And with that, he turned and left, leaving the Synth to carefully contemplate her narrow escape, for just a fraction of a second.

40

Family Business:

Spencer had to admit that Bradlii had done a fine job in setting up a company, bank account, credit history and fictitious owner for 'SE Investments (Automotive) Ltd.' Further, the Galaxy's most conceited AI had transferred Spencer's salary through multiple financial exchanges and commodities before finally depositing more than £400,000 sterling in a bank account controlled by a certain Mr Cornelius Van Der Builder (a nice touch, thought Spencer once Bradlii had explained his little joke to him).

Of course, to Bradlii, as he had taken much pleasure in informing Spencer, the above tasks had been mere child's play, given the 'woeful lack of security around Earth's financial system.'

Some carefully targeted emails, convincing Hassan that he had been recommended as a potential manager with experience of both cars and their insurance, had elicited an enthusiastic response, and the setting up of a meeting at a vacant premises Bradlii and Spencer had identified and then leased entirely online, just two miles from the family home.

Bradlii had repeatedly questioned the ethics surrounding Spencer's instructions, but eventually, he had quietened down after Spencer had stood his ground and explained that once the business was operational, Hassan would have to run it successfully and make a profit sufficient to live on. Spencer was clear, this wasn't charity, it was an investment in a man he had great faith in and would enable the Emperor of the Galaxy to concentrate on being the Emperor of the Galaxy without continually worrying about the welfare of those he loved.

And so, on a slightly rainy Tuesday morning in April, Spencer waited in the office of the used car lot he was now quite incredibly the owner of. He and Bradlii had spent some time perfecting the holoimage of Mr Van Der Builder that the AI was now projecting to surround Spencer, complete with a disguised voice that gave Spencer a rather distinguished yet hard to place accent. Spencer knew that the one thing he must not do was to shake Hassan by the hand because this would disrupt the holographic imaging, but in the aftermath of the pandemic that custom had become less commonplace, so he felt that was a manageable risk.

However, Spencer was still nervous. Hassan was no fool, and pulling off this deception, no matter how benign and well-intentioned, was not going to be easy. Spencer was also, his drama teacher would have confirmed, no actor.

There was a knock at the door. Spencer straightened and whispered, 'Ready Bradlii?'

'Of course,' said the AI. Spencer rolled his eyes and took a deep breath before striding to the door and opening it.

'Good morning, Mr Shah, thank you so much for coming and being punctual. I appreciate that.'

Hassan smiled his broad smile and stepped into the small office.

'Mr Shah, my engagements this morning are pressing, but I hope we may conclude our business quickly and look forward to a long and profitable relationship.'

'I am obviously delighted that you approached me Mr Van Der Builder, but I'm honestly still quite taken aback by all this. Your emails said you heard about me from a mutual friend?'

'Well, yes, more of a friend of a friend of a business acquaintance, but I have contacts throughout many fields and I always look for ambitious but trustworthy businessmen and women to invest in and grow my portfolio of companies.' Spencer was glad that Bradlii had coached him so well, and although Hassan still looked a little puzzled, he was far too polite to press the matter further.

'Well then, how can I be of help to you?'

'As the emails from my assistant explained, I need an honest man with local knowledge, and experience in cars and all things automotive. You would seem to fit that bill most admirably.'

Hassan nodded emphatically, 'I think I do, and this role, I would be helping out with the running of this place?'

'No, Mr Shah, you would be running it yourself. You would be solely in charge. This would be your business as much as mine. I will provide these premises and the initial investment to purchase stock, and then the rest is up to you.

Profits will be split 50/50 between you and me.'

Hassan's jaw dropped, and it was clear he could hardly believe the offer he was being made.

Spencer continued, 'I am a wealthy man Mr Shah, and I have been successful by being a quick and unusually accurate judge of character. I am also a busy and private man, so you would largely be on your own. I can provide some advice and support by email or telephone, and my assistant, Miss Watson, who you have already been in contact with, will be your main point of contact. Once a year you will be required to undergo a full financial audit, and I expect complete transparency at all times in our dealings.'

Hassan nodded that he understood and Spencer felt that he was nearly there. He heard the voice of Bradlii in his head urging him to wrap it up and get out.

'You have my word that I will do all that I can to make this a success Mr Van Der Builder, and I cannot express to you how grateful I am for this opportunity.'

'I do not expect gratitude, I expect results. I am investing in you Mr Shah, and I trust you will not let me down.'

'Sir, I will not, and for my family's sake, I will make this the best and most reputable used car business in the area. I do have one question though, if I may?'

Spencer nodded.

'What name shall we give it?'

Spencer thought a moment, and then asked, 'You have a family I understand? And a young son, Mohammad?'

'Yes, I am blessed with a family, but I have two sons, Mohammad and Spencer.'

Within the holoimage, Spencer felt his voice might

crack, but he swallowed hard. 'Then it is settled, it shall be M. Shah and Sons.'

Hassan beamed and extended his hand, and Spencer nearly reciprocated before catching himself and with a smile, he proffered his elbow for a post-pandemic bump.

41

Death Trap:

'Ready to engage multi-drive in three...two...one... jump.' Zan punched the holobutton and the familiar feeling of momentary disorientation swept over the crew. Every time they did this, Spencer thought to himself, they bent the laws of physics in a way that would appear like nothing short of magic to any human being on earth.

Spacetime rippled and was punctured as *The Infinity* winked out of existence, ready to re-emerge just moments later, light years away on their journey to Ignis, the first port of call on their Ixenarian quest.

Suddenly ship-wide alarms began to sound and *The Infinity* lurched, hard to starboard. The AI's voice spoke with uncommon urgency.

'Jump interrupted, navigation systems off-line.'

Spencer shouted to Zan, 'What the hell is happening?'

'I'm not sure sir, I'm trying...' There was another hard

lurch, and then the sound of something impacting the hull. They all turned their eyes upward, although it was impossible to pinpoint the source of where the noise had come from.

'Multi-drive offline, manoeuvring thrusters compensating for lack of pitch control,' the AI continued to intone. 'Stabilising attitude. Ship is at all stop.' The silence was the first thing they all noticed and then, 'Look!' said Amy, pointing at the main holoscreen, and they all gave a collective gasp.

Outside *The Infinity* was something but it wasn't like any region of space they had become accustomed to. Energy was visible, rippling in boundless sheets and waves, spirals of charged particles appeared, flexed, and then vanished to be replaced moments later with other eerily beautiful tendrils of light.

It was Bradlii who spoke first. 'By my observations, and the data I have accessed from the ship's sensors, our jump was deliberately interrupted, and we are now outside of normal spacetime and fully enveloped in inter-dimensional space.'

Spencer said, 'I don't like the sound of that, Bradlii. You said our jump was deliberately interrupted? Why, and by whom?'

Qarak pointed at the holoscreen, 'I think there lies our answer, Emperor.' A point of light, some distance off in the murk, were just about visible and growing slowly. The holoscreen zoomed, and the crew issued a mutual groan. The pinprick was evidently another ship, and the jagged silhouette could only belong to one space-faring but hostile species.

'Damn!' Galen voiced their thoughts in a manner most unlike him. 'It looks suspiciously like a troop carrier to me, Spencer. Let me just check something.'

He flicked through a few holomenus and confirmed, 'Yes, as I suspected, all our weapons are inoperable here, which at least means those Zylaxxians are not going to be able to blast us from the sky either.'

'Well, that's at least a good thing, isn't it?' Spencer asked, desperately hoping for something positive about their situation.

'I'm afraid not. It means we are almost certainly going to be boarded.'

Spencer felt his stomach tighten. Of course, Galen was right. That ship would be full of heavily armed Zylaxxian combat troops with one purpose in mind. They surely meant to capture *The Infinity* and his friends, and then presumably take them all back to Haxenaar for a less than pleasant meeting that would almost certainly involve public humiliation and execution.

'Okay, we need options and fast. Bradlii, how long before that ship reaches us?'

'Due to the distortions in spacetime, it is not possible to give an accurate assessment.'

'So make your best guess.'

The AI hesitated, 'I would estimate at less than an hour.'

'Then we have a little time,' Spencer turned to the rest. 'Let's go to the conference room. Zan, instruct the ship's AI to monitor and update us if there is any significant change in the situation.'

A minute later, Spencer was standing at the head of the

table, and all eyes were on him. 'We can't overpower them in a direct fight, so we have to assume they will breach *The Infinity*'s hull and get aboard. However, if there is one thing I think I have noticed about Zylaxxians, it is that while formidable fighters, they aren't that quick to adapt or deviate from a plan once it is underway.'

Galen nodded. 'They are highly trained warriors, but they are conditioned to follow their training and mission orders and not to diverge unless instructed to do so. They are highly focused on achieving their objectives and they care little for any casualty rate they may suffer, but...'

'But if we can disorientate them, maybe give them something they can't cope with that is outside of their training...' Spencer continued. 'We might be able to defeat them.'

Yes, it is our best shot, as you might put it,' Galen agreed.

Amy spoke next. 'Zylaxxians are powerful but big and bulky. Despite their strength, they aren't exactly agile, Spencer. What if we could really throw them off balance, maybe by some kind of extreme manoeuvre?'

The others turned to her. 'That's a good idea,' said Galen quickly.

'Zan, could we programme *The Infinity* to undertake a pre-set series of high and low G manoeuvres?'

Zan looked doubtful. 'We could try it, but sensors showed that inter-dimensional space is pretty lumpy. There are lots of different eddies of energy, matter and dark matter here. We could severely damage *The Infinity*, or even rip ourselves apart.'

Bradlii coughed. Spencer had noticed this recent, very human affectation whenever he wanted to draw attention to himself, and somehow it made him seem a little less artificial. 'Yes, Bradlii?'

'I may have an idea, but it is completely untested and the risks are potentially great to the ship and each and every one of us, well, apart from me, obviously.'

'I don't think we have much of a choice right now Bradlii, so whatever your idea is, now is the time to hear it.'

For the next five minutes, Bradlii outlined his plan while the others sat in stunned silence, the dangers immediately apparent to one and all. When he had finished, Spencer gazed around the table. 'Has anyone got any other suggestions?' There was silence. 'Then this is what we have to go with. Bradlii, make the arrangements and then everyone to their assigned hiding places.'

*

Spencer and Aila crouched behind the crystal throne in the formal throne room that made Spencer feel distinctly uncomfortable at the best of times. The throne itself was a thing of wonder, grown as a single crystal of a gem similar to sapphire. Its delicate deep blue was translucent, and yet according to Bradlii, who was in Spencer's pocket, it was almost indestructible. It was this property that they were relying upon to provide a shield from the impending assault just long enough for their plan, possibly the most foolhardy Spencer could have ever imagined, to be enacted.

The artificial gravity aboard *The Infinity*, and indeed any spacecraft, was provided by an almost impossibly small amount of material from the heart of a neutron star. This tiny pinprick of matter had a simply mind-boggling amount of mass, and was held in a forcefield of anti-gravitons that was continually manipulated to provide a localised gravity field that enclosed the ship. Spencer had seen the artificial gravity core when he had first explored *The Infinity*, and marvelled at the technology involved, and then struggled to follow as Bradlii had explained in his most superior tone how it all worked. He couldn't remember much of it, but he did recall the answer to his one question: What if it fails?

Bradlii had explained that the artificial gravity core was the most heavily shielded and strengthened compartment in the ship, even more so than the multi-drive. If a gravity core is destabilised or fails as it would when a ship is destroyed, the mass of the neutron matter can cause the ship to literally collapse in on itself, crushed like a Delanian eggshell.

Yet despite this, they planned to manipulate the anti-graviton field in such a way, and at such speeds, as to create gravitational havoc onboard *The Infinity*. Spencer had to acknowledge it was an audacious, even brilliant idea, and Bradlii conceded that it was the ill-fated game of Vari-G Hyperball that had inspired him. 'What we will do, is turn the entire ship into an extreme version of that game. But we will control it so as to render our attackers, once they are onboard, incapable of carrying out their assault.'

'Contact imminent, contact made.' The ship's AI confirmed neutrally that Zylaxxians had landed on the hull. External cameras showed dozens of dark shapes wearing space-hardened protective suits gathering on the upper outer skin of *The Infinity*. Within moments they could be seen lifting a device into place that Bradlii confirmed was a high-capacity plasma cutter. There was a spark, and then an intense glow that the holoscreens automatically dimmed as the assailants began to cut their way into the ship.

'Hull charging,' Bradlii confirmed. Their first countermeasure was to release a burst of charged ions throughout the hull. Bradlii had calculated that while it wouldn't disable all the Zylaxxians attempting to board, it would fry the circuitry of some of their spacesuits and thus reduce the number of assailants a little.

There was a flash as the charged ions rippled through the outer hull, and nearly half of the Zylaxxians who were working there suddenly stiffened and were flung off into the darkness. Spencer smiled grimly, 'some down, still a lot to go.'

'Hull breached,' the ship's AI intoned. The holoscreens showed perhaps forty or more Zylaxxians rapidly disappearing through the hole they had cut.

'Intruders detected on deck eight. Sensors detect forty-three Zylaxxian life signs aboard.'

42

Enemy at the Gates:

Spencer's heart was in his mouth, and he tried desperately to slow his breathing as the cameras showed the Zylaxxians advancing rapidly through the ship, systematically searching for him and his friends. They were highly organised and had formed into small squads of three. Their guttural voices relayed back via the holoscreens to the throne room. In less than two minutes three squads had merged and were outside the throne room. One of their number advanced and fixed a package to the door.

'Ready to initiate gravity flux programme Alpha One', Bradlii whispered inside their ears.

Spencer took a deep breath. The explosion ripped the door open and nine Zylaxxians rushed in, their weapons drawn.

'Now Bradlii!'

Gravity reversed as if a switch was thrown, and the

Zylaxxians were thrown violently upwards, all nine of them hitting the ceiling some eight metres above with sickening thuds. Spencer and Aila remained anchored to the floor behind the throne, Aila using her own magnetic grips, and Spencer relying upon his pre-programmed smartsuit.

Gravity returned in an instant, and the Zylaxxians fell to the floor. Six staggered to their feet, disorientated, but three were inert, their heads at horrible angles where their necks had been snapped.

Aila and Spencer emerged from behind the crystal throne, plasma pistols in hand, and began firing. They took out the two nearest Zylaxxians who fell with burning holes blasted in their armour, but the remaining four began to return fire, and fanned out to flank them.

Gravity flexed, and the Zylaxxians rose from the floor, still firing, but this time they remained suspended in mid-air while Spencer and Aila ran beneath them, crouching into a forward roll and firing upwards, hitting another two. Gravity shifted again, and the remaining two intruders were flung against the far wall, pinned halfway up. They continued to fire, plasma bursts ricocheting off the smooth surfaces.

One zipped past Spencer's leg as he ran, and he felt an instant searing heat despite his suit's protection. He stumbled but regained his balance.

In a second, Aila was there, grabbing his arm and propelling him toward the gaping cavity where the door had been. As they passed through, gravity flipped once more and the Zylaxxians suspended in mid air plummeted to the floor at precisely the same time as they were hit by plasma blasts from the retreating Aila and Spencer.

'How many, Bradlii?' Spencer gasped as he ran.

'Sensors showing twenty-six Zylaxxian life signs aboard at this moment.'

Seventeen down, but still there were more than enough Zylaxxians to take the ship and complete their mission.

Plasma blasts ricocheted down the corridor, and within seconds they had rounded a corner and Spencer realised they were running full tilt toward a squad of three Zylaxxians. 'Now Bradlii!'

Gravity reversed and both he and Aila and the Zylaxxians fell upwards. Somehow, with the help of his smartsuit, he managed to pivot in mid-air and landed on his feet upside down on the passageway ceiling with Aila next to him. The Zylaxxians were not so fortunate. They landed in a crumpled heap, before beginning to stagger to their feet.

The firefight was intense, with blasts from both directions making the air burn and crackle. Aila was hit, but it was a glancing blow and she didn't even hesitate for a moment, unleashing a volley of shots into the nearest intruder.

Gravity flipped again, and Spencer and Aila landed heavily back on the floor. This time Spencer was winded, but he forced himself onwards knowing they had to clear the ship. 'Update, Bradlii.' He managed to gasp as they ran toward the control bridge. 'Now nineteen Zylaxxian life-signs, but they are advancing toward the bridge and sensors show Galen and Qarak are dug in but engaged in a heavy barrage some twenty metres from the bridge doors.'

'We aren't going to make it, are we?' Spencer shouted to Aila as they pounded forwards, 'There's just too many of them.'

Bradlii then spoke, urgently. 'The ship's AI has just

reported a small ship has appeared a hundred kilometres from our port bow. It is closing to an intercept course.'

Spencer groaned, more Zylaxxians coming to provide backup. The battle was beginning to seem lost. 'How come we've only just seen it now, Bradlii?'

'I'm unsure, the ship appears to be screened in some way. Sensors didn't detect it, possibly due to the distortions in inter-dimensional space. It is now manoeuvring towards our hangar bay doors.'

'Seal the doors, no matter what!'

'Trying, door seals being overridden. Hangar bay opening.' Even Bradlii sounded confused. 'Ship is docking.'

Spencer swore under his breath. This was surely game over. His crew were already losing, but more Zylaxxians hell-bent on taking the ship would quickly overwhelm what little fight they had left in them.

'Incoming message from the unidentified ship, standby. Holoscreen activated.' A screen materialised in front of Spencer and Aila in the alcove in which they had paused to shelter.

The image was corrupted, bits scrambled and dropped out. A silhouette could briefly be seen and Spencer braced himself for the inevitable gloating threat from yet another Zylaxxian.

'Can you stabilise this, Bradlii?'

'Compensating for local gravimetric interference… got it'.

'Greetings sir. We got Galen's message and we shadowed your jump. It looks like we got here just in time.' The image of Astren snapped into focus. 'Standby and take cover, I have twenty chidwas here and we are in a fighting mood!'

And then she did something strangely human and out of character, she winked.

Spencer felt his knees buckle with relief. 'Oh Astren, you have no idea how good it is to see you!'

Her composure regained, she nodded once and the link severed. The holoscreen switched to a high-angle shot of the hangar as the doorway materialised in the side of the stealth ship they had used to rescue Amy, and the chidwas poured out, immediately running in perfect synchronisation for the hangar bay exit and on into the heart of *The Infinity*.

'Track them, Bradlii!' Spencer commanded, and the screen cut into multiple views as it followed the chidwas breaking into squads of three and splitting up to engage the Zylaxxian invaders. He watched in fascinated horror as they cut through the marauders, taking them entirely by surprise. The chidwas were on a mission to save their Emperor, and they eliminated every Zylaxxian they came across without hesitation. Sonic grenades flashed, plasma bolts dazzled the cameras, and on several occasions the Androsian troops engaged in hand-to-hand close conflict with the aggressors, cutting them down with their lances and daggers.

The violence of the Androsian assault was matched only by its discipline. Some Zylaxxians held out briefly, entrenched in positions and unleashing heavy volleys of plasma bursts, but the chidwas were relentless. Even as gravity pulsed, they adapted, continuing their advance against the now collapsing Zylaxxian opposing force. Spencer watched as one of the chidwas ran between two Zylaxxians, a plasma blade in each hand to finish them both without even breaking stride.

'Come on Aila, we still need to get to the bridge.' He knew Amy and Zan were holed up there as a last line of defence, and he would die trying before letting anything happen to them. They began moving forward again, cautiously at first, and then at an increasing pace as they encountered no resistance. By the time they reached the corridor leading to the control bridge, the chidwas, under the command of Qarak, were engaged in a fierce firefight with the last remaining Zylaxxians. A barrage of sonic grenades and then a hot-smoke thermocharge, that Spencer later learned both dazzled and disabled the heat-sensitive imaging built into their helmets, finally allowed the Androsians to subdue the last of the invaders.

The five Zylaxxians in the corridor were either dead or dying. One of the chidwas stepped over one of the prone forms who was still trying to stand, and raised a plasma pistol.

'Stop!' Spencer commanded. 'I want to speak to him.'

The Androsian quickly removed any weaponry still in the Zylaxxian's possession, and then stood smartly back and to attention. Spencer hurried over to the inert body of the Zylaxxian who, he quickly saw, was mortally wounded and struggling for breath. He knelt beside him. 'Why? Why are you doing this?' In that moment, Spencer felt a powerful wave of anger and sorrow well from deep within him.

He looked into the dark eyes of their assailant and saw little there but hatred.

'It is my duty to kill you,' The Zylaxxian gasped.

Spencer shook his head in frustration. 'Damn you and damn Haxenaar!' he cried.

Suddenly the Zylaxxian lunged, a hidden blade flashing in his right hand. Spencer recoiled instinctively, and then there was a shot just as the knife was about to cut his throat.

245

The Zylaxxian slumped back, a hole blown through his massive forehead.

He felt a hand on his shoulder, and on shaky knees, he rose and turned to face Astren, a plasma pistol was crackling in her hand. 'Thank God! Astren, yet again you've saved my life.'

'It wasn't me, it was him.' She gestured toward a prone Zylaxxian, who was breathing heavily. Spencer immediately went to his side. 'It was you who spared me. Why? Who are you?'

The Zylaxxian struggled to speak, his voice a rasp. 'I follow Vortrax, and you must live so that you can defeat Haxenaar in the battle to come...'

And then his body convulsed and was still. Spencer waited for long moments, his mind racing, before he leaned down and whispered in the dead Zylaxxian's ear, 'Thank you, I promise you will not have died in vain.'

Spencer got to his feet and smiled weakly. He felt absolutely exhausted but then on impulse, he hugged Astren, and after a moment she rather awkwardly returned the embrace.

43

For the Love of Hate:

The QEComms newsfeed was horrifying. Spencer and his crew had watched in silence, all sitting around the conference table as Haxenaar had delivered an ultimatum. If they didn't surrender now, he would have all the delegates of the Galactic Council being held by his troops within the enormous Governmental Compound on Eloim III, executed. To ram his threats home, five hapless members of the council had been slain by his order, their bodies cleaved in two in the hideous Zylaxxian tradition.

Astren sat across from Spencer. Her return had been one bright point of light in these dark and difficult times. Spencer's gaze swept across his friends, they all looked as shocked and downcast as he felt himself. It fell to Galen to speak softly for them.

'Awful as this is, Spencer, I believe Haxenaar has miscalculated and made a strategic mistake. By killing those elected representatives, Haxenaar has attempted to strike fear into the worlds of the Galactic Council. However, I think what he has actually done with such a public demonstration of his brutality, is show just how important it is that he is defeated. He may have given us a tactical advantage by helping to solidify resistance against him, and remind the Galaxy that there is an alternative to his reign of terror,' he paused, 'namely, you.'

Spencer nodded slowly. Galen's argument did make sense. If Haxenaar's dreadful acts of violence against unarmed beings from other civilisations could trigger outrage and an alignment of forces against him and the Zylaxxians, then that had to be encouraged and exploited.

All of a sudden, Spencer came to a decision. 'I want to speak to the Galaxy. These threats need to be answered. I need everyone to know that I am not going to accept them and that together we can defeat the Zylaxxians and make Haxenaar answer for his crimes.'

Galen nodded his approval, and Spencer saw the eyes of his friends turn toward him. What was it he saw there? Admiration? Really? Amy gave him a private smile of encouragement. That was all he needed.

He set his jaw, enough was enough. No matter how absurd it may be, he was the Emperor of the Galaxy. He knew he needed to start to be seen to lead the beings of countless worlds against a tyrannical oppressor whose only desires were conquest and oppression.

The QEComms broadcast reached all inhabited member worlds simultaneously. Apparently, Zan explained, *The Infinity* had the ability to override all other galactic communications in times of emergency, and, Spencer had readily decreed, this was such a time.

And so, on trillions of holoscreens across thousands of light-years, Spencer's face appeared, sombre, but resolute. Although it made him uncomfortable, he made this address from the Throne Room of *The Infinity*, wearing the deep blue iridescent tunic with a tasteful gold spiral emblem that was part of his official wardrobe. He had spent more than an hour working on the text with Galen and Amy and then practising his delivery. Public speaking had never been Spencer's strong suit, but he knew that he had to get this exactly right.

He was nervous, but Galen had pointed out this wasn't a live address, so he didn't have to get it right first time. They could make edits if needs be, and even tune his voice.

As it happened though, Spencer, despite his self-doubts, absolutely nailed it.

OFFICIAL TO ALL WORLDS AND GALACTIC
CITIZENS – INCOMING ADDRESS FROM THE
EMPEROR OF THE GALAXY, HIS EMINENCE
SPENCER EDWARDS
THE FIRST OF EARTH

'My fellow citizens of the Galaxy, I extend my hand in friendship to you all.

Just hours ago we witnessed the cowardly murder of five delegates to the Galactic Council whose only wish was to serve and improve the lives of all sentient beings. For this, they were cut down by a violent and dangerous tyrant who would seek to enslave us all, to bend us to his will alone, and to drive division and hatred between us.

He will not achieve this. On the contrary, through his dreadful crimes against us, he will bring us even closer together and strengthen our resolve.

As long as I live, I will not allow this aggression against the peace-loving people of the Galaxy to prevail.

I address you now as your Emperor, and I call you to my, to our, just cause. Together, we will stand united against hatred, against oppression, and against violence as a means to achieve wicked and evil ends.

Therefore, today, I am designating Haxenaar and all those who follow him, to be criminals of the Galaxy. This means that they will be held accountable for their actions, and will be brought to justice so that they may pay for their crimes.

To all those of you who value peace, justice and Galactic law, I must tell you that we face a resolute foe who has shown he has no mercy, no compassion, and nothing but hate in his heart. A great battle is coming, a battle between good and evil for the future of the Galaxy, and we must fight it together.

I am your Emperor, by your consent. I expect all law-abiding citizens of the Galaxy to do their duty, as I will do mine. Even if I must pay the ultimate price.'

Spencer paused, and then leaned forwards towards the camera menacingly, 'I am coming for you Haxenaar, with the Galaxy at my side. I suggest you run, now.'

The camera ceased recording and Spencer leaned back in his throne. 'How did I do?'

Amy smiled, and so even did Galen. 'That was good, but are you sure about the direct challenge to Haxenaar at the end? Won't that just provoke him further?'

'That's what I am counting on, Amy. If there is one thing I have noticed about Haxenaar, intelligent and resourceful as he is, it is that his hatred of me can be used against him. He *needs* to kill me, not just for his cause, but for his own personal satisfaction. A person with an all-consuming hatred can be blind to other dangers, and I think that when the final battle comes, he will take risks and make mistakes because of his overwhelming desire to destroy me. I believe we can use that to our advantage.'

Galen was surprised. 'That is leadership thinking Emperor, a very impressive strategy.'

Spencer was flattered, but retorted sombrely, 'I hope so Galen, I genuinely do, because we are going to need every possible advantage we can find to defeat him.'

*

The effect of Spencer's QEComms was electrifying. Across the inhabited worlds, endless newscasts devoted countless hours to discussing, debating and analysing his words. The planetary and interplanetary social networks lit up with discussions and posts from all the spiral arms and star clusters.

For a frightened Galaxy, many found them reassuring, but there were doubts from some. How could this unknown boy from a technological backwater hope to defeat a massive and hardened militaristic state led by a warrior who had no hesitation about killing anyone who got in his way?

And then came a broadcast from Haxenaar himself. He stood and glowered aboard his flagship now lying several million kilometres from the immense scientific research station of Valandese, home to more than a hundred thousand scientists and researchers from across the Galaxy, and a key communications hub for the inner systems. Countless scientific and technological advances had been born from the station over the many millennia since it was first established by one of the most respected scientists in galactic history. Over the centuries it had grown and become one of the most recognisable and powerful symbols of galactic cooperation.

'Spencer Edwards of Earth,' he growled in his most menacing guttural tone. 'I will not run, I will not hide. I will destroy you and your pathetic dreams. Mark this moment, for this, is your doing. You alone have brought destruction down upon the Galaxy, and now you will watch as we obliterate this symbol of so-called "cooperation and unity,"' he spat the words with utter contempt.

The holoscreen view pulled back to show attack waves of Zylaxxian ships bearing down on the enormous scientific outpost while the hundreds of linked asteroids that spanned out into space, each housing research facilities, accommodation, and precious knowledge along with many of the most brilliant minds of the era, glittered in the starlight. It was, Spencer thought, quite beautiful and a truly inspiring vision of the shared values of the thousands of planets that comprised the Galactic Council. And it was, of course, because of what it represented, the reason that Haxenaar would destroy it.

The crew watched in horror, some of them struggling not to sob as Valandese was blown to smithereens, its defences overwhelmed in minutes. Swarms of escape pods ejected, and some of them were mercilessly picked off by fast-moving Zylaxxian assault craft, the amazing intellects within forever erased from the cosmos.

But Spencer did not cry. Instead, he sat transfixed in total silence, his eyes never moving from the holoscreens. When it was done, and Haxenaar had appeared again, gloating and telling the citizens of the Galaxy that their Emperor bore responsibility for this act because of his resistance, he looked up and spoke, his voice steady as a rock.

'He will pay for this. I swear it.'

44

Ixenarian Quest:

Satyvrat, the ancient Ratarian, had instructed Spencer that *The Infinity* must first visit the volcanic moon of Ignis in the Cantalesian system, some five hundred light-years from their encounter.

And so, once the jump was complete, Spencer joined Zan and Galen on the control bridge. The sight that met his eyes was unlike anything he could have imagined. The Cantalese planetary system was small, but there were many bodies within it. The orbital radius of the most distant was still less than that of Venus to Earth's sun, and the central star burned with intense heat, more than three times the 5600 degrees radiating from the surface of Sol. This amount of radiation ensured that the crusts of the orbiting planets were both scorched and in dynamic flux, heating when faced towards their tormentor, and then rapidly cooling as the planet revolved and half of its face went dark.

The moon designated Ignis orbited the third planet from the parent star, and to Spencer, it looked absolutely hellish. The holoscreens zoomed to show highly active volcanoes spewing lava high into the atmosphere that, Bradlii cheerfully informed him, was mostly comprised of sulphur and other superheated poisonous gases.

'So basically, what you are saying Bradlii, is that if we go down there we are either going to get cooked, fried, poisoned or suffocated?'

'Correct, but even if you don't die from any of those threats, the intense radiation will almost certainly ensure you do not survive more than a few hours after return to *The Infinity*.'

Spencer raised his eyebrows at the others who had joined him on the control bridge. 'I'm very open to ideas here!'

Surprisingly it was Astren who spoke first. 'It would make sense to assume this is some kind of test. The Ixenarians would know how inhospitable and dangerous this place is, so we can assume that the information we need is accessible without costing us our lives, or there would be little point in them bringing us here.'

Galen nodded his agreement. 'Your reasoning is very sound, Astren. The Ixenarians have carefully chosen this place because they don't want anyone stumbling upon their message, or directions, or whatever it is they have placed down there. But for those they do want to communicate with, it would make little sense for them to kill them off at the start of their journey.'

'So are we looking for an entrance to some kind of underground cavern, or a building or something like that?' Amy asked.

'The problem with that is the extreme stresses that the crust is under – caves could easily collapse, and any buildings would be quickly destroyed.' Galen paused thoughtfully, 'Unless we can determine that there is a place on the moon that is geologically more stable than the rest.' He spoke to the ship's AI, 'Please enter the ship into an orbital pattern that will allow you to scan the moon to a depth of ten kilometres.'

'Complying, standby. Scan will begin in twenty-seven minutes and will take five hours and sixteen minutes to complete.'

*

Spencer and Amy returned to his quarters, while the others did likewise to their own. Everyone felt tired beyond reason. The relentless events of the past few days threatened to catch up with them all and there was little to do until the scans were completed.

The Emperor's quarters were both beautiful and comfortable, and most importantly to Spencer, they were quiet, like a peaceful oasis surrounded by the chaos and turbulence of a Galaxy on the brink of war. Standing in front of the huge virtual window that when activated covered the entire surface of one wall of the principal chamber, Spencer and Amy were silent, their hands entwined. It was rare moments like this, Spencer thought to himself, that brought him some calm in the face of what seemed to be never-ending trials. But the certain knowledge that he would have to face Haxenaar in a final, desperate battle was never far from his thoughts.

He turned to look at Amy, her head level with his shoulder, but she was looking out into the vastness of space. To Spencer, she was still the most beautiful thing he had seen, on any world.

Ten minutes later they were both asleep, side by side on the plush couch that had become their favourite place to sit. Amy was snoring softly, Spencer's arm around her shoulder. The Emperor of the Galaxy was, for a short while, oblivious to it all.

*

'Wake up! Spencer, Amy, you need to wake up, now!'

Groggily, Spencer felt the welcome embrace of sleep slip away and he struggled to sit up. Amy stirred, yawned and rubbed her eyes.

'Bradlii, what is it?'

'You need to get to the control bridge, you are going to want to see this.'

Just a couple of minutes later, Spencer, Amy and the others were standing with their mouths agape, not quite sure what they were looking at.

Galen tried to explain. 'I didn't wake you until the scans were complete and I was certain of what they showed, which is if I say so myself, quite remarkable. What you are looking at is a much smaller moon inside of Ignis, buried more than a hundred kilometres beneath the surface inside a colossal cavern. The outer surface is of course unstable and highly volcanic, but the inner sphere is considerably more stable and appears to be held in what is essentially a bubble of atmosphere and gravity. It is also revolving independently of the outer shell.'

'Artificial?' Spencer asked, his brain struggling to take in what he was seeing.

'Almost certainly. I've checked and there are no records anywhere in the galactic archives of such natural phenomena, but it begs the question as to what kind of civilisation could create such a marvel. If it is Ixenarian in origin, then their technological prowess must be truly impressive, because according to our scans this structure is at least a million years old.'

'Okay, well it certainly is incredible, but we wouldn't be here unless the Ixenarians wanted us to be, so I guess we have to go down there and get to that inner moon somehow. Have you been able to find a way in?' Despite the spectacle, Spencer felt a sense of urgency. They had to press on, find the Ixenarians, and then somehow persuade them to help defeat Haxenaar. There was little time for sightseeing.

'Scans do confirm one possible route to the interior, but it is highly hazardous,' Bradlii said ominously.

Spencer smiled inwardly to himself. Of course it was. There hadn't been more than a few hours since he became Emperor that he hadn't felt his life was in immediate peril. And yet somehow, he almost marvelled to himself, he had become rather used to it.

'We have identified one of the active volcanoes that has a defunct lava tube leading from the caldera down into a network of tunnels that eventually lead to the void space between the outer and inner spheres,' Galen confirmed.

'So basically we need to fly into an erupting volcano, then find this tunnel and navigate into the interior of a boiling planet,' Spencer paused for effect, 'and somehow get onto the surface of the other moon hidden inside, find whatever it is the Ixenarians want us to find, and then get out without being killed in the process?' He almost laughed, 'Okay, who's with me?' Everyone's hand went up and for a delicious moment, they all stood grinning at each other over the lunacy of it all.

*

The good news, if that weren't too optimistic a term, was that Bradlii had calculated that a heavily screened Lander would fit through the subterranean tubes and tunnels. With skill and a lot of AI assistance, it could feasibly then be piloted through the inner void space and enter into an internal scanning orbit before landing on the small inner moon.

Maintenance drones, under the guidance of Bradlii and the ship's AI, had immediately set to work fixing additional hull plating and armour to the second Lander that Spencer had (in a visible change of heart much to the relief of his crewmates) named *Harmony*. Once it was finished, Spencer stood and regarded it thoughtfully. The Lander wasn't pretty, as most of its sleek lines were now buried beneath a multitude of overlapping composite plates, hastily fixed together using flexible smart alloy seams and even, Bradlii informed him, hyperthermic glue. The end result, Spencer observed dryly, was something akin to if the Lander had been magnetised and crashed into a scrap heap. But Zan, who stood alongside, reassured him that the modifications would hold. Or at least they would provided the stresses Bradlii had calculated would be encountered were accurate.

Spencer turned to Zan and spoke quietly so that he wouldn't be overheard. 'Zan, I am going to pilot this,' he raised his hand as Zan began to protest, 'I need you here, taking care of *The Infinity* and the rest of the crew, including the chidwas. If something goes wrong, your orders are to leave as quickly as possible, and find a safe place to regroup.'

'But we cannot leave you there sir, that would be a grave dereliction of duty.'

'Zan, I am aware of the risks, and I will be taking Aila and Qarak with me. Look, we don't have time to debate this. Those are my orders, and I do expect you to carry them out.'

'Of course, sir!'

Spencer nodded. 'Okay, well, I think we might as well get underway, the Galaxy still needs saving.' And then he grinned. 'Don't worry Zan, I definitely don't intend to end up burnt to a crisp on a moon inside another moon, ten thousand light-years from home.'

*

Amy was training with the chidwas in *The Infinity*'s fitness centre when *Harmony*, with Spencer, Aila and the inscrutable Qarak aboard left the hangar with Spencer at the controls. Minutes later he executed a graceful arc and roll to align the ungainly Lander with the volcano identified as the only entry point to Ignis' interior space. Amy closed her eyes momentarily, and said a quick prayer for their safe return, before wheeling and connecting a nearly perfect roundhouse with an advancing chidwas' left cheekbone.

Onboard *Harmony*, Spencer took a deep breath and

flexed his hands around the control grips. It had been agreed that he would manually pilot the craft, but that Bradlii, who was firmly ensconced in his smartsuit pocket, would continually monitor all systems including the local environment and could take control if circumstances required it.

'Alright everyone, hold on, here we go.' The tiny craft dove towards the boiling crater spewing columns of fire and ash, and in moments the viewscreens went dark as they flew directly into the eruption. The augmented targeting systems kicked in, showing a graphical representation of the flight path Spencer had to hold to if they were to reach the mouth of the lava tube that would take them into the moon's interior. The tiny *Harmony* began to shake violently as it was buffeted by the heat and turbulence of the eruption, and then there was a loud bang and the ship was knocked off course for a moment before Spencer was able to wrestle the controls and bring it back onto its trajectory. 'Rock impact,' Bradlii explained matter of factly. 'Outer left hull shielding took a sizable impact, but is holding, just.'

Then came something that sounded initially like rain, but rapidly grew in intensity to become a deafening roar. 'We are travelling through an ejection of thousands of smaller rock projectiles and the hull is now taking damage.'

But moments later, just as Spencer thought the little ship wouldn't be able to stand much more, the crescendo eased and for a moment the viewscreens cleared to show the boiling lava lake at the base of the volcano's caldera. He gasped, and swerved the Lander around a plume of molten rock. 'We are locked on to the access point.' Aila informed him, and the augmented reality holoscreen in front of him highlighted the entrance to the tube, overlaid with an indicated flight path.

'Just stay with it, sir,' Qarak encouraged him, 'We're nearly there.'

There was a deafening crash, and the Lander shook so violently that Spencer felt certain it was going to come apart, but somehow the valiant little craft, protected behind its hastily installed shielding, held on and he was able to quickly right it. 'That was a big rock!' he muttered under his breath. 'A bloody big rock!'

The mouth of the lava tube loomed large in the viewscreen, green arrows appeared, guiding Spencer in his flight, and red warning data streamed, showing proximity alerts and distances to the rock face they were now swooping towards. And then suddenly they were inside, and the darkness enveloped them for a moment until the viewscreen switched to a night-vision setting and the walls of the tube were revealed in a ghostly grey.

On the small ship flew past columns of basalt and then through a stretch, many kilometres long, of spectacular pyro-formed stalactites and stalagmites. The three were quiet, and only Bradlii occasionally spoke to inform them of their progress. 'We are now sixty kilometres below the surface, temperature dropping to 338 degrees above zero.'

Still, they flew on, over a small lake of bubbling lava, pausing only occasionally to use the plasma cannons to clear a path where a rock fall made progress too difficult. Spencer focused entirely on his controls and felt a strange sense of calm. He could do this. They could do this together.

After nearly an hour had passed since they entered

the tube, Bradlii spoke more urgently. 'My calculations, correlated with sensor readings, indicate that we should be approaching the void space in the next two minutes.'

Spencer found he was almost holding his breath as the viewscreen began to resolve the end of their passageway to the interior.

However, as their brave little ship burst through, nothing could have prepared them for the sight they saw. Spencer gasped, and Qarak, usually implacable, said something in his own language that could only have been an exclamation of astonishment. Even Aila stiffened, her clear blue eyes widening in disbelief.

45

The Traveller Within:

The sight that filled the holoscreen was difficult to comprehend. The inner moon was glowing, like a vast orb with a light source deep within. Colours seemed to merge and then fade as if on some kind of cycle, but the pattern was very hard to comprehend. Snaking up from all over the sphere were tendrils that appeared to connect it in some way to the outer shell of the enormous cavern within which it was suspended.

Spencer turned to his companions and raised his eyebrows in what he had discovered was a fairly universal expression of 'What now?'

'I think we should do a slow and careful flyover of the surface with scanners set to collect the maximum data load possible, and then retreat for a few minutes to allow Bradlii to process it. Then we can then decide our next move,' Aila suggested. Spencer nodded, that seemed eminently sensible and he didn't have an immediate plan anyhow. He gently eased forward on the manoeuvring thrusters and then levelled off just a hundred metres above the glowing surface.

Immediately the colour progressions changed, becoming more rapid and intense.

'All systems nominal, no threats detected,' Qarak reassured them from his seat where he was monitoring weapons systems and any hostile intentions.

'Okay then, here we go.' Spencer set the craft on a low altitude elliptical orbit around the little moon's equator. The surface seemed to be flawless and highly polished, and at times reflected the Lander as it drifted overhead. As they flew, the glowing lights changed seemingly at random, but with an increased tempo and complexity that faded as they passed by. He carefully avoided the tendrils, gently easing around them whenever they blocked their path.

Within ten minutes, Spencer had completed three orbits, each at a slightly different latitude, and then moved them off to a comfortable distance where they could analyse the data gathered and discuss whatever they learned.

'So Bradlii, what did you make of that?' Spencer leaned back in his seat, and sipped a hydropouch that was not entirely dissimilar to mango juice from Earth.

'I have collected a great deal of data, Spencer, and I am just checking my findings both internally and with other AI's because I want to be certain in my conclusions.' And then just a couple of minutes later, 'I have shared the sensor readings and my conclusions with 14,212 of my colleagues, and discussed them at length. There was a lively debate, and some of them have written academic papers as a result. We have conducted thirty-eight polls and the presentations from more than a hundred AI's were quite fascinating. I have rarely experienced such a lengthy debate amongst my peers.'

Spencer wasn't sure where this was going, but he felt it was somewhere significant. 'And you did all this in the past two minutes?'

'Oh no, it was all completed within approximately eight of your seconds, the rest of the time I've just been chatting and catching up on the gossip while you had a drink.'

Spencer sighed in only slightly exaggerated frustration. 'So what have you all discovered then?'

'It's quite simple, yet also quite remarkable. Nothing like it exists in any of the galactic records or databases. That was why we took so long to agree.'

'And?'

'The moon is alive and sentient. And it has been expecting us.'

*

The lights that flashed across its surface were the moon's preferred means of communication, and Bradlii had rapidly determined the key to decoding them. The moon was ancient, far older than the Earth, he explained, and over the next hour, Spencer and his friends learned that it had wandered through space countless millennia ago, before becoming caught in the gravitational pull of their own Galaxy. But it soon became clear that this was not the result of an accident. This moon, and many others like it, had been sent out into the cosmos by an ancient and advanced civilisation as part of a never-ending quest to collect knowledge from across the known, and unknown universe. The moons were in many ways, as Bradlii pointed out, the ultimate in deep space probes. Intelligent, extremely hardy to the point of being almost indestructible, and virtually immortal compared to any biological life-form.

This one, whose name and designation was Sala B-214a, had made contact with a civilisation that recognised its importance and determined to provide it with safe shelter in a time of galactic strife.

Sala confirmed that the civilisation was Ixenarian, and that working with them the small moon had been transplanted into this immense cavern more than a million years previously, or as Sala explained patiently, almost yesterday given the immensity of a moon's life-span.

A thought, or rather more a question, suddenly occurred to Spencer.

'Did you have anything to do with the response to the Zylaxxian invaders on Balairen?'

'Not directly,' came the response, 'but I was aware of it. Balairen is a sentient planet, not as developed as I am, nor as old, but it is aware of hostile intent and responded to the threat accordingly.'

Spencer followed up. 'Are all planets "alive" in the same way?'

'No, many are simply barren lifeless rocks or gas giants. But some, a small proportion that have either nurtured large biospheres or developed in proximity to other sentient travellers (Sala would repeatedly refer to itself as a traveller the team noted), do evolve to become deeply aware of the universe and their role within it.'

'And what is that role?' Bradlii asked.

'To exist, to perpetuate, and to sustain.'

Spencer was puzzled. That sounded rather vague to him. 'Bradlii, what does that mean?'

'I believe Sala is telling us that its purpose is to continue to live for as long as possible, maybe even billions upon billions of years, and to ensure the survival of the knowledge it has gained, and use that to help, in some way.'

'Well, I like the sound of that. Can Sala point us towards the Ixenarian homeworld?'

'Sala has agreed to give us the coordinates and is also going to transfer some information to me that it thinks may be useful. Standby.'

Bradlii fell silent for nearly four minutes, before speaking again. Spencer was alarmed. 'Bradlii, what happened? Are you alright?'

'Sala has transferred approximately nine zettabytes of information to me, from the many yottabytes it holds.'

'That's a lot, right?'

'Yes, to give you some context, it is billions of times more information than flows across your entire primitive internet in a year. Spencer nearly asked the AI what he had just learned, but stopped himself as even to him it was obvious there was no possible way Bradlii could summarise such a staggering amount of information. So instead he said, 'What do we need to know right now?' Bradlii paused for just a moment. 'Two things. First, the location of Ixenar, and second, where Sala originates from.'

Somehow Spencer knew the answer to that one before Bradlii said it.

'It's Andromeda, isn't it?'

'Correct.'

46

GALACTIC DATABASE FILE:
Adrastea

The Sol System where Earth resides comprises a single star, approximately 4.6 billion years old and of medium brightness, and eight planets. Mercury, small and scorched, orbits closest at just 60 million kilometres. Next comes Venus, its dense atmosphere thick with carbon dioxide and sulphuric acid, and a surface temperature of 475 degrees centigrade that is hot enough to melt lead. Then comes Earth, an oasis of life in an otherwise now barren system, followed by Mars and then, in turn, the gas giants of mighty Jupiter, the largest in the system, Saturn with its beautiful rings, mysterious Uranus and finally remote Neptune, more than thirty times as far from the Sun as Earth.

The early life of this solar system was one of violence and tumult, as the inner planets formed from spinning discs of dust and debris, first coalescing into roughly spherical conglomerates of matter before gravity began to fuse them together. Then followed many millions of years of intense bombardment, as billions of meteorites, leftover from the nascent formation of the system rained down on the lifeless planets. Some of those meteorites and comets bore the organic chemicals that would become the building blocks of primitive life on Sol 3, known as Earth to the inhabitants, a rocky planet just the right distance from the star to harbour and nurture these biological reactions.

Along with the eight major planets, there exist many smaller, or dwarf planets, including Pluto, and more than two hundred moons and countless asteroids. In some limited respects, the Sol System is of passing interest to observers from afar, but it is mostly unremarkable with little of particular note.

Jupiter, with a volume of more than 1300 Earths has a large number of moons of varying size and mass, more than eighty in total by the most recent count of Earthly astronomers. These moons are held in largely stable orbits, many of them captured aeons ago by the colossal gravity of their parent planet.

The moons of Jupiter are grouped. The outer larger moons include volcanic Io, Ganymede (itself the largest moon in the solar system and larger than the planet Mercury), and Europa, a frozen ocean world. The smaller, and more plentiful inner moons are also named, and the Amalthea Group comprises four small moons, each of less than 200km in diameter.

END OF ENTRY.

*

It was here, in the Amalthea Group, that the small Zylaxxian fleet emerged undetected from interdimensional space. Three frigates (fast, lightly armed vessels) and one heavy tug-ship, designed to retrieve and move large ships or asteroids.

For several hours, the ships maintained a motionless position relative to Adrastea, the smallest of the group. A tiny moon just 20km across, Adrastea orbits Jupiter at high velocity. Indeed the moon is so small it was only discovered by Earth astrophysicists in 1979 when the Voyager II space probe captured an image of it during a flypast.

Onboard the Zylaxxian ships, computers crunched massive amounts of data, calculating the orbital mechanics of Adrastea and simulating trajectories. Finally, once satisfied, the large tug-ship moved in close and anchored itself to the moon using carbon nanotube tethers.

At a signal from the captain of the lead ship, the mighty engine of the tug fired for two minutes and forty-two seconds, and for the first time in more than three billion years, little Adrastea left orbit and broke free of its parent's gravity before heading off into deep space and an eventual rendezvous with the third planet from the small star whose light was much diminished by the distance, but was still the brightest object in the sky.

47

Suspicions:

Aboard *The Infinity*, the mood was subdued but expectant. Spencer, Amy and other members of the crew had taken the opportunity to eat, shower and get some much-needed rest while Galen and Zan planned a route to the coordinates Sala had given them. Due to the distance, it would require three M-drive jumps, and they were keen to avoid the possibility of being detected by any Zylaxxians on the journey.

It was more than three hours later that Galen had called them to the conference room, and bade them all sit down.

'We have a problem.' Galen said softly. Spencer had never seen him look so concerned.

'Our M-drive system is down. Zen was running routine checks ready for our departure, when he found that the matter injectors that focus the energy on the singularity at its heart are out of line.'

'How did that happen?' Spencer asked, frustrated, 'and how long will it take to fix?'

'To answer the second part of your question first, it will take at least another six hours to re-align, calibrate and then check,' Spencer groaned. To be this close to finally reaching Ixenar, and be thwarted by a technical failure was deeply frustrating.

Galen continued, 'But the answer to the first point is more problematic I'm afraid, because the only way the injectors can be this far out of alignment is if someone has deliberately moved them.'

Spencer felt his blood run cold.

The atmosphere in the conference room was electric because they were all thinking the same uncomfortable thought. The friends looked around at each other, knowing that someone must have betrayed them. Somebody must have given the Zylaxxians the location they had learned from Sala, and had sabotaged the ship to delay them getting there.

Spencer was still reeling, but all eyes were turned to him. He waited a moment to compose his thoughts. 'Galen, I refuse to believe that anyone in this room could be a Zylaxxian agent if that is what you are saying?'

Galen nodded slowly. 'I'm afraid it is Emperor. There is no other explanation.'

Spencer's stomach was a knot. 'No! This must be some kind of misunderstanding.'

Amy gently placed her hand on his arm. She sensed how upset he was, and he was grateful for the reassurance.

Spencer felt like the room was spinning. 'Are you telling me that Haxenaar knows where the Ixenarian homeworld is, and may already be on his way there to snatch the Spear of Rigel?'

'I'm afraid I think that is very likely. Indeed he may have already visited.' Galen fell silent. The implications of his words were not lost on anyone present.

Spencer slumped back in his chair. For a moment he felt beaten. Haxenaar, his blood foe, had out-smarted them all. While Spencer and his crew had congratulated themselves on their small victories it was now obvious that Haxenaar had been playing a longer game, perhaps even deliberately lulling them into believing that they could succeed and so make mistakes and tactical errors. If Haxenaar hadn't already won, he was pretty damn close to victory.

But of course, it was even worse than that. If Galen was right, then Haxenaar had somehow compromised Spencer's crew. Someone sitting at that table was a traitor, and, Spencer realised grimly, an immediate threat to them all. He raised his eyes to the softly glowing ceiling. He knew he had to do something. He had to lead.

'Everyone to their quarters, now, and remain there until I say. Nobody is to speak to anyone else. That is an order.' Spencer spoke quietly and as calmly as he could manage, but his voice carried the full authority of his position. ' Yes, Amy, you too. Sorry. Galen, you remain here with me.'

In shocked silence his friends trooped out, leaving him alone with the old man. 'Galen, I have to trust someone here, and although I cannot be certain, you are the one who has brought this to our attention, so it is probably less likely that it is you who has been betraying us.'

Galen nodded slowly. 'Your logic is sound, and I can only give you my word that it is not I who has knowingly passed information to the Zylaxxians.'

'For now, I am going to have to accept that,' Spencer acknowledged. 'So that leaves us with three possible scenarios. The first is that the Zylaxxians have infiltrated the ship's AI and have obtained the information that way.'

Galen shook his head decisively. 'Shipboard AI's have never been compromised in such a way, and are designed from the ground up to be impervious to external attack. They have several trillion levels of continually monitored security algorithms to prevent precisely such an event. There would simply be too many ways for such an attempt to fail.'

'Alright, so if we accept that, there are two scenarios left. The first is that one of us has been knowingly gathering intelligence and transferring it to Haxenaar somehow. Surely it should be possible to determine whether there have been any outgoing QEComms transmissions?'

'Possibly. Provided that is the means being used. We could check for all outbound transmissions, but we may not be able to decrypt them or know where they were going or to whom.'

Spencer nodded. 'The final scenario though is perhaps in some ways the most frightening. One of us, and it could even be me, has somehow been manipulated by the Zylaxxians and has been communicating with them without realising it.'

'Your reasoning, Emperor, is impeccable.' Galen, despite the circumstances, was obviously impressed.

'Good. And that's as far as I have got Galen, I need your help now. We are dead in the water until we have figured this out. We daren't go to Ixenar, in case the Zylaxxians haven't ascertained the precise location and are watching and tracking us. In fact, who knows, that could be their plan all along, to trick us into revealing the location.'

Spencer's head hurt. If this was what leadership was about, having to make impossible decisions and judgment calls, then he certainly wasn't enjoying it in the slightest anymore.

Galen saw his confusion and self-doubt, and in a welcome display of warmth and empathy reached out and rested his hand briefly on Spencer's shoulder. 'If I may say so, Emperor, you are doing just fine. If there is one thing that is true across the entire Galaxy, it is that you cannot know what you do not know. So trying to second guess yourself based on a complete lack of information is never going to be much help.'

Spencer smiled wanly. 'Right. So we are going to act on what we do know and can find out. Let's start with some facts, or at least as best we understand them.' Galen agreed and Spencer continued.

'One, I don't believe any of us would deliberately betray each other. I just don't. I know that is based on my feelings and emotions, but it just doesn't make sense. If Haxenaar had an agent amongst us, he, or she, could have killed me at any time thus fulfilling Haxenaar's deepest desire and ending this war some time ago. Instead, every single person aboard this ship has risked their lives to save me, over and over again.'

Galen nodded to show he accepted that argument. 'That does make sense. Your death is what Haxenaar so desperately needs to secure his control of the Galactic Council.'

'Two, if the agent is betraying us against his or her will, or even without knowing they are, then the Zylaxxians must have had direct contact with that person in order to brainwash them, or maybe implant something?' As he spoke, Spencer began to feel truly ill. There was, he realised, one person who had been in prolonged contact with the Zylaxxians where something like this could have happened.

'It's Amy, isn't it?' he whispered.

Galen looked grave. 'I am so very sorry Spencer, but she would seem to be the most likely candidate. She was aboard the Zylaxxian ship for some time before you rescued her. They could have compromised her then.'

'So if she does know, then everything since has been an act. Being part of this crew, me...' His voice trailed off. It was too horrible to contemplate. He loved Amy deeply, and the thought that she might not love him back was painful beyond words.

'If I may, sir?' Galen spoke gently, his voice surprisingly tender, 'I don't believe she is that good an actress. Amy wears her heart on her sleeve, to use an old Earth expression, and she loves you, too. I have no doubt of that.'

Spencer looked up into Galen's kindly eyes, tears were pricking at his own and betrayed his inner turmoil. 'Thank you, Galen, I have to believe that. Or at least I want to believe that.'

The old sage stood up. 'What we need to do now is decide what we know, and what we believe to be true, and then act. Therefore the third point I believe you were going to make is this; it is still possible that this compromise happened recently, and that the subject has not been programmed to assassinate you because there wasn't enough time to do so. Our most recent direct contact with the Zylaxxians happened when they boarded the ship. Therefore it is conceivable that they either planted some kind of device in the ship when they did so, or even a device in one of us.'

'So can we simply scan the ship, and ourselves and find out the truth?' Spencer's voice was full of hope. Perhaps this could be resolved quickly after all.

'Well, that isn't quite so simple. Any device would be carefully hidden. If it is electronic, then a range of scans should be able to detect it. If it is a biological device, then it is much harder, but not impossible. I will begin work on calibrating the sensors.'

'In the meantime, I am going to find a quiet place to do some research of my own.' Spencer informed him, and without further comment, he left the conference room and headed to the ship's library.

*

Spencer's smartsuit chimed and Amy appeared as a holoimage a few feet in front of Spencer. It was evident that she had been crying, and was in considerable distress. 'Spencer, I know you can't trust me right now, but I need you to know that I would never willingly do anything to hurt you or anybody on this ship.'

Spencer tried to give a reassuring smile. 'I know that Amy, I promise I do, but I've got to be able to prove it beyond any doubt whatsoever because all of our lives depend on it.' She rubbed her eyes, and nodded, even attempting a watery smile back. 'Are you making any progress with finding out who it is?'

Spencer gave a non-committal shrug. 'I'm still working on it.'

Amy nodded. 'I love you Spencer, I want you to be

absolutely sure of that, and I always will, no matter what happens.' Her image disappeared, and Spencer sat back in his chair, disturbing thoughts running through his mind. Was Amy trying to manipulate him? Was her purpose in calling him to try and find out what he knew?

He pushed the thoughts aside. He hated this. As if he hadn't done enough damage already, now Haxenaar had him doubting the one person he was closest to.

But still, the thoughts wouldn't go away.

Spencer spent the next two hours examining the video feeds of the Zylaxxian attack and boarding of *The Infinity*. He wasn't at all sure what he was looking for, but he had to do something while Galen conducted a shipwide scan for any hidden devices. It was only after he had watched the same footage of Zylaxxian intruders advancing along the corridor toward the command control centre perhaps a dozen times, that he thought he spotted something.

He isolated and replayed a ten-second segment. Then instructed the AI to zoom in. It wasn't clear at all. He tried multiple angles, nothing. It wasn't until he instructed the computer to display a high-angle enhanced view that he saw it.

Spencer thumped the extruded desk in front of him. 'Yes!' That had to be it! And then his heart sank as he summoned Galen to his quarters.

The elder man quickly confirmed that he had scanned every atom of the ship and found no electronic devices out of the ordinary at all. Spencer bade him sit, and then showed him the footage. The elderly scientist was silent, studying the holoimages closely. 'Again!' he requested, and then once more.

He turned to Spencer, 'I think you've got it.'

*

At Spencer's command, the rest of his team returned to the conference room. Their surprise was immediate for on the table in front of each chair was a pair of electronic cuffs.

'Everyone, please sit down and put your hands in the cuffs.' Amy, Spencer saw, looked terrified. He felt awful.

At a nod from Galen to confirm that all had been secured, Spencer began. 'Galen and I have conducted our investigations, and he was able to eliminate the possibility of some kind of electronic bugging device being planted on the ship. So that meant it had to be one of us. I discounted Galen because he was the one who brought this to our attention, so it would make absolutely no sense for him to betray himself and possibly hinder Haxenaar's plans.' He paused, everyone's eyes were locked on him.

'I also discounted myself, because if Haxenaar had been given any opportunity to get close enough to me, well, I wouldn't be standing here talking to you now.' The others nodded, it was clear they understood that.

Spencer waved his hand and a holoimage appeared above the conference table. It showed three Zylaxxians advancing down the main ship's corridor. Moments later, a firefight ensued as they encountered Androsian troops. After a fierce exchange of plasma bolts, the intruders were felled, and the chidwas moved forward. It was here that the footage slowed, and zoomed in on a fallen Zylaxxian.

An Androsian foot came into view, striding past the inert form. As it passed, the hand of the Zylaxxian twitched, and as the camera zoomed again, and then froze the image, it was clear that it was holding some kind of syringe injecting device.

'Camera to wide view.' The image expanded to show the victim of the Zylaxxian assault.

Everyone gasped, and Spencer clicked his fingers. All the restraining cuffs sprang open except one.

'Qarak, it wasn't your fault.' The mighty Androsian looked stunned, but then roared in fury, attempting to wrestle the restraints from his wrists. Galen stepped forward to quickly place a small device against his temple and Qarak slumped forward, unconscious.

Astren was horrified, but Spencer raised his hand to her. 'Astren, he is the victim here. He was injected with what we suspect is an advanced Zylaxxian bio-weapon, cleverly designed to take control of his subconscious and cause him to carry out their wishes. Once we had realised who it was they had infected, we were able to determine that he had sent an encrypted message just minutes after we received the first half of the coordinates from Sala. We can't decipher the contents of that message, but it no longer matters because it obviously sent the Zylaxxians to Ixenar where they arrived some hours before we did.'

Amy asked, 'Is he going to be alright?'

'Now I know what to search for, and where to look, I can use the bioscans that I have of him to identify anything that shouldn't be in his body. I am certain I can then purge it from his system. He will be fine in a few hours.'

Amy smiled, and Astren looked greatly relieved.

Spencer exhaled loudly. 'Okay, well Zan, now I need you to lay in the coordinates for Ixenar and hyper-jump us there as soon as you can.' He gazed around the table, and spoke the words everyone was thinking, 'I wish I could say something inspiring here, but I have a very bad feeling about this.'

*

At the same time as *The Infinity* broke orbit and unbeknownst to Spencer and his crew, the small moon Adrastea, travelling at more than a hundred and twenty kilometres per second, crossed the orbit of the planet designated tetrahelio by the Zylaxxians who had unleashed it. To the entirely unaware occupants of trihelio, whose planet was Adrastea's ultimate destination, it was known by a different name: Mars.

48

Ixenar:

The Infinity emerged from interdimensional space on the outer edge of the Ixenarian system. Spencer had instructed Zan to approach with extreme caution, and his entire team now stood together on the control bridge, watching the expansive holoscreen. At a gesture from Zan, the walls and floor also became transparent, and Spencer stifled a gasp as they stood, seemingly suspended in space.

There were six planets, four of them rocky and two gas giants, and many small moons, but what surprised Spencer the most was the close proximity of them all. This was a small solar system but in some ways all the more astonishing and impressive for that. A holographic diagram appeared above them, showing the orbital paths of the celestial bodies, and how they intersected with each other. It really was very beautiful.

'I am detecting very little in the way of electromagnetic transmission' Zan called out. The system is quite silent.

Some of these planets and moons show signs of previous habitation, but not for a very, very long time.'

It was Galen who then dropped the bombshell, looking up from a small holoscreen he had been studying. 'I believe the entire system is artificial. This has been carefully constructed. The orbital mechanics are too complex, and too perfectly balanced to have occurred naturally.'

They flew on and began to head in toward the inner planets, the unnatural silence began to become a little unnerving.

'Sensors are detecting substantial residual plasma energy readings from the second and third planets,' the ship's AI informed them.

'Take us closer, Zan,' Spencer ordered, and they flew silently onward, sweeping past the rings of one of the gas giants and smoothly easing around a couple of the small moons.

The collective mood on the control bridge was tense. It felt as if they were flying into a system full of ghosts, a place eerily quiet where at any moment a monster might suddenly leap out and attack them.

'This is all wrong,' Spencer muttered. There was a general murmur of agreement.

'Sensors detecting multiple life forms on the second planet,' the ship's AI informed them.

'Lock on and take us there,' Spencer instructed Zan, who signalled his compliance.

Suddenly a proximity alarm sounded, and Zan took immediate evasive action as the ruined hulk of a destroyed ship hove into view, shortly followed by another and then even more.

'We are entering a debris field,' Zan told them. 'Many of these ships are still burning, and I am detecting faint life signatures aboard several.'

Spencer's feelings of dread intensified. There had been a battle here, perhaps just hours ago. 'Keep scanning for any Zylaxxian ships that might still be in the area.'

'Nothing detected sir,' Spencer frowned. It was clear that a Zylaxxian battle fleet had been in action here very recently, and Haxenaar would have surely taken the opportunity to lay a trap for him.

A part of a jagged hull spun into view, faint sparks still glittering in the twilight between the worlds. Astren gave a little gasp, 'That definitely looks Zylaxxian to me.'

Bradlii cut in, 'I'm linked into the sensor arrays, and I can confirm that was a Zylaxxian battle cruiser. There are more wrecks, most of them confirmed Zylaxxian, ahead of us.'

Spencer voiced what everyone was thinking, 'So the Zylaxxians came here and attacked, but they met with strong resistance from the Ixenarians. It looks like both sides have suffered appalling losses. The question is, what is left of the Ixenarians, and do they still have the Spear of Rigel.'

Galen concurred. 'We are also detecting highly unusual energy readings within the system. I've never seen anything quite like them before. I don't yet have enough data to make an assessment as to their origin.'

'Entering geosynchronous orbit around the second planet, directly above the most active source of life signs and electromagnetic transmissions,' Zan said quietly, as a wrecked satellite hove into view for a moment, before speeding off back into the dark of the planet's terminator.

'Galen, Aila and Amy, you're with me. We are going down there. Astren, you too, and bring four chidwas, because we have no idea what might be waiting for us.' Spencer was experiencing a strange sense of fear mixed with expectation. Despite all the struggles and challenges, they had made it to the Ixenarian homeworld, and whatever now lay in store would have to be tackled head-on. He reflected momentarily on the extraordinary journey that had brought them to this point, and, he admitted only to himself, he was surprised at how much more comfortably the mantle of leadership had been sitting with him recently.

*

In the dark and unforgiving cold of deep space, Adrastea continued its lonely journey. Advanced orbital mechanics and calculations of its trajectory had ensured a precision perfect alignment. In the distance, a tiny blue pinprick of light was growing almost imperceptibly slowly as the little moon's final destination, home to more than seven billion human beings, existed in blissful ignorance of its approach.

49

Revelations:

The Harmony Lander flew over a landscape that could only be described as a never-ending scene of destruction. Buildings once intricately beautiful were reduced to charred rubble. Spires that would have towered over ornamental lakes and perfectly manicured gardens remained only as grotesquely twisted tributes to a once powerful and advanced civilisation.

Mile after mile of death and carnage eventually led them to what would have recently been an impressive compound. The walls were partially demolished and small fires were still burning. An immense dome rose from ornate balustrades, soaring more than a hundred metres into the air, pockmarked where plasma bolts had seared its polished marble skin, and mortally wounded where a disfiguring hole had been blown in the side.

'This is where we are detecting the largest concentration

of life signs,' Aila informed them all. 'Approximately six, to be exact.'

'I have a very strange feeling about this,' Spencer voiced the concerns they all shared. 'These planets look like they were mostly deserted a long time ago. Even with a massive Zylaxxian bombardment, there couldn't be this amount of life lost.' The others muttered their agreement.

The touchdown was barely felt, and within moments the chidwas had disembarked and spread out, crouching down with weapons drawn.

'Four life forms approaching from the south-west,' Aila alerted them, 'a hundred metres and closing.' Spencer, Amy and Aila carefully stepped out of the craft and drew their weapons.

A figure, dressed in a flowing white gown appeared from behind an intersecting wall, quickly followed by three others.

In unison the chidwas raised their plasma rifles and cocked them, ready to open fire at the first sign of a threat.

But the figures were walking directly towards them, hands raised in the universal symbol of peaceful greeting. As they neared, Spencer began to be able to determine their features. There appeared to be three males and one female. All were dark-skinned, slim and moved with poise and grace.

The party stopped just ten metres away, and one, perhaps the most senior stepped forward, his arms stretched wide. 'Welcome Emperor, we have been expecting you.'

Spencer stepped forward warily, and all the chidwas tensed.

'Greetings, to whom am I speaking?'

'I am Nitona, and I am your humble servant.'

'Are you Ixenarians?' Spencer had to know.

Nitona smiled gently, 'Yes, we are Ixenarian Emperor. We are honoured by your presence, for we have much to talk about.'

Spencer was sure that might be the understatement of all time, but a wave of welcome relief washed over him that not only had they finally managed to make contact with the Ixenarians, despite the tragic circumstances, but that they also appeared to be friendly. Or at the very least they weren't another hostile species intent on killing him.

The chidwas stood, never taking their eyes from Nitona and his companions, and remained between the two parties as they walked, at the invitation of an Ixenarian named Sumedh, towards the shattered dome.

Inside was cool, the rather intense heat of the outside being banished by the scale of the dome. Far above their heads, the jagged hole allowed the baleful light of the Ixenarian sun to stream in, illuminating countless dancing dust motes that helped contribute to a sense of almost overwhelming age.

As if sensing his thoughts, Nitona turned to Spencer and said, 'This dome was constructed more than ten million of your years ago. It has stood, unchanged until just earlier today.'

'How many Ixenarians do you think have perished in the Zylaxxian attack?' Galen asked.

'Far fewer than you might think. This planet and this system were largely abandoned a very long time ago. Just a small defence force remained, guarding the planets, and of course the spears.'

Spencer gave a visible start. 'You said spears, plural. More than one?'

Nitona gestured him and his friends to some polished stone benches and they all sat down. 'Yes, there were two. One of which we used to repel the attack.'

So that explained the vast debris fields in the system, Spencer thought to himself, 'And the other?'

Nitona grew grave. 'I'm afraid the Zylaxxians took it.'

Spencer closed his eyes to try and compose himself. This was precisely what he, and his crew feared most.

'Tell us what happened, and, if you can, how we can neutralise the remaining spear. We don't have much time though, so please be as brief as you can.'

Nitona indicated he understood. 'The attack was brutal, but most of us who remained to defend the spears were able to return to our Galaxy, or transmute into our ethereal forms.'

Spencer raised an eyebrow. 'You are going to need to explain that.'

'A long time ago, my people developed technology to the point where we were able to exist within an artificially constructed reality that could intersect with the corporeal universe whenever we chose. Our physical manifestation, such as the version of me you see before you, is no longer our natural state. I choose to appear to you in this way, as a young man, but my consciousness has existed for many millennia.'

Spencer didn't react. Curiously this didn't surprise him.

'We exist now purely to learn and acquire knowledge and wisdom. Sala, who you have already visited, is one of our repositories of knowledge.'

'Where are you really from?' Spencer asked.

'I think you know, Emperor.'

'You're Andromedan, aren't you?'

Nitona smiled. 'Yes, and that is where we have returned to, but we are also much, much more than that.'

Now Spencer was confused. He turned to Galen and saw the old man's eyes were shining.

Nitona nodded. 'We are you, Emperor, all of you. Our Galaxy is younger than yours, but sentient life evolved there much earlier. Millions of your years ago we journeyed out, and your Galaxy, the Milky Way as you call it, was our first destination. We found only primitive insentient life. So our elders decided that it was our duty to bring consciousness to some of the worlds we encountered. Yours, Earth, was genetically seeded in an area you now know as The Rift Valley. To you, it is the cradle of humanity,' he paused, 'and so it is also to us.'

Spencer's mind was reeling. 'You are saying that we are your...your children?' He could scarcely believe what he was hearing, and yet somehow it made sense.

'In a way, yes. Evolution has played a part and created great diversity across the Galaxy, but wherever you go, you will find beings with a form similar to us, and to you. It is not an accident that we all mostly share two arms, two legs, a head, a brain and a body, even though millions of years have given birth to wondrous variations.'

'If you have been watching and learning, then you know just how bad things have become.' Spencer cursed that he didn't articulate himself better at times, but Nitona clearly understood his meaning.

'Indeed. Ever since we founded the Galactic Council, we have kept a watchful eye on a number of species, knowing it was likely that some of our children would ultimately rebel against the peace that we sought to bestow.' Nitona's face grew sorrowful. 'One species learned of their heritage earlier than we had anticipated, and it fundamentally challenged their view of themselves as the supreme beings in the cosmos.'

'The Zylaxxians,' Spencer said. A lot was beginning to make sense now.

'Yes. Some of them took a more enlightened view, but others, well, it shook their beliefs about Zylaxxian supremacy to the core and started them down a hate-filled path.'

Sumedh then spoke, 'Emperor, before we talk further, there is one here that you must meet.' And at his gesture, a figure stepped out of the darkness. Spencer gasped, and the chidwas immediately raised their rifles, stepping in front of him.

Into a pool of soft light strode an enormous Zylaxxian, his great head erect and his eyes burning like embers amid the destruction his kind had wreaked.

For a moment Spencer stood frozen to the spot. And then the Zylaxxian knelt, and in a deep rasping voice said, 'Emperor, forgive me for my presence, but I must talk to you most urgently.'

*

Aboard his flagship, Haxenaar was exultant. He regarded the captured Spear of Rigel almost as someone might contemplate the most beautifully exquisite piece of artwork. He gently ran his gloved hand across its flank, admiring the seamless workmanship of its casing. Within, he was certain, lay the device that would bring the Galaxy to heal, and anoint him, finally, to rule as its supreme leader. In just a few hours he would be Emperor of the Galaxy, and, in time, ruler of the galaxies beyond.

*

The Zylaxxian was named Vortrax, and he sat quite calmly, his palms open on his knees while two Androsians flanked him, their plasma pistols held to either side of his head.

'Emperor, you probably believe that all Zylaxxians are warlike and have sworn devotion to Haxenaar?'

Spencer was wary. 'I've not yet met a Zylaxxian who isn't.'

Vortrax nodded slowly, 'And that makes me sadder than you can imagine, sire. Zylaxxian culture, while built upon conquest is also not devoid of art, poetry, literature and music. In the past, all of these things have made us more than we are now. Some of us believe these to be the fundamentals of Zylaxxian civilisation, but now they are treated as worthless irrelevances by Haxenaar.'

Spencer shrugged, 'I am aware of some of your history, but I'm not sure that I have the time to discuss it with you now.'

'Please sire, I beg of you. Haxenaar does not speak for all Zylaxxians. I am a dissenter, or as he would describe me, a traitor. I lead a small but growing resistance movement.' He sighed deeply. 'The Zylaxxian political system is complex and almost entirely factional. As one group rises, so they must crush their opposition in order to maintain their power. Haxenaar is from a powerful faction, the Reexaran, who have managed to maintain their grip on power for decades through their sheer brutality and ruthlessness.'

Spencer was regarding him closely, "Go on.'

'But they are only secure as long as Haxenaar continues to demonstrate his military prowess through conflict and conquest. He has to give the Zylaxxians an enemy to fight and victories to celebrate. His followers believe they are destined to rule the cosmos, and he knows that can never happen as long as the Ixenarians, or rather the Andromedans as they truly are, wait in the wings, watching and perhaps ready to one day challenge him. Haxenaar has realised that in order to secure his rule of this Galaxy, he must also defeat Andromeda, and he has been able to convince his subjects that by doing so and destroying those who claim to be their creators, they are fulfilling their destiny and asserting themselves as the supreme species in all of existence.'

Spencer whistled softly. A lot of pieces of the jigsaw were now falling into place. Haxenaar's objectives were far greater than any of them had yet realised, and the implications if he were able to fulfil his plan were so profound as to be beyond comprehension. Haxenaar was intent on no less than rewriting the shared history of all sentient beings. If nothing else, this was the one thing that Spencer had learned bound them all together. If he succeeded, Haxenaar would create a new reality, one that would persist and change everything for everyone, forever.

'So what's his next move?' Spencer asked the Zylaxxian, although the pit in his stomach confirmed he probably already knew.

'He must destroy you, and your home planet as a very public demonstration of his ruthlessness and will. He needs to send a message to all the corners of the Galaxy that he will not be defied. Unless you defeat him, he will assume the mantle of Emperor of the Galaxy through force and dissolution of The Galactic Council.'

The Zylaxxian hesitated, and then as if stiffening his resolve, continued. 'He will simultaneously use the intergalactic jump system he has been constructing at Eta Carinae. He'll launch the Spear of Rigel that he has into that massive star, and at the point of detonation, the energy of that sun will be converted and channelled into the jump grid instantaneously transporting his invasion fleet to Andromeda.'

This came as a surprise to Spencer. 'But I thought he would be using his spear to destroy Sol, my sun?'

Vortrax shook his great head, and his voice was full of sorrow. 'I regret to inform you, Emperor, that the fate of your planet was sealed some time ago when one of the moons of your gas giant, the planet you call Jupiter, was wrenched from orbit by a Zylaxxian task force and sent on a collision trajectory with Earth.'

Spencer felt as if he had been gut-punched. 'Oh my God, are you saying that I have to choose between trying to save my planet and trying to prevent Haxenaar from taking control of the Galaxy and declaring war on Andromeda?'

The Zylaxxian said nothing but lowered his eyes. Spencer was in turmoil though. He looked around, Amy's face conveyed her shock, and even the usually implacable Galen looked distraught.

'How can I make that choice? How can I possibly be expected to choose?' Spencer was desperate, and in that moment he understood with appalling clarity what it meant to be Emperor. He stood, suddenly he needed some air. The chidwas immediately moved to surround him, but he waved them away. Almost stumbling, on legs that felt as if they might give way at any moment, he made it to the entrance of the dome, and stood there, blinking in the light, and trying not to throw up.

The extraordinary events of the past, what was it, less than two months, came crashing into his head, swirling around, vying with each other for his attention. Why me? Why me? Why me? He must have been speaking out loud because there was a sound and he turned. Amy was standing there. 'Why you, Spencer?' He nodded, looking at her in despair. 'Because you are the Emperor of the Galaxy, Spencer, and these people,' she gestured in the direction of the dome, 'and every single person we have met on this insane journey, has come to respect and trust in you. And I know you well enough by now to be absolutely certain that you aren't going to let them, or me, or the Galaxy down.' She drew near. 'It feels like a lifetime has passed since we sat in Yum Burger, doesn't it?' Spencer forced a small smile at the recollection of the happiest night of his life. 'And I wouldn't change a single moment of any of it, because I have been with you.' She leaned in and kissed him tenderly.

'Now, get a grip, Spencer, because we have a mad Zylaxxian to defeat, and a Galaxy to save.' Amy said firmly.

And somehow he felt some certainty returning. Yes, *dammit*, yes! He wasn't beaten yet.

*

Spencer and Amy headed back to the group, and as he walked alongside her a plan began to form in his mind. It probably wasn't a great plan, but it was better than nothing.

By the time they had reached the others, Spencer felt a little better.

'We need to return to *The Infinity*, right now. Nitona, thank you for your hospitality and help, I hope we might meet again one day.'

'Emperor, before you depart I must speak with you alone. It won't take long.' The Ixenarian said quietly.

The rest of the landing team sat and watched as for perhaps five minutes Spencer and Nitona were out of earshot, evidently engaged in earnest conversation. More than once Spencer appeared to express surprise, but it was difficult to tell from a distance.

50

The Final Battle – Part One: Sacrifice

The shipboard AI guided *The Infinity* out of the Ixenarian system without incident, while Spencer and his crew assembled once more in the conference room.

The Emperor stood at the head of the table, his hands leaning on the highly polished dark stone that was cool to the touch. He straightened and spoke in carefully measured tones.

'There are, as far as I can see, three factors at play. The first is that a small moon is bearing down on Earth and if it strikes it will create catastrophic damage, probably ending human civilisation as we know it. The second is that the Zylaxxians intend to launch an invasion of the Andromeda Galaxy. The Third is that Haxenaar intends to kill or capture me, and declare himself Emperor of the Galaxy.

'None of these things can be allowed to happen.' Spencer slammed his fist down on the unforgiving stone to emphasise his determination. 'I have a plan, and it is complex and dangerous, but having discussed it with Bradlii and run some simulations, there is a slim chance we could succeed. However, I have to be completely honest with you,' he paused, and his voice wavered before he cleared his throat. 'All of you are my most precious friends. In the short time we have known each other, I have come to value each of you more than you can possibly know. Every single one of you is brave beyond belief, probably much more so than I am, and there is a very good chance we may not all survive this. So take a good look around you. It is not just for Earth's sake, or the Galaxy's future that we do this. It is for each other.'

*

Two days later, the Zylaxxian ship "Azvagarde" made contact with Adrastea long after it had crossed the orbit of Mars and continued its inexorable silent journey toward the bright blue planet known by its near seven billion inhabitants as Earth.

Speed in space is all relative, but objects and even planets tend to move at velocities that are rather difficult to comprehend.

Travelling at more than a thousand kilometres per second relative to Earth, little Adrastea contained enough kinetic energy to smash its target to smithereens. Put simply, it was as if a grain of sand was fired at a travelling bullet from a thousand miles away, and yet the Zylaxxian computers had made their calculations with such total precision that it would indeed impact planet Earth in the mid-Atlantic, causing the near-total destruction of the world and almost every living thing upon it.

Vortrax stood on the command deck of his ship from where they were tracking Adrastea and regarded it thoughtfully. As a Zylaxxian, he marvelled at the ingenuity of Haxenaar's plan, and perhaps even admired the tyrant for it, but he was also his sworn enemy, and for the sake of the Galaxy he knew he must be defeated.

He turned to his Scientific Adviser, 'Can we deflect it?'

'No sire, its mass and velocity are too great. We don't have sufficient engine power.'

'Then can we destroy it with our weapons?'

The adviser looked down sadly. 'We might damage it, but even with all our missiles and plasma cannons concentrated upon it, we would most likely only succeed in splitting it into several large pieces which would then rain down on Earth and still cause total devastation. Rather than a single artillery shell, we would create multiple bullets but the result would be the same.'

'Then I need options or Earth is lost and with it the chance for peace in the Galaxy.'

Their eyes met, and each knew what the other was thinking.

The Infinity re-entered normal space, less than a million miles away from the Zylaxxian energy grid orbiting Eta Carinae, at precisely the coordinates and time they had planned for.

'We've been detected.' Zan informed them. 'As expected, the Zylaxxian fleet is powering up and going to battle stations.'

'I'm registering over four hundred Zylaxxian cruisers and frigates, and twenty battleships,' Qarak glanced up from his holoscreen. 'It's an invasion fleet, no question about it.'

Spencer turned to Zan, 'Open a comms link to the Zylaxxian fleet.'

Haxenaar's face appeared on the main holoscreen. Upon recognising his hated foe he twisted his face into a cruel smile. 'Spencer Edwards of Earth, I have been waiting for this moment for a long time. Whatever plan you may have will fail, as you can now see the might of my war fleet. In a moment we will blow you and your pitiful friends out of existence.'

'Are we alone?' Spencer asked Qarak quietly.

'Yes. No. I'm detecting another ship behind us, and another, two, no, five, more coming out of phase-space now... all different species.'

'How many now, Qarak?'

'Three thousand two hundred and sixty-seven.'

Spencer's eyes went wide. 'My God!'

'You did this, Spencer! You did it! That's the whole Galaxy behind you!' Amy's eyes shone.

On the holoscreen Haxenaar could be seen barking urgent orders to his subordinates.

'All allied ships are now synchronised to our communications system. You can speak to them now, Spencer,' Bradlii informed him.

Spencer cleared his throat, 'My honourable friends, I thank you for coming. With you at my side, we can, and must prevail, to bring peace to the Galaxy.'

He looked Haxenaar directly in the eye. 'Still fancy your chances?'

With a curse, the Zylaxxian cut his comms link and moments later the two fleets engaged. The heavily armed and armoured Zylaxxian ships fought viciously and destroyed many of their opponents, but slowly they began to be overwhelmed by sheer force of numbers.

Without warning *The Infinity* was hit a glancing blow from a Zylaxxian plasma cannon broadside, nearly shaking them off their feet and strafing a burning scar across her gleaming hull. But still, they fought on, driving hard towards Haxenaar's flagship.

'We aren't going to be able to penetrate his defensive perimeter in time, Spencer.' Galen said. 'He has too many heavy cruisers surrounding him.'

Spencer nodded. He had anticipated this. 'Then we execute plan alpha echo. Amy, Astren, you are with me.'

Aila spoke quickly, 'I still recommend against this sir, it is too high risk.'

Spencer nodded, 'Noted, but we have no choice. If we are to die, then we'll bloody well die setting the best example to the rest of the galaxy we possibly can. Right, Amy?'

'Damn right, babe!'

'Besides Aila, this is personal now, between me and him.'

They ran from the bridge and within moments joined Galen in the ship's science centre. 'Activate it!' Spencer shouted, and at a gesture from the scientist, a wormhole began to form in the centre of the lab.

'Spencer, I have managed to target the arrival point and the wormhole is stable for the moment, but it's very dangerous. This has rarely ever been attempted, and most times it has failed.'

'We're out of options, Galen,' and then he gripped the old man's arm, 'If anyone can do this, it's you.'

And with that, Spencer, Amy and Astren ran into the glowing portal and vanished.

'The Galactic Armada has engaged the Zylaxxian battle fleet at Eta Carinae sire.' Vortrax's communications officer informed him. 'There is heavy fighting.'

Vortrax nodded that he understood. They too were out of time. For the past several hours they had studied Adrastea's composition and structure, and run countless simulations. Every time, no matter what variables were changed, Earth was destroyed.

The errant moon was now closing in on the final vector of its long journey, less than half a million kilometres out from Earth's own ancient satellite that it would very soon sweep past before striking the homeworld of humanity just four minutes later.

'We must intercept at precisely the right moment so that Lunar acts as a partial shield to the planet below. The coordinates are locked and matched, sire,' the science adviser said softly.

'Open a link to the crew, and broadcast on QEComms to all points.'

The communications officer saluted to signal compliance.

'My beloved crew, we stand together as the best of Zylaxxians, and to show to the Galaxy that we are not all as Haxenaar and his faction. We are noble and selfless, and we do this for the Emperor of the Galaxy and his homeworld, a place we do not know and have never visited, but that gives life to seven billion sentient souls.' He stood straight, put his fist to his heart and said, 'For the Galaxy, and for our

Emperor!'

Onboard *The Infinity*, on holoscreens across all the ships of the armada, and on countless worlds across the Galaxy, beings from all races watched Vortrax smile as the Asvagarde jumped out of space-time for an instant, her course plotted for the dead centre of Adrastea.

The little moon flashed once as the Asvagarde re-entered normal space at its heart, discharging incalculable amounts of kinetic energy as it did so. And then Adrastea detonated, shattering into billions of tiny fragments, some colliding with the dark side of Earth's moon, while others swept by, entering the planet's upper atmosphere just minutes later.

On Earth, seven billion people gazed skywards as countless tiny meteorites burned up in the outer atmosphere making the most spectacular and unexpected meteor shower ever witnessed by humankind, and wondered what had just happened.

Haxenaar stood silently, his gaze never wavering as he regarded the vast and ever-changing holoscreens that floated in the dome of his flagship. He watched, transfixed as they showed the live feeds of the intense and brutal battle raging between his fleet and the Galactic Armada when Spencer, Amy and Astren emerged from the wormhole just metres away from him.

A look of surprise immediately turned to a snarl as he realised that his nemesis now stood before him. 'You! I will kill you all!'

The three friends were poised ready to fight, their faces set with utter determination. 'This is your last chance, Haxenaar, to stand down.' Spencer stared directly into his eyes and suddenly realised he was no longer afraid of this monster.

The Zylaxxian cursed, and then he drew his hideous scimitar and lunged. All three ran forwards, their smartsuits in full combat mode. They landed blow after blow and Haxenaar staggered under the onslaught. Astren crouched and threw a barrage of the tiny glowing stars the chidwas so favoured, piercing his body armour and sending paralysing arcs of energy between them.

In Spencer's ear, Bradlii spoke urgently. 'The wormhole is collapsing, Spencer! You must get out now!'

But Spencer wasn't finished. He and Amy executed perfectly synchronised roundhouse kicks to his chest, flinging the mighty Zylaxxian warlord backwards.

'Stay down!' Spencer commanded, but Haxenaar was already struggling to his feet. His armour was heavily damaged and dark purple blood dripped from his mouth. At his gesture, a glowing red forcefield materialised between them.

He laughed, a hideous choking bellow. 'You cannot win, Spencer Edwards of Earth! I curse you, and I spit on your childish dreams of peace in the Galaxy!' He wiped the blood from his chin and smiled cruelly.

At that moment a muon burst from a Horovian gunship struck the dome, smashing it open to the stars. Instantly, as the air began to rush out into the cold vacuum of space, Spencer, Amy and Astren's smartsuits extruded clear plastic domes over their heads and their shoes gripped onto the smooth deck beneath their feet.

'You have less than ten seconds to transit the wormhole!' Bradlii's voice was desperate in all their ears.

The deck began to split as a chasm opened up beneath the forcefield that separated them from Haxenaar. Metal groaned and shrieked as the Zylaxxian flagship slowly broke in two.

Haxenaar stood staring defiantly as the forward part of his ship began to drift away from the trio, sparks of energy flashing and snaking across the void where the two halves of the massive craft had been ripped apart.

Spencer grabbed Astren and Amy and rushed them towards the wormhole, throwing them in and then diving through himself just as it closed and vanished.

The battle was still raging as Spencer, Amy and Astren made it back to the command bridge of *The Infinity*, with Galen following closely behind. The relief of the rest of the crew at their return was short-lived as Qarak shouted, 'He's launched the Spear!'

Spencer wheeled around, 'All ships, target the Zylaxxian grid now!'

On the holoscreen, hundreds of ships of all shapes and sizes immediately moved towards the colossal spider's web construction orbiting Eta Carinae, their weapons unleashing a firestorm of directed energy toward it.

'Zan, engage the clamp and jump now!'

At his order, the pilot punched a holobutton and *The Infinity* smashed through the spacetime barrier, hurling itself towards the Spear of Rigel as it sped towards the supergiant star.

'Closing in, clamp active. We're not gonna make it!'

Spencer and his crew watched in horror as the electromagnetic bottle extended, but missed the rapidly moving Spear as it entered Eta Carinae's heliosphere.

'Get us out of here, now!' Spencer shouted. Then a moment later, 'All ships, full retreat!'

Zan pulled up hard, and *The Infinity* rolled over in a loop, engines pushed to the maximum and accelerated away from the grid. The Galactic Armada fell back with them, ships closing in to form a protective bubble around their Emperor.

Eta Carinae emitted an intense pulse and then went instantly dark as if an immense hole had suddenly opened in space.

The Zylaxxian grid dissolved into searing white light as, in a fraction of a second, more energy than had ever been released in the entire known history of the Galaxy arced across space, and for a moment Haxenaar's crazed face appeared on their holoscreen before the transmission cut.

As the dazzling light faded, what remained of the Zylaxxian fleet was gone.

'Where are they?' Spencer asked.

'Unclear,' Galen responded. 'They may have been vaporised along with the grid, as they were all linked to it, but I can't be sure.'

The Armada remained in the sector where Eta Carinae had shone for billions of years, conducting intense sensor sweeps for several hours, but no sign of the Zylaxxian battlefleet could be found. There were multiple ripples in spacetime, and the massive drifting wreckage of the battle returned many resonances, as survivors were picked up from both sides, the Zylaxxians placed in holding cells at Spencer's command to be returned to their homeworld in due course.

Finally, Spencer gave the order for all ships to make their way to Eloim III.

51

The Final Battle – Part Two: Return to Eloim III

As the Armada arrived in orbit around Eloim III, the news from the ground was not good. Chaos had broken out amongst the Zylaxxian troops tasked with holding the Grand Hall of the Galactic Council underguard and its inhabitants from all the worlds across the Galaxy as hostages.

'By defeating Haxenaar, you've cut the head off the snake,' Galen advised earnestly. 'Zylaxxians are entirely hierarchical in their militaristic structure. With their leader gone they have dissolved into inter-factional fighting, pitting Zylaxxian against Zylaxxian, with tens of thousands of members of the council caught in the crossfire.'

Spencer grasped the situation instantly and made his decision.

'I'm going down there. We need to get to the council chamber, and I must assert my authority while offering amnesty to the Zylaxxians.'

Astren looked aghast. 'Sir, these are killers! They have already slain numerous dignitaries, and given the chance will carry out Haxenaar's last orders and kill you!'

'I'm not so sure, Astren. I learned a lot about Zylaxxians from Vortrax, and I think that given the chance, I can appeal to them rationally. And besides,' he added, 'I'll have you, Qarak, your chidwas and several platoons drawn from our escort ships to help persuade them.'

Astren sighed, 'Alright, I know by now there is no point in arguing this further with you, Emperor. It will be as you say.'

Spencer winked at Amy, who shrugged resignedly. 'Well, we've got this far, we might as well see it through to the end.'

Aila said, 'Shall I prepare a Lander for you?' Spencer shook his head. 'Not this time. We've been through this together, and one way or another we'll finish it together. All of us.'

Spencer turned to Zan, 'You once said *The Infinity* was probably the most famous ship in the Galaxy, or words to that effect?'

'No question about it, she is.' Zan's pride was evident whenever he talked about her.

'Then, in that case, take her down, and make sure everyone gets a really good look at us.'

Zan grinned, 'Yes sir!'

Escorted by four heavily armed assault craft from the armada, *The Infinity* swooped down through the lower atmosphere of Eloim III. Once again, Spencer was struck by the sheer beauty of this most revered planet. The wide-open seas glittered and sparkled, and the lush dense forests gave birth to spectacular mountain ranges capped by pure white snow. As they closed to within five hundred kilometres of their destination, the ship's AI sounded an alarm tone.

'Sensors are showing heavy fighting in the area surrounding the Capital. Council Guards and Zylaxxian forces are directly engaged.'

Galen looked up from his holoscreen, 'We need to be careful.'

Spencer inclined his head to show he had heard but instructed Zan to fly directly over the melee. 'Make as much noise as you can while you're doing it, too.'

'Afterburners on, Sir.' *The Infinity* shook as anti-matter was injected directly into the exhaust ports of the ship's mighty engines whose usual faint hum quickly built into a deafening roar as the ship blazed over the Zylaxxian ground forces, scattering many of them as they dashed for cover.

'Landing struts extending, bringing us to Landing Pad One.' And with an almost imperceptible bump, *The Infinity* docked at precisely the same place where just a couple of months before, Spencer had fled from the council chamber following the death of Volaria, with Haxenaar's henchmen in murderous pursuit.

Their escorts ships remained to hover over the battlefield, an implicit threat as they guarded the Emperor's docked ship.

Spencer, Amy, Aila, Astren, Zan, Galen and Qarak stepped out of *The Infinity* and into the corridor that led to what was once Volaria's chamber. Chidwas immediately fanned out in front and behind them, securing the area before signalling the party to move forwards.

Bradlii warned that there were armed Zylaxxians in the Council Chamber but Spencer didn't break step for even a moment.

Galen walked alongside Spencer. 'What is your plan Emperor?'

'I don't have one Galen, not this time. I'm just going to speak to them.' The sage raised his eyebrows quizzically, and then smiled but said nothing.

As they reached the anti-chamber, Spencer stopped and turned to his friends. 'This ends now. Agreed?'

They all nodded.

At his gesture, the wall opened and Spencer strode out into the spectacular auditorium, his friends one step behind him. There were audible gasps as he made his way to the lectern where not long before his predecessor had been obliterated along with the faithful Nomo.

He turned to face the audience of delegates and saw numerous Zylaxxians raise their plasma rifles and train them on him. But this time he was not afraid. Drone cameras began to broadcast across all the news feeds and media platforms of the Galaxy, and an audience of many trillions watched as Spencer held up his hand and addressed the Zylaxxians directly. 'Enough! Haxenaar is gone and with him his hold over all of you.' He paused to let his words sink in and then spoke more gently.

'I knew a Zylaxxian, and he was the noblest and bravest being I ever met. His name was Vortrax, and I believe you will have heard of him.'

One or two of the Zylaxxians lifted their eyes towards Spencer, and he recognised their anguish.

'I had grown to hate Haxenaar and all Zylaxxians, but Vortrax taught me there is so much more to you than I ever believed. I learned that like every species and civilisation there are those who are inherently good and others who are not, but I was guilty of thinking the worst of all of you.' He paused again and stretched out his arms towards the Zylaxxians. 'Vortrax showed me the best of you, and the nobility in all of us. His name and the names of his valiant crew will forever be remembered by me and by the Galaxy. That I promise.'

The auditorium was now silent, save for a growing murmur of approval from the thousands of delegates present.

'So I ask you, as your Emperor, to lay down your weapons and join me in a new era of galactic peace. I stand here with my cherished friends, and to you all, everywhere, I hold out *my* hand in friendship.'

The largest of the Zylaxxians, evidently their leader, stood straight and his eyes bored into Spencer. Then he slowly lowered his weapon. With a bound, he leapt onto the stage and advanced toward Spencer until he was standing just a few feet from him. The chidwas, waiting in the wings were already responding but Spencer, his eyes never leaving the huge Zylaxxian, waved them back.

'I am Klaarax, of Zylaxxia.' His deep rasping voice was amplified throughout the hushed chamber.

And then he knelt and bowed his head. 'Spencer Edwards, Emperor of the Galaxy.'

52

Aftermath:

The days following the battle against Haxenaar were a time of reconciliation and new beginnings for the Galaxy. The Zylaxxian forces on Eloim III stood down, and returned to their own system, while The Galactic Council was reconvened, this time with Spencer acknowledged by all delegates as the new Emperor.

Spencer posthumously awarded Vortrax and the crew of the *Asvagarde* the medals of Heroes of the Galaxy, and wrote to each of their families personally to express his profound gratitude for their sacrifice. Many of the responses he received back moved him deeply.

Astren and Qarak returned to Androsep at the request of their families. They seemed unsettled, but neither Spencer or Amy could get much out of them and so gave up, deciding to respect their privacy for now.

Galen settled quickly into his new role as Counsel to

the Emperor – a fancy title for being Spencer's most trusted advisor. He was clearly delighted when Spencer told him there was no-one whose wisdom he trusted more.

Zan prepared to take *The Infinity* to the Alpha Cassiopeia Orbital Shipyards for a full service and long planned refit. The valiant ship had taken a pounding the past few months, and everyone, Spencer included, was keen to give her a rest. Besides, Zan promised some impressive upgrades to her capabilities.

Aila remained with Spencer, acting as his personal assistant. At times, Spencer felt rather spoilt by her ministrations, and made sure he took the time to do some things for her, even though she usually protested.

Amy stayed too, and she and Spencer even found some time to relax and visit some of the sights of Eloim III. The waterfalls of Dizara were truly spectacular and became a special place for both of them.

Spencer also learned that in the grounds of the Grand Hall was a mausoleum that doubled as a museum. It was here that previous Emperors and Empresses were interred or remembered if they so chose, and records of their service were retained for future generations. Spencer made a special request, and was able to visit late one evening after all the other visitors had departed.

He sat for more than an hour, alone, and contemplated the wall-mounted holoscreen that displayed a picture and significant events and achievements from the life of Volaria 18th. He hoped that she would have approved of all he had done.

When he left, he placed a single yellow flower, of a kind unique to Eloim III beneath the screen and bowed his head for a moment.

Naturally, the Galaxy-wide QEComms media were desperate to know more about Spencer, and requests for interviews, public appearances and the opening of events and new schools, hospitals, spaceports and even stadiums came thick and fast. Spencer felt obliged to agree to do as many as he could, but the rather extensive staff of his personal office at the Grand Hall of the Galactic Council seemed well able to handle his public profile.

He did agree to one interview, with Amy and Galen alongside him. According to Aila, it was well-received across the Galaxy, and messages of support came from the governments of the hundreds of thousands of inhabited worlds.

But all the time there was the shadow of Haxenaar. His disappearance, along with that of his battlefleet made Spencer very uneasy. Even though some scientists believed he and his warships had been vaporised, Spencer had his doubts.

Before *The Infinity* departed for her refurbishment, she made one last journey and arrived at the ruins of Valandese, the galactic research hub that had been virtually obliterated by Haxenaar. Through QEComms streams, the Emperor of the Galaxy was seen placing a memorial in the space above where once had been housed some of the greatest and most inquisitive minds in the cosmos, and on countless holoscreens, he pledged to rebuild it for the benefit of the entire Galaxy.

And then, out of sight of the drone cameras, he touched his badge and opened the space-time portal to go home.

53

Epilogue:

As Spencer and Amy stepped out of the wormhole and into his bedroom, Spencer tripped over the skateboard he had left carelessly on the floor. He froze.

'Spencer, Spencer, is that you?' Mum's voice came floating up the stairs.

'Quick Amy, under the bed,' and without hesitation she rapidly concealed herself.

'Yes Mum, sorry.'

'Can you come down here for a moment please?' Mum paused.

'And bring Amy with you.'

Spencer groaned and helped Amy out from her hiding place. She was grinning, 'Aw, Spencer, that was so sweet of you!' and clutching the snacks and little note he had placed there, days, or was it weeks previously, for just this eventuality.

Slowly, they made their way down to the kitchen, Spencer bracing for a proper telling off.

Mum was sitting at the table, smiling. Hassan was standing behind her, leaning on one of the kitchen units, smiling also. And there was another figure, sitting at the table next to mum.

Spencer's jaw dropped. 'Galen! What on earth are you doing here?'

Mum spoke, 'Spencer, Amy, sit down dears. We need to have a little talk. Oh, and you can put Bradlii there on the table too.'

Spencer was staring hard at Galen, who shrugged and said, 'She knows pretty much everything Spencer, and now I guess it's only fair that you do too.'

Spencer reached for Amy's hand under the table and squeezed it before replying, 'Believe me, I'm all ears, Galen.'

The sage nodded and then began. 'I have known, or rather knew Volaria for a very long time and she was truly dear to me in so many ways. She was a remarkable woman and leader. She was wise, resourceful, perceptive and kind.' He paused, 'Her loss is an immense tragedy for us all and I feel it deeply still.' Spencer nodded slowly, as Galen continued.

'About twenty of your years ago, Volaria began to realise that the Galaxy was in greater jeopardy than it had been for a millennia, as the terms of the Orion Treaty that had held the Zylaxxians in check for five centuries began to falter. She knew that her term of office was drawing to a close, and she was determined to ensure that there was continuity.'

'And so she made a plan,' Spencer stated.

'You knew?' Galen asked quickly.

'Not until I talked with Nitona, but he confirmed a few things that I had begun to suspect.'

Galen nodded slowly. 'Volaria was not a leader to leave the entire fate of the Galaxy to chance you know.'

Mum reached across the table and patted Spencer's arm reassuringly while Galen continued.

'Volaria and I were, well, let's just say close. She confided in me her ideas, and I helped her to realise them. You, Spencer, are one of the results of that plan.'

Spencer looked straight at Galen and asked the one question that he knew he must. 'Are you my father?'

Galen's eyes flickered for a moment, 'No, I am not. But if I were, I would be truly proud to be so Spencer.'

Mum interjected. 'You could think of Galen as more like an uncle, and,' She paused for a moment, 'Volaria as perhaps your aunt.'

Spencer's confusion was evident, and so Galen explained further. 'You and twenty others like you spread across the Galaxy, are a little more than you may have suspected. Along with the DNA of your parents, you contain the combined genetic code of Volaria, me, and several other trusted and valued scientists and leaders, all chosen for their strength of character and a strong sense of moral purpose.'

'Mum?' Spencer had to know.

'Oh Spencer, I am absolutely your mother, in every single way.' She stood and crossed over to hug him. 'Galen first came to see me more than fifteen years ago. I'm not entirely sure why, but maybe someday he'll explain. I thought he was some kind of lunatic at first, but then I listened, and he took me to see Eloim III and meet Volaria.'

Spencer couldn't contain his surprise. 'You've been to Eloim? You've known all this time?'

'Yes, but my job, and that of Hassan, when he was told, was to keep you safe and hidden.'

Hassan reached over and ruffled Spencer's hair. 'It wasn't always easy, not telling you, but we knew it was the only way. You had to become your own person Spencer, and besides, any one of twenty others could have become Emperor in which case you would never have known,' he said gently.

'What about these others?' Spencer asked Galen directly.

'Yes, there were some possible candidates but after assessments, you were the obvious choice, although the pace of events meant we had to bring Volaria's plan forward by quite some years. We hadn't expected to need you to become involved until you were quite a bit older, but the Zylaxxian threat was growing more rapidly than anyone had foreseen.'

'Why me though?'

'Bradlii has been monitoring you since you were born. He has been there, one way or another, throughout your life. In a bit of a masterstroke, he even wrote BattleBlast for you.'

Spencer was dumbfounded. 'Bradlii, you wrote BattleBlast?'

'Oh yes,' the AI responded cheerfully, 'It didn't take long, but it has proved to be a great training programme and a way for me to see your ethical decision-making skills develop. I just gave the source code to some gaming company, I believe they have done quite well out of it actually. And, if I may add, you have exceeded even my best projections.'

'How so?' Spencer could barely believe what he was hearing. All his life he had been Mr Average, hadn't he?

Galen cut in, 'We knew you were the one when you

repeatedly demonstrated your willingness to sacrifice your own chances of winning for the collective benefit of your team. That, along with many other factors, showed that you consistently put the collective good above your personal success. And that is an essential quality in any great leader.'

Spencer let out a deep breath. This was a lot to take in. 'So when Volaria asked the galactic AI's to choose someone at random from all the sentient beings across all the inhabited worlds, it wasn't at random at all?'

'That's correct,' Galen nodded. 'As I said, Volaria was never going to risk the safety of quadrillions of beings across the Galaxy to luck. The one person we hadn't reckoned on though was Amy.' He turned to her, 'You have been truly remarkable in every way Amy, and the Galaxy owes you a great debt of gratitude also.'

Amy grinned in the way that always melted Spencer's heart.

'You are more than welcome, mate. I did it for Spencer, because I love him.'

Galen nodded, 'I know that you do, and he loves you, of that there can be no doubt.'

Spencer desperately wanted to hug her but resisted the urge. After all, it was still mum, Hassan and well, now his sort-of uncle apparently that were sitting across the table from him, and such overt displays of affection in front of your family aren't cool when you are fourteen.

'So what happens now?'

Galen's face turned grave. 'Now, Bradlii plays you a message that was received just some hours ago.'

At his instruction, a holoscreen appeared over the kitchen table. It displayed a complicated multi-faceted symbol and then a mechanistic voice spoke. 'Andromeda has received your emissary designated Haxenaar, and he has communicated Valius' declaration of war upon us. We will respond to neutralise the threat.'

Spencer felt his heart sink, but then his resolve stiffened and he looked at each in turn. 'Well, that confirms our worst fears. So I guess we'd better get back to work and save the Galaxy again, hadn't we?'

Coming Next – Spencer Edwards: Andromeda

Galactic Databank

Key technologies:

Bradlii – an incredibly powerful AI that disguises himself as Spencer's Smartphone. He can project himself as a fully holographic lifeform of any type as required.

Command Bridge – on board *The Infinity* the entire bridge is virtual, and can turn transparent to give the occupants a full 360 degree view outside the ship – including above and below – as if they are literally standing in the vastness of space.

Graviton – an elementary particle that mediates and controls the effects of gravity.

Holford Clamp – a device that produces a highly energetic focused magnetic field that can be used to attract or recover items in space.

Holoscreens – projected screens that operate and display in mid-air without physical form.

Multi-dimensional inter-phasic drive (Multi-drive) - a singularity powered space-time drive that channels vast amounts of energy into the space of a single atom to jump out of our dimensions and then instantly re-enter at another point in space-time.

Muon Launcher – a muon is a heavy particle that when a charge of them are packed into a super-dense pulse can cause devastating damage to a target. Or acts like a cutting beam, scything ships in half.

Nano-air – in the event of extreme manoeuvre, the ship's atmosphere can be instantly turned semi-solid to cushion the occupants from excessive g-forces.

Nanoswarm – millions of tiny medical robots that can repair severely damaged tissue and organs.

Plasma pistols and guns – handheld and larger ship born, that fire a charged burst of super-heated plasma to vaporise the target.

Portable Wearable Wormhole Initiator – uses quantum entanglement to link Spencer to the entry and exit point hidden in his bedroom on Earth. Allows almost instantaneous return to Earth at any time.

QEComms – Quantum Entanglement has been used to enable communication over the vast distances of the Galaxy. QEComms is the established galactic standard.

Self-e-scan – a small badge that performs an immediate assessment of the wearer's health, strength and vitality, and warns when any are dropping (works in conjunction with the smartsuit).

Smartsuits – able to adapt to the environment, including intelligent camouflage and even colour and lighting effects. Smartsuits take professional pride in not letting the wearer die. They have multiple modes all designed to protect their owner, and can significantly augment muscle and the wearer's capabilities.

Sonic grenade – detonates with a sonic shockwave, knocking any creature off their feet and temporarily stunning or disorientating them.

Spear of Rigel – a mysterious device that has the ability to halt all fusion within a star.

The Infinity – the Galactic Emperor's personal starship. It is the most famous and recognisable ship in the Galaxy – sleek, fast and well armed. *The Infinity* is not a new ship, but it has been continually updated over the several centuries since it was first built in the Cassiopeia Orbital Shipyards.

Wormhole – a shortcut through time and space created by the linking of two points on the quantum level. Visits to planetary surfaces or other ships are usually conducted by landing craft but under certain emergency circumstances short space-time tunnels can be opened through which life forms can transit.

About the Author

Alex Prior attended the University of Manchester and then pursued a career in Television and Film for the next decade or so, eventually ending up at Elstree Film Studios. He has written scripts, commercial copy and even musicals.

He slowly changed career to education after being asked to deliver some guest lectures, and became a school leader and then Principal and Head teacher of several challenging schools.

He has a lifelong interest in space science, geology and palaeontology, and lives in Central Bedfordshire and Somerset with his wife Emma and son Jamie.

He is a huge fan of Blackadder, Star Trek, Sherlock Holmes and collecting weird and wonderful ephemera.

"The Lost Case Files of Sherlock Holmes" was his first book, published in November 2020, and it went on to become a bestseller and received rave reviews.

"Spencer Edwards: Emperor of the Galaxy" is the first of a new series.

www.alexpriorauthor.com
tiktok: @alexpriorauthor
Instagram: alexpriorauthor
X: alexpriorauthor

About the Cover Artist

Adi Granov is a visionary artist and designer who first arrived on the comic book scene with his painted art on Marvel comic covers and Iron Man - Extremis comic series which redefined the character for the current era.

His designs and art style set the tone for the first Iron Man movie which started a relationship with the Marvel Cinematic Universe that carries on to this day through his contributions to the Iron Man Trilogy, Avengers and Black Panther movies as well as Spider-Man: No Way Home and Moon Knight.

Adi started his career as a concept artist at Nintendo and an editorial illustrator. He illustrated for RPG games Star Wars, Shadowrun, and Wheel of Time and illustrated a story in Metal Hurlant which was adapted for Television.

His relationship with Marvel started in 2003 and he has provided countless cover illustrations, video game designs (Spider-Man PS4 and Iron Man VR both feature original designs by Adi), interior pages, licensing, and merchandising art. He has created artist series toys and collectibles from his original designs of Marvel and Star Wars characters as well as his own creations from the Sova universe. He has a longstanding relationship with the legendary band Tool for whom he has provided original artwork and designs for posters, album art, and a wide range of merchandising and promotional material.

He was awarded a Master of Arts honor by the Leeds Arts University for his contributions to the popular arts."

www.adigranov.net
Instagram: adigranov
Facebook: AdiGranovIllustration